Leonardo Padura was born in Havana in 1955 and lives in Cuba. He has published a number of novels, short-story collections and literary essays. International fame came with the *Havana Quartet,* all featuring Inspector Mario Conde, of which *Havana Black* is the second to be available in English. The *Quartet* has won a number of literary prizes including the Spanish Premio Hammett. It has sold widely in Spain, France, Italy and Germany.

D0035967

HAVANA BLACK

Leonardo Padura

Translated from the Spanish
by Peter Bush

BITTER LEMON PRESS
LONDON

BITTER LEMON PRESS

First published in the United Kingdom in 2006 by
Bitter Lemon Press, 37 Arundel Gardens, London W11 2LW

www.bitterlemonpress.com

First published in Spanish as *Paisaje de Otoño* by
Tusquets Editores, S.A., Barcelona, 1998

Bitter Lemon Press gratefully acknowledges the
financial assistance of the Arts Council of England

A CIP record for this book is available from the British Library

ISBN 1–904738–15–X

Typeset by RefineCatch Limited, Broad Street, Bungay, Suffolk
Printed and bound in Great Britain by Bookmarque Ltd,
Croydon, Surrey

For Ambrosio Fornet, the best reader of the history of Cuban literature.
For Dashiell Hammett, because of *The Maltese Falcon*.
For friends, near and far, who are part of this story.
And, happily, for you, Lucía.

Author's Note

In 1990, when I started to write the novel *Pasado Perfecto*, Detective Lieutenant Mario Conde, the protagonist of that book, was born. One night a year and a half later, after the novel had been published, the Count whispered something in my ear that, when I'd thought about it for several days, seemed in the end like a good idea: why don't we write more novels? And we decided to write three other works that, together with *Pasado Perfecto* (which took place in the winter of 1989), would make up the four season tetralogy of "The Havana Quartet". And thus were conceived *Vientos de cuaresma* (spring), *Máscaras* in the original, *Havana Red* in the English edition (summer) and this *Paisaje de Otoño* or *Havana Black*, which we finished writing in autumn 1997, a few days before the Count's and my birthday, for we were indeed born on the same day, if not in the same year.

I want to note just two things via this confession: that I owe to the Count (a literary, never real, character) the good fortune to have meandered through a whole year of his life, following his every hesitation and adventure; and that his stories, as I always point out, are fictitious, although they are quite similar to some accounts of reality.

Finally, I must thank a group of reader-friends, for their patience in absorbing and analysing each of the versions of *Havana Black*, an exercise without which the book would never have been what it is – for better or for worse. They are, as loyal as ever, Helena Nuñez, Ambrosio Fornet, Álex Fleites, Arturo Arango, Lourdes Gómez, Vivian Lechuga, Beatriz Pérez, Dalia Acosta, Wilfredo Cancio, Gerardo Arreola and José Antonio Michelena. My thanks also to Greco Cid, who presented me with the character of Dr Alfonso Forcade. To Daniel Chavarría, who inspired me with the story of the Manila Galleon. To Steve Wilkinson, who saw the mistakes nobody else had seen. To my publishers, Beatriz Moura and Marco Tropea, who forced me to write with an axe, as Juan Rulfo recommended. And, of course, my gratitude to the person who sustained and tolerated this whole endeavour more than anyone: Lucía López Coll, my wife.

Autumn 1989

She reflected. "I prefer stories about squalor."
"About what?" I said, leaning forward.
"Squalor. I'm extremely interested in squalor."
J. D. Salinger

Hurricane, hurricane, I feel you coming
José María Heredia

"And get here quick . . .!" he screamed at a sky that seemed languid and becalmed, as if still painted from October's deceptive palette of blue: he screamed, arms crossed, chest bare, bellowing a desperate plea with every ounce of strength his lungs could muster, so his voice would carry and also to check that his voice still existed after three days without uttering a single word.

Punished by cigarettes and alcohol, his throat at last felt the relief of creation, and his spirit thrived on this minimal declaration of freedom, soon to bubble up in an inner effervescence leading him to the brink of a second exclamation.

From the heights of his terrace roof, Mario Conde had surveyed a firmament devoid of breezes and clouds, like the lookout of a lost vessel, morbidly hoping his crow's nest would allow him to glimpse, at the horizon's end, two aggressive crosses he'd been tracking for several days as they journeyed across the weather maps, as they approached their prescribed destination: his city, his neighbourhood and that very terrace from which he was hailing them.

Initially it had been a distant, anonymous sign on the first plotting of a tropical depression, heading away from the coasts of Africa and gathering hot clouds before entering its dance of death; two days later it won promotion to the worrying category of cyclonic disturbance, and now was a poisoned arrow in the side of the mid-Atlantic, hurtling towards the Caribbean

and arrogantly claiming its right to be baptized: *Felix*;
yet, the previous night, swollen into a hurricane, it
had appeared in a flux grotesquely poised over the
archipelago of Guadalupe, which it crushed in a devastating, one hundred and seventy mile an hour embrace,
advancing, intent on demolishing trees and houses,
diverting the historical course of rivers and overturn-
ing millenary mountain peaks, killing animals and
humans, like a curse descended from a sky as omin-
ously languid and becalmed as ever, like a woman
ready to betray.

But Mario Conde knew none of those incidents or
illusions could change its destiny or mission: from the
moment he saw it born to life on those maps, he felt a
strange affinity with that freak of a hurricane: the bastard's coming, he told himself, as he saw it advance
and swell, because something in the atmosphere outside or in his own inner depression – cirrus, nimbus,
stratus and cumulus rent by lightning, though still
unable to transform themselves into a hurricane – had
warned him of the real needs of that mass of rain and
rabid winds cosmic destiny had created specifically to
cross that particular city and bring a long anticipated,
necessary cleansing.

But that afternoon, tired of his passive vigil, the
Count had opted to issue verbal summons. Shirtless,
his trousers barely secure, with a skinful of alcohol
fuelling his hiddenmost energies, he clambered out
of a window on to the terrace and encountered an
autumnal, pleasantly warm twilight, where, however
much he tried, he couldn't detect the slightest trace of
a lurking cyclone. Beneath that cheating sky, and
momentarily oblivious to its designs, the Count began
to observe the topography of his neighbourhood,
populated by aerials, pigeon-lofts, washing-lines and

water tanks reflecting simple, rustic routines from which he, however, seemed to be excluded. On the only hill in the area, as always, he espied the red-tiled turret of that fake English castle his grandfather Rufino Conde had laboured to construct almost a century ago. He thought how the stubborn permanence of certain works that outlived their creators and resisted passing hurricanes, storms, cyclones, typhoons, tornadoes or even whirlwinds seemed the only valid reason to exist. And what would remain of him if he threw himself into the air there and then like the pigeon he had once imagined. Infinite oblivion, he must have reflected, a rampant emptiness as lived by all those anodyne individuals weaving along the black snake of the Calzada, weighed down by their bundles or hopes, or empty-handed, minds a mess of uncertainties, probably unaware of the inexorable approach of an awesome hurricane, indifferent even to death's void, with nothing to remember or look forward to, now alarmed by the desperate cry he unleashed at the most distant point on the horizon: "Get here quick, you bastard . . .!"

He imagined the cork's possible pain as if it were live flesh he was penetrating with his implacable metal corkscrew. He sunk it in as far as he could, with a surgeon's precision and determination not to fail: he held his breath, pulled gently, and the cork surfaced like a fish embracing the hook that was its perdition. The alcoholic vapour rushing from the bottle rose full and fruity to his nostrils, and, not a man for half-measures, he poured a large dose into a glass and downed it in one gulp, with the panache of a Cossack haunted by the howls of winter.

He gave the bottle an anguished look: it was the last from the stocks he'd hurriedly assembled three days earlier, when Detective Lieutenant Mario Conde abandoned Police Headquarters after he'd signed his request for a discharge and decided to lock himself in to die of rum and cigarettes, grief and bitterness. He'd always thought that when he'd achieved his wish to depart the police he'd feel a relief that would allow him to sing, dance and, naturally, drink, but without remorse or pain, for he was after all realizing a desire for emancipation he'd postponed for far too long. At this late stage in life he told himself he'd never really understood why he'd said yes to joining the police, and then that he could never fathom at all clearly why he'd deferred his escape from that world where he'd never really belonged although he'd found it infectious. Perhaps it was the argument to the effect that he was a policeman because he didn't like bastards getting off scot-free that had seemed so convincing he'd eventually believed it himself. Perhaps it was his inability to be decisive that had guided his whole erratic life, tying him into a routine crowned by satisfaction at his more than dubious successes: catching murderers, rapists, thieves or fraudsters who were already beyond redemption. But he was in no doubt whatsoever that it was Major Antonio Rangel, his chief for the last eight years, who was mainly to blame for his almost infinite postponement of his wish to make an escape. The relationship of feigned tension and real respect he'd established with the Boss had functioned as an overactive delay tactic and he knew he'd never find the necessary courage to go up to that office on the fifth floor clutching his release papers. So he rested his hopes of making a break for it on the retirement of the Major, now fifty-eight, with possibly only two years to go.

But all the real and fictitious parapets fell at a single

4

strokc that last Friday. The news of Major Rangel's replacement had spread around the corridors at Headquarters like wildfire, and, when he heard it, the Count felt fear and impotence grip and score his back, spread to his brain. The Boss's much debated, always inconceivable departure wouldn't be the last chapter in that history of persecutions, interrogations and punishments to which detectives at Headquarters had been subjected by other detectives entrusted with the unnatural act of spying on other police. The long months of that inquisition had seen apparently untouchable heads roll, while fear thrived as the prot-agonist in a tragedy that smacked of a farce prepared to see its three obligatory acts through to the bitter end: an unpredictable end dragged out to a grand finale, and the sacrifice of something everybody had believed invulnerable and sacred.

Mario didn't have to think twice before he decided to go once and for all. He refused to listen to any of the poisonous explanations going the rounds in relation to the Boss's departure, wrote down his request to be discharged on personal grounds, waited patiently for the lift to take him to the fifth floor and, after signing his letter, handed it to the woman officer he met in the lobby to what had been – and would never again be – the office of his friend, Major Antonio Rangel.

But, rather than relief, the Count was shocked to find himself overcome with sorrow. No, of course not: that wasn't the path to the triumphant, self-sufficient escape he had always imagined, but a reptilian slither-ing out of sight that not even Rangel would forgive. And so, instead of singing and dancing, he simply decided to drink himself silly, and on the way home spent all his savings on seven bottles of rum and twelve packets of cigarettes.

"Hey, you giving a party?" asked the Chinese sales assistant in the liquor store with a knowing smile, and Mario Conde looked him in the eye.

"No, friend, a wake," he retorted, and back he went into the street.

While he got undressed, drinking a glass from the first deflowered bottle, the Count noticed how the death foretold of his fighting fish, Rufino, had been enacted: he was floating in the middle of water a dark, sickly ink colour, his gills open, like an aged flower about to drop its petals.

"For Christ's fucking sake, Rufino, what made you die now and leave me all alone . . . just when I was about to change your water?" he asked the motionless body, before gulping down his drink and casting corpse and liquid down his voracious lavatory.

Already clutching his second glass and unaware that he wouldn't say a word for three days, Mario Conde took his phone off the hook, picked the folded newspaper up from under the door and put it next to the lavatory in order to give that ink-stained paper the use it deserved when the time came. That was when he spotted it, tucked away on a corner of page two: it was an as yet unnamed flurry, drawn west of Cabo Verde on a map whose cold latitudes sent an electric shock of prescience through him: the bastard's heading this way, he thought immediately, and began to desire it with all his might, as if he could mentally attract that catastrophic, freakish engine of purification. And he poured himself a third glass of rum, and waited calmly for the cyclone to hit.

He woke up sure the hurricane had arrived. The thunder resounded so close by he couldn't fathom how he'd seen such a becalmed sky only a few hours before. The short-lived autumnal evening had given way to darkness and, convinced it was thunder he was hearing, he was surprised by an absence of rain and wind, until a voice came on the heels of the last rumbling echoes: "Hey, Mario, it's me. Come on, open up, I know you're in there."

A flash of lucidity pierced the hangover fogging his brain and a warning light winked in his consciousness. Not thinking to hide his naked parts reduced by fear, the Count rushed to open his front door.

"What you doing here, wild man?" he asked, the door open, feeling uneasy in his heart. "Something happened to Josefina?"

An explosion of laughter brought the Count back to the idea of his irrevocable acts, and skinny Carlos's voice alerted him to the magnitude of the disaster he'd just committed: "Fuck me, you animal, you've got a right titchy cock ..." prompting more laughter, which was boosted by Andrés and Rabbit, whose heads had peered round the corner to check out Skinny's observation.

"And your mother's is even titchier," was all he could manage, as he beat a retreat, mooning a pair of incongruously pallid buttocks at his adversary.

The Count had to swallow two analgesics to see off his impending headache, which he preferred to blame on his scare rather than the rum: skinny Carlos's unexpected appearance, in his wheelchair, had made him afraid something must have happened to Josefina. His best friend hadn't been to his place for a long, long time and he thought that the visit could only be triggered by some unhappy event. The morbid vision he'd had that evening, when he'd seen himself cast into the void unsupported by any wings, seemed definitely out of reach: could he go and abandon his friends like that? Leave Carlos alone in his wheelchair and kill off old Jose with an attack of sadness? The water running down his face washed away the last cobwebs of sleep and doubt. No, he couldn't, least not for now.

"I thought the worst," he said when he finally returned, cigarette between lips, to his living room and saw that Carlos, Rabbit and Andrés had helped themselves to the mortal remains of his last bottle of rum.

"And what do you think we thought?" rasped Skinny swigging away. "Three days not knowing where the fuck you'd got to, your phone out of order, not giving any damned warning . . . You went too far, you bastard, you went too far this time."

"Hey, hold it, I'm not a kid." The policeman rallied to his own defence.

Andrés, as usual, attempted reconciliation. "That's enough, gentlemen, nothing dire's happened." And looking at the Count: "The fact is Josefina and Carlos were worried about you. That's why I brought him here. He refused to let me come by myself."

The Count observed his best and oldest friend, transformed into an amorphous mass, overflowing the sides of his armchair, where he vented his anger like an animal destined for sacrifice. Nothing now remained of the lean figure skinny Carlos once was, because a mean bullet had mangled his destiny, had left him an invalid for ever. But there also, intact and invincible, was all the goodness of a man who increasingly persuaded the Count of the injustices of this world. Why did it have to happen to a guy like Carlos? Why did someone like him have to fight in a dark and distant war and ruin the best of his life? God cannot exist if such things occur, he thought, and the policeman's distressed soul felt moved, almost to the point of splitting in two, when Skinny said: "You only had to ring."

"Uh-huh, I should have rung. To tell you I resigned from the police."

"Just as well, my son, you had me really worried," sighed Josefina, and gave him a kiss on the forehead. "But look at your face. And that smell. How much rum did you drink? And you're so thin it's scary . . ."

"And guess what *we* found out," interrupted Carlos, his fingers pointing up the Count's visibly reduced virility, and he laughed again.

"Conde, Conde," interjected Rabbit anxiously, "you who are at least half a writer, please: elucidate a problem of meaning I have, tell me, what is the difference between pity and pithy?"

The Count looked at his interrogator, who could barely hide his outlandish teeth behind his upper lip. As usual he couldn't decide whether the grimace hid a smile or just his buckteeth.

"No idea . . . the aitch, ain't it?"

"No, the size," replied Rabbit, releasing his dentures to laugh long and sonorously, and inviting the others to join in the joke.

"Don't take any notice of him, Condesito," said Josefina, coming to the rescue and holding his hands. "Look, as I imagined these three who claim to be your friends would bring you here, and as I also imagined you would be hungry, and because anyone can see you are hungry, I started to think hard, now what can I cook these lads? And, you know, I couldn't think of anything special. The fact is it's really difficult to get things . . . And there and then a light went on and I chose the easy option: rice and chicken. What do you reckon?"

"How many chickens, Jose?" enquired the Count.

"Three and a half."

"And did you add peppers?"

"Yes, for decoration. And cooked it in beer."

"So three and a half chickens . . . Do you think that'll do for us?" The Count went on with his questions, as he pushed Skinny's chair towards the dining room, with a skill acquired from years of practice.

The final judgement from those round the table was unanimous: the rice could do with green peas, although it tasted good, they added, after ingesting three big plates of rice transfigured by chicken gravy and juices.

They shut themselves up in Skinny's room for their after-supper rum and chat, while Josefina dozed in front of the television.

"Put something on the deck, Mario," insisted Skinny, and the Count smiled.

"The same as usual?" he asked, purely for rhetorical pleasure, and got a smile and a nod from his friend.

"You bet . . ."

"Now then, what do you fancy?" asked one.

"The Beatles?" responded the other.

"Chicago?"

"Formula V?"

"Los Pasos?"

"Credence?"

"Right on, Credence," they both chorused perfectly as in a routine rehearsed a thousand times, over countless, knowing years. "But don't tell me Tom Foggerty sings like a black. I've told you often enough before that he sings like God, haven't I?" And the two nodded, revealing a deeply rooted accord, for they both knew that was right: the bastard sang like God, and started to show it when the Count pressed play and

Foggerty, with the Credence Clearwater Revival, launched into his unique version of "Proud Mary" . . . How often had he lived that scene?

Sitting on the floor, a tot of rum by his side and a lighted cigarette in the ashtray, the Count yielded to pressure from his friends and told them of the latest developments at Headquarters and his irrevocable decision to leave the force.

"I really couldn't care less what happens to those sons of a bitches . . . Every day there are more of them. Battalions of sons of bitches . . ." "Regiments . . . armies," was the opinion of Andrés, who extended the quantitative, logistical power base of invaders, more resistant and fertile than roaches.

"You're crazy, Conde," concluded Carlos.

"And if you leave the police, what will you do?" came the question from Rabbit, a viscerally historical individual, always in need of reasons, causes and consequences for the slightest incident.

"That's the least of my worries. I want out —"

"Hey, wild man," interrupted Carlos, putting his glass of rum between his legs. "Do whatever you want, whatever, it'll be fine by me, because that's what friends are for, you know? But if you're going, enjoy, don't hide in a cloud of alcohol. Stand bang in the middle of Headquarters and shout: 'I'm going because I fucking well want to', but don't slip out the back, as if you owed something, because you don't owe anybody anything, do you?"

"Well, I'm happy for your sake, Conde," commented Andrés, looking at the hands he devoted three times a week to cutting open abdomens and sickly voice boxes, with a view to repairing what could be and excising and ditching what was worn out and useless. "I'm glad one of us is prepared to call a day on this load of shit and sit it out and wait for whatever shows up."

"A hurricane," whispered the Count, taking another gulp, but his friend carried on, as if he hadn't heard him.

"Because you know we are a generation that obeyed orders and that is our sin and our crime. First, our fathers gave us orders, to be good students and citizens. We were ordered around at school, also to make us be good, and then we were ordered to work where they wanted us to work. But nobody ever thought to ask us what we wanted: we were ordered to study in the school they thought best, to pursue the degree it was our duty to get, to work at the job it was our duty to do, and the orders kept coming, nobody ever asked us fucking once in our damned lives if that was what we wanted. Everything was pre-planned, wasn't it? From playschool to the spot in the cemetery assigned for us, everything decided for us, and they didn't even ask what disease we wanted to die of. That's why we are a pile of shit, because we don't dream, we just exist to carry out our orders . . ."

"Hey now, Andrés, don't exaggerate," said Skinny Carlos, trying to salvage a crumb of comfort, as he poured himself more rum.

"What do you mean 'don't exaggerate'? Weren't you ordered to the war in Angola? Wasn't your life fucked up and you stuck in that shitty chair because you were a good little boy who always said yes? Did you ever dream of saying you wouldn't go? They told us that historically we had to obey and you didn't even think to refuse, Carlos, because they always taught us to say yes, yes, yes . . . And as for this fellow –" he pointed at Rabbit, who had performed the miracle of hiding his teeth and for once seemed really serious at the threat

12

of the imminent lethal salvo – "apart from playing with history and changing women every six months, what has he done with his life? Where the fuck are the history books he was going to write? At what point did he give up on everything he said he wanted to be and never got to be in his life? Don't piss me off, Carlos, at least grant me the right to believe my life is a disaster . . ."

Skinny Carlos, who had long since ceased to be skinny, looked at Andrés. The friendship existing between them had been cementing for twenty years and there were very few secrets between them. But recently something had turned in Andrés's brain. That man they'd first admired when he was the best college baseball player, applauded by all his comrades, with the manly merit of losing his virginity to a woman so beautiful, so crazy and so desirable that they all would have loved to give up everything, even their lives, to her. The very same Andrés who would become the successful doctor they'd all consult, the only one who had managed an enviable marriage, two children included, and had been privileged to have his own house and private car, was now revealing himself as a man full of frustrations and rancour, which embittered him and poisoned the atmosphere around him. Because Andrés wasn't happy, was dissatisfied with his lot and made sure all his friends knew it: something in the projects he held most dear had failed, and his path in life – like all of theirs – had taken predetermined undesirable turnings to which they'd never consented as individuals.

"All right, let's assume you are right." Carlos nodded resignedly, drinking a long draught and then adding: "But you can't live thinking like that."

"Why not, wild man?" the Count intervened, puffing

out smoke and recalling that afternoon's alcoholic suicidal impulses.

"Because then you have to accept it's all a load of shit."

"And isn't it?"

"You know it isn't, Conde," declared Carlos, looking at the ceiling from his wheelchair. "Not everything, right?"

He collapsed on his bed, head thick with alcoholic vapours and Andres's lament for a generation. Lying there, he started to undress and throw each garment on the floor. He could already predict the headache he would have at daybreak, a just punishment for his excesses, but he felt his mind racing along enjoyably, strangely active, spawning ideas, memories and obsessions endowed with a feverish fleshly quality. With a supreme physical effort, he abandoned his bed and went to the bathroom in search of the analgesics that could thwart his recurrent migraine. He reckoned two would suffice, and dissolved them in water. He then walked to the lavatory, where he piddled a weak, amber trickle that splashed on the bowl's already stained edges and made him consider the proportions of his member: he'd always suspected that it was on the small side and now he was certain – pitifully so – after the strip show he'd offered his friends that evening. But mentally he shrugged his shoulders at its non-importance, for, even as it was, the currently moribund strip of meat had always been an effective companion to his binary or solitary erotic outings, even rising up rapidly when necessity required it to be on a war footing. Ignore those sons of bitches, he told it, looking at it head on, right in the eye: don't feel pathetic,

14

because you're a good'un, aren't you? And he gave it a last shake.

He was pleasantly surprised when he realized he didn't have to go to work the following day, and, lungs full of the air of freedom and cigarette smoke, he decided to waste no more time in that lonely bed. You are going to change your life now, Mario Conde, he reproached himself, and decided on a useful wakefulness. The exercise of independence was one of the privileges of his new situation. He quickly went into the kitchen and put a flame under the coffee pot, ready to drink his morning infusion in order to trick his body and restore the energy necessary for what he wanted to do: sit down and write. But what the fuck are you going to write? Well, about what Andrés said: he would write a story of frustration and deceit, of disenchantment and futility, of the pain of discovering you had taken the wrong turning at every point, whether you were to blame or not. That was the great experience of his generation, which was so secure and well nourished that it grew with every year, and he concluded it would be good to put it in black and white, as the only antidote against the most pathetic oblivion of all and as a practical way of reaching once and for all the diffuse kernel of that whole unequivocal equivocation: when, how, why and where had it all begun to fuck up? How much were they each to blame, if at all? How much was he? He sipped his coffee slowly, now seated in front of the white sheet, bitten by the platen of his Underwood, and realized it would be hard to transmute those certainties and experiences, twisting in his gut like worms, into the squalid and moving story he needed to tell. A tranquil story like that of the man who tells a child about the habits of the banana-fish and then blows his brains out because he can't

15

find anything better to do with his life. He looked at the unpolluted paper, and realized that his desires alone wouldn't suffice to defeat that eternal eight and· half by thirteen inch challenge into which the chronicle of an entire wasted life should fit. He needed an illumination like Josefina's, able to provoke the poetic miracle of extracting something new from a daring mix of lost, forgotten ingredients. And so he started to think of the hurricane again, still only visible in the newspaper: something like that was necessary, ravaging and devastating, purifying and righteous, for someone like him to regain the possibility of being himself, myself, yourself, Mario Conde, and for that deferred state to be resurrected that could beget a little beauty or pain or sincerity on to that mute, empty, defiant paper, where he finally wrote, as if overcome by an irrepressible ejaculation: "The youth slumped to the ground, as if pushed, and rather than pain he felt the millenary stench of rotten fish issue forth from that grey, alien land."

"What are you doing here, Manolo?" asked the Count when he opened the door to see the unexpected, skeletal face of Sergeant Manuel Palacios, his companion in detection over recent years.

Something about his face revealed a state of shock – the squinting eye more lost than ever behind an ample nostril – and the Count knew immediately that his own face was the cause.

"You ill, Conde?"

"Like hell I'm ill. I was up writing all night," he replied, and felt an aesthetic well-being as he offered that explanation: he imagined the marinated bags under his eyes and the exhausted eyelids, but was happy to have the poetic justification, even if it wasn't altogether true: various badly scarred sheets of paper were the only real fruits of hours of application.

"Ah, so you're back on that track. So be it," declared the sergeant, wagging a finger at him.

"And might one enquire what brings you here?"

Manolo smiled sweetly.

"I came to get you."

"But I left the force three days ago."

"That's what you think. The new boss says he wants to you to come in and discuss your departure with him."

"Tell him I can't today, tell him I'm writing."

Manolo smiled, broadly this time. "He told me not to accept any excuses."

"And what will they do to me if I don't go? Kick me out of the police?"

"Or put you inside, for lack of respect. That's what he said . . ." went on Manolo, spelling out the details of his orders before finally finding his own voice. "Do you really want out, Conde?"

"Yes, I really do. Come in, I'll make us some coffee."

They sat in the kitchen waiting for the coffee to percolate, while Manolo recounted recent events at Headquarters. Only eleven out of sixteen detectives remained and it was like an angry hornets' nest. The files of all those who still survived were under review yet again, and there was talk of a fresh round of interrogations of each and every one of them: it was a merciless hunt to the death, as if someone had decreed the necessary extinction of a dispensable species.

"And what's the line on Major Rangel?"

"That he did nothing, and that's why he's guilty. I don't think he's been back there, but I heard he'll be retired with full honours."

"He won't want that kind of honour," rasped the Count.

Finally, Manolo related, the new chief had gathered them together that morning to ask them to make an effort until the situation returned to normal. What was happening at Headquarters didn't stop life on the outside from going on the same – more or less the same, perhaps worse – and all manner of crimes were being committed . . .

"It never will be normal," said the Count, pouring out two big cups of coffee. "At least as far as I'm concerned."

"But come with me, Conde, talk to him and then do what you want. Don't throw overboard what you've achieved in ten years. Didn't you like people saying you were the best detective at Headquarters? Don't fuck about, Conde, show them what you're made of . . ."

"And what do I get out of it, Manolo?"

The sergeant looked at his friend and attempted a smile. They knew each other too well and the Count was perfectly well aware of the scares Manolo had suffered in the recent months of investigations, purges and expulsions, during which they'd all been questioned several times, and the most unexpected hares had been flushed out: colleagues of twenty years, bitter mutual betrayals, old policemen beyond suspicion revealed to be outright scoundrels, cases buried under incredible piles of loot, favours exchanged for the most unlikely goods: from a youthful, throbbing sex to a university degree awarded to someone who never went to class, via a simple handshake from Somebody able to repay a favour at an opportune moment, and the fuse was still lit, apparently set to burn everybody in its path. Manolo looked at the Count, downed his coffee and gave the best possible reply: "You get to leave without being kicked out. You get to leave the shit smelling of roses. You get respect. And you get a bonus when they find out that Major Rangel wasn't wrong about you . . . or me."

The image conjured up of the lonely Major, gazing at the twilight in the backyard of his house, in his slippers, smoking a long cigar and deciding on the best way to spend his enforced leisure, once more shook the Count's sensibilities. After working so hard the man didn't deserve an end like that.

"All right, I'm coming . . . but tell me just one thing: Where's Felix got to today?"

"Felix? Felix who, Conde?"

"Felix, the hurricane, my friend."

"How the hell should I know"

Manolo shook his head after drinking the last drop of coffee.

"What kind of policeman are you if you don't even know where that bastard has got to! You're a disaster. Manolo . . ."

He could be forty-five. Maybe slightly older. The grey hair aged him, but his smooth waxen face – mulatto white or bleached-white mulatto, carefully, even frenetically shaven – suggested a subtraction might be in order. He sported a uniform that looked made to measure by a tailor and not off the peg: the bolero, neatly shaped to his chest, descended over his flat belly to cover the belt to his fine cotton, elegantly hanging trousers, which were in the wrong time and place . . . And then there was the smell: he wore a delicate but very definite scent, creating around him a dry, manly, exquisite aura ten inches from his oh-so-stylishly uniformed silhouette. As he observed him, the Count thought this man could lead him to bury all his prejudices: he had expected to meet an ogre, not this fragrant, preening fellow; he had wanted to see a despot who refused to grant him his independence and found a man of pacific mien; he was sure he was going to meet an irate prosecutor in the spot now filled by this human being ready to disarm him with a smile and a question: "Do you smoke, Lieutenant? Ah, good, so I can smoke as well," and he took a cigar out of his export box of H. Upmanns, after first offering one to Mario Conde.

"Thanks, Colonel."

"Colonel Molina. I'm Alberto Molina . . . But please take a seat, as I think you and I have lots to talk about. But first let me order two coffees."

"Lieutenant, I don't think you slept very well last night, did you . . .? Well, I can tell you I didn't. I tossed and turned in bed till my wife got angry because I wouldn't let her sleep and she sent me to the living room. I threw the bedspread on the floor and started to think about everything that's happening and the situation they've landed me in. Because to be honest I don't know whether I'm going to be able to go through with it. I almost think I can't . . . And it's very disagreeable to know one is replacing an officer like Major Rangel, the man in the country who knows most about investigations, trials and the work you people do. And I don't. You know where I come from? From the Executive for the Analysis of Military Intelligence, and that has nothing in common with what you do. And you know something else? For years I dreamed of being a spy. But a real spy, not like the ones in John Le Carré novels, who seem genuine but are only fictional. It seemed the best possible future, and I spent twenty years with this dream, office-bound, processing what the real spies found out: in a word, I was the bureaucrat who seemed like a character out of Le Carré . . . But if you start playing this game, you soon learn you're obliged to obey orders, Lieutenant, and when you're under orders, you have no choice but to belt up and obey. That's why I'm here and not in Tel Aviv or New York, and that's why I decided to talk to you, for it can't be through choice that you have such a reputation as a detective, although there is the odd rumour . . . Not that these things bother me, I swear: I didn't come here to judge anyone, but to ensure things keep working more or less the same way they did under Major Rangel . . . The others out there have come to pass judgement, and let me tell you that I, personally, deeply regret that several of your companions have done the things they did and provoked the investigations that led to all this and to Rangel losing his post. And though I regret it, I fully understand the need to proceed in this way: because a corrupt policeman is the worst of criminals, and I think we must be agreed on that, mustn't we? The fact is that recently the most peculiar things have been happening ... Besides, Lieutenant, if you ask to be discharged in the middle of all this business it may give rise to suspicions, and you should be aware of that. Although I must say I'm not here to suspect anyone and that's why I want to hear your reasons for asking to be discharged. This place is no longer what I imagined it to be, although it should continue to be what it used to be: a headquarters for criminal investigations, and that's precisely why I've called you in. Right now I've got all the detectives on the payroll, old and new, on some job or other, and I need you, Lieutenant. And you won't think what I'm about to say is very orthodox; I brought you in to offer a straightforward deal: solve this case for me and I'll sign you off ... Please don't imagine for one minute that I'm using your discharge as blackmail: let's say rather that I'm compelling you to help me, because I need your assistance now and because you know that if I don't sign the paper here on my desk, you won't be discharged for several months ... I told you I didn't sleep well last night, didn't I? I should tell you that the truth is it was your fault I didn't sleep properly: I couldn't think how to suggest something to you that might sound like blackmail and persuade you in the nicest possible way to take on this specific case. So I decided the best thing was to be completely frank with you ... But first of all I'll run through the case and you can say yea or nay, and we'll see what happens, because although you're hearing me being so polite and calm, I can also dig my heels in and make things difficult. Believe me . . . The problem is that on Saturday night they found a man's corpse, a Cuban with US citizenship who'd come to visit his family . . . A real problem, you know? The man went out for a drive by himself on Thursday evening in his brother-in-law's car; he'd said he wanted to see a bit of Havana, and that was the last that was seen of him, he didn't appear until eleven p.m. Saturday when some fishermen found the corpse on Goat Beach, at the exit to the bay tunnel. You with me? According to the forensic, the man was dead before he was thrown into the sea, a blow to the head from a blunt instrument. He died of a fractured skull and brain haemorrhage. From the nature of the blow, the forensic thinks the object could have been something like a baseball bat, one of the old wooden sort . . . So far, so reasonably mysterious and politically complicated, but one can't overlook a detail that makes things even more difficult: the dead man's penis and testicles had been cut off, evidently with a blunt kitchen knife . . . What do you think, then? Doesn't the story grab you? Of course, it must be revenge, but we have to prove it and find the guilty party, before the scandal blows up in Miami and the government's accused of doing the evil deed. Because the man who died from several blows to the head, the man whose genitals were mutilated comes with a name and a history: he was Miguel Forcade Mier, and in the sixties he was deputy head of the Provincial Office for Expropriated Property, and national deputy director for Planning and the Economy until he stopped off in Madrid in 1978, on his way back from the Soviet Union . . . Now, doesn't this case really grab you?"

In his ten years working as a policeman Mario Conde had internalized a few basic lessons to guarantee his survival: first of all came the concept of loyalty. Only by preserving the group spirit, by protecting the other members of the police tribe to which he himself belonged, could he guarantee that the others would provide him with similar protection and that their unity was really genuine. Even when he never felt like a real policeman, and preferred to operate without a pistol or uniform and even hated the idea of employing violence, when he dreamed he would soon jettison all that to embark on a normal life – now what the fuck was normality? he would also wonder, imagining a log cabin with a tiled roof facing the sea, where he would live and write – the Count always practised that code, perhaps to excess, as Major Rangel also did, only to end up betrayed by those bastards he'd stubbornly defended, even to the point of putting his own neck on the block when sentences were meted out. Consequently at that moment Mario Conde's police and street ethics walked a dramatic tightrope: either he kept to his decision to leave Headquarters because they'd removed Major Rangel, or he took on that rancid-smelling case he'd already started to like the sound of and would thus earn the freedom awaiting him when it was solved and demonstrate into the bargain why the Boss had singled him out from all his detectives. As he listened to the alternatives offered by his new sweet-smelling, smartly uniformed chief, the Count lit another cigar and looked at the white folder on his lap, which contained the known facts about the life of defector Miguel Forcade Mier and the part of his death that had been revealed. He looked out of the big office window and noted that the sky was still blue and quiet, oblivious to the existence of Felix, and decided to negotiate a way out: "Colonel, as we are forging a deal between gentlemen, before I respond I want to ask you a question or two, and make one demand."

The well-shaven and better-dressed man who was now his boss, smiled.

"You are mistaken, Lieutenant, it's no gentleman's deal, because I'm now your boss. But I'll go along with you . . . What's your first question?"

"Why had a man like Miguel Forcade been let back in the country? From what you tell me he was a pretty high ranker and defected when he was coming back from an official mission? As far as I know, it's not usual for someone like that to attempt a comeback and even less to get permission to return to Cuba. I know of people who've been refused entry for much less . . . When this man left, did he take with him documents, money, something to incriminate him legally?"

It was now Colonel Molina who lit up one of his cigarettes, before responding. "No, he was incredibly clean. But the fact is they let him back in to keep an eye on him and see what he wanted to do. He sorted his re-entry through the International Red Cross, as his father is sick. And it was decided it was best to let him come back in."

"I more or less expected an answer like that, so I will now ask my second question. Did he throw off his minder?"

"Yes, regrettably from our point of view and his, he slipped the tail that had been put on him. Are you equally happy with that answer?"

The Count nodded, and raised his hand like a suspicious pupil.

"But now I want to ask a third question: did anyone ever find out or suspect why Forcade stayed in Madrid?

Because this kind of man isn't the type to defect for the usual reasons, I assume?"

"There were several suspicions, as there always are in such cases. For example, at the end of '78 they discovered a case of fraud in Planning and the Economy, but they could never prove he was involved. People also thought he might have taken something when he worked in Expropriated Property, but he was never known to sell anything valuable. There was also a suspicion he had information to give, though nothing was ever proved and Forcade never made any public declarations . . . I told you already: he seemed clean and that's why he dared to return. Now I want to hear your request and I'll tell you if I can agree to it."

The Count looked the Colonel in the eye and placed the folder on his desk, before answering: "I don't think it's anything too difficult to grant me: I just want to speak to Major Rangel before I give you my reply. And if I accept, I want him to help me if need be . . ."

Colonel Molina put his cigar out gently, extinguishing the embers against the walls of the metal ashtray, and scrutinized Mario Conde.

"You're an admirable man, Lieutenant . . . The fact is I thought such loyalties were a thing of the past. Of course, speak to your friend the Major, consult him to your heart's content and tell him from me that I regret what has happened and apologize for not going to tell him so personally, but that might be awkward, particularly for me. As things stand now . . . Well, I'll expect you back in two hours, Lieutenant," and he stood to attention, giving a precise, fluid military salute.

Surprised by his martial gesture, the Count stood up and moved his hand across his forehead, in an attempted salute that was more like a farewell or, perhaps, merely a flick to see off the buzzing fly of doubt.

Ana Luisa looked surprised when she opened the door and found herself face to face with Lieutenant Mario Conde.

"Now what are you doing here, my boy?"

The Count looked at her, pleased by the initial effect provoked by his visit, then he tried a familiar gambit: "I came to see if one of your daughters will marry me. Either would do nicely and I quite like the father-in-law who comes in tow."

The woman finally smiled, as she let him in and patted him on the shoulder.

"With that face, I don't think either will fall for you."

"I must look terrible: you're the third person to say that today," said the Count resignedly. "Where's your husband then?"

"Go through. He's in the library. I'll bring your tea in a moment."

"Hey, Ana Luisa, has anyone been to see him?"

The woman glanced at him and he saw affecting pools of sadness in her eyes.

"No, Conde, not one of those who were his friends has dropped by. Well, you know what it's like: if you fall by the wayside . . . Just as well you . . ." she stammered before rushing into the kitchen.

The Count walked across the dining room, stopped in front of the sliding door to the library and rapped twice with his knuckle.

"Push it, Mario, come in," spoke a voice from beyond the closed doors.

He pushed one of the doors and found Major Rangel

behind his desk: the situation was like a slightly altered replay of their encounters at Headquarters, but on this occasion the Count wondered how the Boss could have known it was him: the doors were wooden and not opaque glass like at the office and his dialogue with Ana Luisa had been too distant to reach the Major's almost sixty-year-old ears.

"Just tell me one thing, Boss. How do you know when it's me? Do I smell or something . . .? You know I'm not a man to use cologne."

"Forget the bloody cologne: I saw you arrive from this window," and he pointed to the shutters that looked over the garden. "Did Ana Luisa say she'd bring a coffee?"

"No, she mentioned tea."

"Fuck, fuck, fuck," shouted the Major as if he were in pain. "Do you know what that woman has decided, Mario? That she must keep telling me to lead a healthier life, that I smoke a lot, drink a lot of coffee . . . And now she makes tea: and makes it from all sorts, orange leaves, lemongrass, crushed aniseed, whatever, because she reckons real tea constipates and stresses . . . As if I was ever stressed."

"And what about your cigars?"

Rangel smiled expansively: a twitch of the upper lip, which didn't even reveal the glint of a tooth.

"Of course, of course. Help yourself," and he opened the small mahogany humidor on his desktop. "You know what these are? They're a truly wonderful set of Cohibas Lanceros. I can tell you they're the best cigars in the whole world. Go on, choose one. Take a good look, what sheen, what colour, what works of art . . . Beautiful, aren't they?"

The Count studied the cigars, arrayed in strict formation in the humidor, shiny and straight-backed like healthy animals, their necks ringed, and thought how the Major's premature retirement must be driving him mad: he never reckoned he would see the day when he'd give away a cigar of such distinction. When it came to cigars, the Boss was an eccentric connoisseur and incredibly tight-fisted.

"If you say so." He nodded and took one of the Lanceros, the first in the set, while the Major eyed the rest and opted for one in the middle, after weighing up two or three other possibilities.

"Now be careful how you prime it," Rangel warned when he saw him bite the end of the cigar. "That decides everything: if you don't prime it properly, you will certainly ruin the cigar . . . Tell me, how do you prefer to do it? With scissors or the guillotine?"

"I don't know, I always use my teeth, you know."

"Fine, but wet it first so you don't break the outer layer. Look, like this," and he continued his lesson, moistening the cigar and twisting it between his lips, finally tweaking it like a nipple, with the delicacy of an experienced lover. "You see?"

Ana Luisa brought in a sweet infusion of unknown provenance, and after drinking it, the two men lit their havanas, the blue clouds from which perfumed the atmosphere in the library. Only then did the Count decide to speak up: "How you feeling, Boss?"

"Can't you see? Fucked, and on boiled water, as if I had diarrhoea. But don't worry . . . I won't die from what happened. These are the risks that go with the job."

"What damned risks? It's a load of crap," blurted the Count, almost choking on the smoke from his cigar. "You're the best head of criminal investigation the country has . . ."

"You think so, Mario? And how do you explain the

fact that several of my detectives were criminals and used their positions to further their own ends?"

"There was no reason why you should have known . . ."

"Yes, I ought, Mario, that much is obvious . . . But I never thought so many could do so much. And don't start telling me about human nature or skeletons in the . . . The fact is I burned my fingers on their behalf and look," he held out his arms, "I got singed."

"And why did you trust someone like me?" the Count queried, hoping to hear Major Rangel bestow rare praise.

"Because I must be mad," replied the Boss, smiling once more: he now shifted only his upper lip from the edge of the cigar. "Hey, Mario, in all these years you never once damned well told me why you joined the police. Will you tell me now?"

The Count nodded, relieved to find the Rangel he'd always known and not the defeated, crestfallen man he had imagined. He still seemed young for his age, in that tight pullover emphasising the pectorals of a practised swimmer and squash player. Not even rejection or fear of those who were once his friends and colleagues seemed overly to affect the true grit of a man born to be a policeman.

"Not right now. But I can tell you now it is down to you whether I remain a policeman or not."

"What are you on about, Mario Conde?"

"It's quite simple: when I heard they were kicking you out, I handed in my resignation, and now they'll accept it if I solve just one more case. And it's a really tasty case. But I'll only take it on if you tell me to . . ."

The Boss stood up and walked over to the shutters. He looked out at the quiet street, shimmering under the midday sun, and looked at the garden, in need of some attention, and drew gently on his Cohiba Lancero.

"Mario, do me a favour," his voice started off quite amiably but suddenly switched tone with that facility the Count had always envied, "stop talking nonsense and tell me what this tasty case is all about. Remember I was also a policeman until only three days ago. Why is it so tasty? Come on. I'm all ears."

A single, well-aimed brutal blow had been enough to put an end to the life of Miguel Forcade Mier: like a ball angrily repelled by a powerful hitter, his brain burst inside his skull, putting an end to the ideas, memories and emotions of the man who in a moment made the transition from life to death. But then the second part of that savage sacrifice was performed: his penis and testicles were excised at the root by a clumsy, furious hand, which scored the flesh, pulled at it, sawed at it, till the entire masculinity of a man who'd returned from the beyond was severed. His body was finally thrown into that turbid sea, a possible offering to certain lethal gods, at a spot where water black with shit, urine, vomit and menstruation issued forth from the city to which Miguel Forcade had returned quite unsuspecting he would never leave it again.

The Count and Major Rangel exchanged looks of disgust: the infinite cruelty of that murder smacked of enraged sacrifice, livid revenge perhaps years in the planning and finally executed when oblivion had apparently buried for ever the unpredictable source of a hatred unleashed now like an October cyclone on the tropics.

And they thought: Miguel Forcade Mier must have died from some ancient crime; perhaps from his time as a repossessor of expropriated goods, when so much wealth abandoned by the Cuban bourgeoisie running for cover with such a hue and cry was confiscated in the name of the people and its government, who should now own everything. Furniture, jewels, works of art, coins ancient and modern, accumulated over more than two centuries by a dialectically defeated social class, had now to pass through the hands of the Official Expropriator charged with the mission of assigning them a more just destiny. Would he always do that? Logic began to suggest not: the bewildering temptations offered by those historically doomed fortunes might have corrupted the vanguard ideology of the man who almost thirty years later, the sign of a traitor cut into his forehead, would die castrated. One could imagine that a part of those recycled riches, minimal no doubt but very valuable (say a Degas that never reappeared, a Greek amphora lost to an oblivious Mediterranean, a Roman bust lost to memory, or collection of Byzantine coins never again exchanged by merchant owners of every temple there ever was?), passed through his hands with the promise of a revolutionary redistribution that never happened and that he perhaps finally paid for in that death of blood, wood and iron . . . But, why was it necessary to castrate him?

Although the crime may not have been that distant or remarkable, perhaps it was no less forgettable for a memory perversely trapped by the physical or moral consequences of that sin: Miguel Forcade Mier had later climbed the ladder of power via the technocratic route, under the hospitable shadow of five-year plans imported from Asian steppes littered with efficient *kolkhoses* and *sovkhoses* – neither the Count nor the Major could remember the difference – infallible

German Democratic economic organization, so perfect it seemed eternal, transplanted to an underdeveloped, one-crop Caribbean island that was nevertheless ready – or so it was often said – to make the great leap into a veritable socialist economic miracle ... That power wielded by the National Office for Planning and the Economy was no small power: there passed through the hands of the man who would become a sexless cadaver with fish-eaten eyes decisions on trade and people's lives, on the investment of millions and possibilities for collective and individual futures, the authority to give, to move, to place, take away and defer, from almost Olympian heights. But Miguel Forcade had leaped fatally into exile from that brilliant National Office, at the peak of its glory though soon to sink to depths of infamy, for no apparent overriding motive: they never discovered what had impelled him to defect, for he was never heard to express sentiments in public, like those usually voiced by people at his level: they always fled a dictatorship, aspired to freedom and democracy, no longer wished to be accomplices, now they had seen ... And how did he ruin the life of whoever at the time, so ruthlessly his victim never found the peace of oblivion or balm of forgiveness?

The origins of such a perverse murder contained all the ingredients of revenge, but the most important item remained unknown: what recipe had created that stew and who had done the cooking?

"What if it was just a matter of jealousy and cuckoldry?" asked the Count, and Major Rangel looked him in the eye from behind his Lancero's infernal glow, before declaring: "Then best not tangle with the wife of the guy who cuts the balls off everyone else, right?"

Whenever he travelled by bus, Mario Conde tried his best to get a window-seat. In his university student days, he would get up twenty minutes earlier than necessary to queue for an empty bus. Unhurriedly, he would randomly choose one of the two sides of the vehicle and keep close to the metal to defend the privilege of the window-seat. Far from the aisle, he enjoyed the material advantages of not having his shoulder knocked by unattractive appendages, his foot trodden on or banged by crates. But there were two much more valuable rewards, which he would alternate according to need, state of mind and interests: he either read for the thirty-five minutes the journey took from his neighbourhood to the stop nearest to the faculty (he only did that on exam days or when he had a really good book), or devoted himself (as he preferred) to studying the buildings the bus encountered on its route, enjoying the second or third floors on the old roads of Jesús del Monte and la Infanta, hidden to anyone not prepared to raise their eyes toward their elusive heights. The Count had acquired that habit from his friend Andrés – who learned it in turn from beautiful Christine, that sexual being with whom they had all fallen in love – and it became such an organic need that when he looked at the buildings he would feel body and mind separating out their most connected atoms, releasing part of his self from his seat to float several yards above the street's dark, greasy surfaces, to penetrate forgotten mysteries, remote histories, dreams wandering behind the walls of places with which he communed, as if they were other souls in distress, also liberated from perishable, onerous matter. That was how he'd discovered the most beautiful, audacious balconies, sculpted on city façades with the most extravagant motifs, eaves decorated with wedding-cake piping, anti-neighbour wrought-iron grilles forged by blacksmiths militant in every baroque art, and he had also discovered that death hovered, nearer every minute to all those centennial wonders of iron, cement, plaster and wood, which turned their best faces to the road, filthy from neglect of historic proportions, from petrified dust and apathy immemorial, whose inhabitants crammed into houses that had lost their dignity and character, degraded by the need for living quarters bereft of water, with communal bathrooms and congenital promiscuity. And although he knew that the pleasure at car level wasn't the same as from the dais of a bus window-seat, which favoured more spiritual outpourings, on that afternoon the Count made of Sergeant Palacios two special requests for which he would be eternally grateful to him: first, for him to keep quiet; second, for him to drive at twenty miles an hour. He wanted only silence and humane speeds in order to observe yet again those elusive landscapes he knew and loved, as he felt afraid it might be his last encounter with the most abandoned, ill-treated architecture of his city of birth: the raging hurricane that at midday was heading towards the South of Hispaniola, after it had devastated tiny Guadalupe – even uprooting some of the trees Victor Hugues himself had ordered to be planted there two centuries ago in a Place de la Victoire dedicated to revolutionary ideals – that same bastard of a cyclone might enter these streets in a few days and demolish the decrepit beauty of second and third floors, which he alone – he was convinced – contemplated, reflecting on their inevitable, regrettable demise, prepared by years of neglect. What other destiny could that city expect if not violent death forged by the protracted agony of oblivion? Or would it also die castrated, a new

Atlantis submerged beneath the sea by an unforgivable yet still unknown sin? Fuck it, he told himself from the gloomy depths of such reflections: it doesn't matter how it dies: we all die in the end. Even you will die. And to usher that transition a little nearer he lit another cigar and puffed with relish as if it were the last wish granted a man on death row.

When he got back to Headquarters and told Colonel Molina: I'll take the case on, his new boss patted him gleefully on the back and agreed to another request: Sergeant Palacios could work with him. But now the Colonel began to name his conditions: he had a maximum of three days to solve the mystery of the castrated death of Miguel Forcade; he must act with the utmost discretion, because he already appreciated the new political implications of what would be a juicy item for the international press, always keen to discredit the government; he should report to him personally twice a day – though he could talk to Major Rangel to his heart's content – because every evening he had to phone Somebody who in turn had to phone Someone charged by the Ministry for Foreign Affairs with speaking to the American consul to report on how investigations were progressing; and he should try to be as orthodox as possible in his methods, though he had carte blanche to do whatever was necessary: everything on the condition that within the three prescribed days he should get to the truth, what-ever that truth might be: the affair could become another international scandal, which the yellow press would feast on, the Colonel emphasized, apparently obsessed by the taste and colour of the mass media, and the only way to cut it dead was by coming up with the truth. And he repeated his organic military salute.

Standing in front of the Vedado mansion from which the currently American, now deceased Miguel Forcade had set out to an unforeseen fate and whither he had returned eleven years later, Mario Conde wondered what might be the price for finding the truth required by his boss . . . First of all, why did they kill Miguel Forcade like an animal?

"What's our way in going to be, Conde?" Sergeant Manuel Palacios asked eventually, after slotting away the aerial and locking the car under the irritated gaze of his superior.

"The dead man's parents live here and his wife must be here as well, as she came on the trip to visit . . . For the moment let's just try to find out a bit about Miguel Forcade the man."

"Who was a bastard?"

"We can take that as read, but we need to know the brand and type," the Count emphasized as he opened the gate leading to the '20s mansion, equally a victim of neglect and apathy, crying out for a new lick of paint.

The surrounding garden was a damp, bushy arbour, with a peculiar mixture of shrubs, flowers, creepers, exuberant trees and grasses, although all that floral disorder seemed exquisitely cared for, as witnessed by the tracery of clearly marked paths through the undergrowth that spread across the whole plot. The work of a hand both rigorous and tolerant in relation to the desires of plants was evident in that small tropical forest, where the Count registered the majestic crest of a silk-cotton tree, the dark, gnarled fruits of a *mamey* and the prehistoric miracle of two *anonales*, still laden with their violently green pomegranates, owners of delicate, white hearts divided into a hundred black seeds. As he walked along the path to the house, the Count came across an overgrown *picuala* and, as he passed by, he dared pick up one of its tiny flowers, which existed in a strange melding of colours, between red and white.

"Josefina loves the scent of the *picuala*," he said, knocking on the door after he'd put the flower in his pocket.

The face of the old lady who opened the door was as exhausted from lack of sleep as the Count's: the wrinkles around her eyes were a deep brown and her gaze was veiled by a grey mist from prolonged insomnia or several hours of sobbing. There were remains of white magnesia at the corners of her mouth, fit to turn Mario Conde's stomach. The policemen introduced themselves, apologized for coming without prior warning and explained why they were there: to speak to the family of Miguel Forcade.

"I am his mother," responded the old lady, whose voice seemed younger than her face. Much to the Count's relief, the woman's tongue executed a precise cleaning exercise and the white cream disappeared. "Come in and sit down, I'll get his wife. My husband is the one who can't come down, he's feeling very poorly today. He is very sick, you know. And this has made him feel much worse, poor man," she concluded, as her voice faded away, but without losing that youthful spark that so surprised the Count.

"And which of you is the gardener?"

The old lady smiled, as if some of her lost energy was flowing back. "He is . . . Alfonso is a botanist and that garden is his. Pretty, isn't it?"

"A poet I know would say it is the place to be really happy," said the Count, recalling his friend Eligio Riego.

38

"Alfonso would be delighted to hear you . . ." conceded the old lady, her eyes moistening.

"Who is it, Caruca?"

A voice emerged from the passage that must lead to the bedrooms and was soon joined by the figure of its owner.

"Oh, forgive me," said the newcomer, in whose wake came a ruddy, frowning man, coughing slightly, with the dry, uncontrollable persistence of a smoker.

"This is Miriam, my daughter-in-law," noted the old lady. "And this is an old friend of hers . . ."

"Adrian Riverón, at your service," said the man, his cough erupting again.

Even before he said hello and introduced himself, the Count's first reaction was to start counting on his fingers, but he restrained himself from a sense of arithmetic politeness: according to the report he'd read, Miguel Forcade was forty-two years when he left Cuba, so he must have been fifty-three when he died, right? But now he was looking at a blonde woman, perhaps with an excess of blonde, which he suspected might be the result of vigorous bleaching, with sturdy thighs barely hidden by shorts and prominent breasts under a thin top, poked by nipples set on perforating the material. But the Count also had to look at her decidedly youthful face, where (grey, green, or were they blue?) eyes glinted from between her curly black eyelashes: thirty at a pinch, estimated the policeman, now able to think straight again, swallowing, counting on mental fingers and calculating that in his forties before he left Cuba Forcade had married a woman not yet in her twenties. Basically, he shouldn't give up hope, he started to speculate, before he called himself to order.

"I was telling your mother-in-law how we have come

39

to ask a few questions about Miguel . . . I know it's a bad moment for you, but we are very keen to solve this case as soon we can."

"You are really very keen?" said Miriam, distilling irony, as she sat down in one of the armchairs.

Her friend, coughing again, swung round like a bewildered seagull trying to find his bearings and found respite against the high back of the chair Miriam had chosen, as if he felt a need to guard the young woman's back. The Count's gaze, inhibited by protectionist Adrian, drifted from those handsome legs, and it was only then the policeman realized he hadn't carried out his customary detailed study of the scene and discovered, unusually, that the room merited the same scientific attentions he'd devoted to the woman. Because it contained the clearest proof of Miguel Forcade's past as the deputy provincial director of Expropriated Property: furniture in different historical styles, mirrors in carved frames, porcelain from various eras, locations and schools, two enormous grandfather clocks, alive and kicking, a number of canvases with hunting and mythological scenes, still lives and nineteenth-century nudes – which could be dated by the area of flesh exposed – as well as a couple of – Persian? flying? – carpets and lamps that only had to cry Tiffany to prove that was exactly what they were: particularly one on a metal stand, in the guise of a tree trunk supporting a glass frond that was open and weary, perhaps from a visible surfeit of warm fruit ripening from red to purple. Impressed by the accumulation of so many undoubtedly valuable relics, the Count surmised their source to be the expropriation of treasures abandoned by the Cuban bourgeoisie and then abandoned again by Miguel Forcade when he inexplicably defected. A man who knew how to take his chances, he thought, corroborating this conclusion with another glance at Miriam's handsome flesh, to whom he decided to return the ball soaked in irony: "It's good to see how a family can bring together so many nice, valuable things, isn't it?" And his hand described a circle that ended on the woman.

"I expect you'd be interested to know where it all came from?" she riposted, and the Count then realized she would be a difficult mouthful to swallow.

"Of course I would. It may help us find out that truth, an interest in which so much excites your suspicion."

"I'm not suspicious, Lieutenant. I only know they mutilated Miguel and killed him, here in Cuba. And that's a fact."

The Count observed Miriam's hardened face and the tears beginning to run down the old lady's rotund cheeks. The silent maternal lament might disarm him so he concentrated on the beautiful widow.

"That's precisely why we are here . . . And because this deed reeks of revenge we need to know more about your husband's past . . . My colleague and I have a responsibility to find out the truth, and I think if you help us it will be much easier, don't you?"

Miriam gave a long, tired sigh. She seemingly accepted the truce, but didn't grant the Count the benefit of a momentary hesitation.

"What I think is hardly the issue now. Just tell me, what would you like to know?"

"Where did Miguel say he was going and why did he go alone?" asked the Count, looking into the young woman's eyes, though it was the old lady who replied.

"From the moment he got here, he hardly went out into the street, because . . . well, you know the story: he was afraid they'd keep him here, or something similar, because of the way he left . . . But that Thursday he said he wanted to go for a drive, to see a bit of Havana, and that he preferred to do so alone, because Miriam was going to be at her sister's, in Miramar. And he left here around five."

Manolo looked at the Count, as if seeking permission and the lieutenant's eyes acceded. He knew his colleague was more skilful in that kind of verbal enquiry and besides if he were silent he could study at leisure the riches gathered in that room: that's why he looked at the Tiffany lamps again and then at Miriam's eyes, breasts and legs, all hot and anxious because it was now he could best evaluate the woman: Miriam was surely a ripe fruit, her shiny, smooth skin, like a beautiful peel protecting all those fleshly assets fashioned over time: and now she was ready to be eaten, her flavours, scents and textures at their zenith, beyond which it was impossible to scale higher. Her disturbing, full ripeness risked possible degeneration into flab as soon as the climactic moment passed: in the meantime it could be a banquet for the gods. A pity the fruit wouldn't fall into his hands, the Count concluded, trying to pick up the thread of the conversation, driven by the insistent gaze of Adrian Riverón.

"Could there be someone who wanted to take revenge because of something that happened in Cuba before Miguel left?"

"That is very difficult to know, comrade," replied the old lady, and she looked to her daughter-in-law for support. "He worked in important areas here, but as you know he took nothing from Cuba, and didn't create a fuss over there . . ."

"He didn't want to come," interjected Miriam, uncrossing her legs: a vampirish Count studied the red circle of blood visible on the thigh that had borne the weight of the other leg. "He came because his father is very ill and Miguel always loved him deeply. But he came fearing they'd get at him. He knew only too well he hadn't been forgotten. And he was right, wasn't he? That's why what happened to him makes one think –"

"Please, Miriam," hesitantly interjected the man called Adrian Riverón, not coughing on this occasion, though he remained on his feet, efficiently protecting the woman's possibly vulnerable rearguard.

"Let me say what I want to say . . ." she demanded, keeping her eyes on the Count.

"Please, forgive her," intervened Adrian, rushing to her defence again, smiling at the policemen. "She's upset and she's always been strong-willed." And he cleared his throat a couple of times.

"There's nothing to forgive," said the Count, smiling, his gaze captivated by Miriam's eyes: dry, magnetic eyes. "Señora, since you suspect so much, I want you to be frank and tell me something: whom did your husband go to visit that Thursday afternoon? And why did he prefer to go by himself, if he was really so afraid to venture out into the street?"

Like another hurricane, the name of Gerardo Gómez de la Peña stirred Mario Conde's Ocean of Sunken Nostalgia. He still remembered him, in his cool, light blue *guayabera* and pale pink trousers, made from soft but strong material, descending with elegantly microscopic precision to his shoes: that unforgettable pair of shoes. The Count closed his eyes and saw them again: moccasins that were comfortable just to look at, a mahogany shading furiously to brown, hand-stitched edging and the lightest of soles, origins beyond dispute: they just had to be Italian. That afternoon

43

Gerardo Gómez de la Peña entered the university theatre, and his feet entered the Count's desires for ever: *those* were the shoes he wanted, he concluded, dismissing the thought, as he contemplated his stiff, heavy Russian boots, (like the heads of our Russian brothers, they would say), which they had to wear to school every day given the terrifying emptiness of their shoe cupboard. His father had died a year earlier and the family was totally broke. The idea he should abandon university and look for a job was not a possibility but an urgent necessity, and now Mario Conde wondered whether those shoes he saw walk by him – still a subject of dreams; he'd never owned anything remotely similar – weren't the reason he became a policeman, who needed to make some money as quickly as possible and give his Russian boots, more suited to walking the steppes, tundra or taiga, to some less proletarian colleagues.

Gómez de la Peña climbed to the podium, followed by the Dean of the Faculty and the Secretary-General of the Youth. The super-minister was the protagonist of the evening, since from the peaks of his historico-economic responsibilities he was apparently the wondrous genius charged with giving material form to all the island's productive miracles: to take the socialist economy to its final, magnificent conclusions till – through these conclusions and that economy – the country was transformed into a land free of under-development, monoculture, unemployment, shortages, social differences and even potholes in its roads, euphemistic gaps in its gastronomy or waiting lists at bus stations.

And the alchemist of Planning, the prophet of prosperity expounded on that promised land to an audience that was literally captive: anyone who didn't attend would have a black mark inserted on his record, the course directors had made clear, and the Count wasn't that sorry to hear for almost two hours about the future realities he would enjoy, after a maximum of two five-year plans, because, according to the comrade minister's speech, it was a fact that comrade Mario Conde would very soon possess all the shoes he needed, was it not?

Twelve years later history had demonstrated there wasn't the remotest possibility that any of those promises would be kept, and not even several tons of faith and preferential trade would have been enough to spark the miraculous salvation. So that is why Gerardo Gómez de la Peña now wore pyjamas and beach sandals that displayed his thin, misshapen, irredeemably ugly toes. The power of shoes, thought the Count, and only then did he look at the smile on the man's face as he saw the two policemen arrive. Of the abundant but greying hair that he remembered, the Count now saw only unkempt fringes, which had been allowed to grow to incredible lengths and then combed from above his left ear to cover his smooth pate and fall over his right ear before descending to the nape of his neck, as if that act of hairy trickery prevented its owner from being merely a bald man who accepted his state in a stoic, dignified way. The pink face of yesteryear had turned into a very ancient, poorly preserved parchment, rent with cracks and crevices: ten years of political, social and nutritional marginalization had been enough to age that fallen angel, mutated from one day to the next into the devil behind economic imitation and commercial surrender that had devastated any planned growth in the productive spheres, by introducing Australian techniques for cutting sugar cane, Czech bottling into the breweries and Siberian

45

methods into agriculture, among the many horrors one still recalled but which people never now mentioned. The thunderous dismissal of Gómez de la Peña had resonated for a couple of weeks because the entire blame for the predictable catastrophe had fallen on that cold, hated technocrat's head: all in all the economic bonanza had never been planned for present generations, who were required only to demonstrate inexhaustible austerity and a continually renewed, almost Christian spirit of sacrifice. Besides, it was a nonsense to copy foreign models, with the constant sun and heat of the island, wasn't it? We should work looking only to the future and independently, was the conclusion of the summary sentence that took Gerardo Gómez de la Peña out of circulation and decreed the end of any possibility that a fellow like Mario Conde could ever wear a pair of shoes like the ones he'd seen on that unforgettable night: brown, supple, Italian . . .

Nonetheless, the dethroned leader had clung to some of a super-minister's old privileges: the house in Nuevo Vedado, for example, which the Count pledged to pay more attention to, for it really warranted it, with its structure of asymmetric blocks, brick walls, multi-coloured windows, the unusual spaces designed by fifties futurists who found one of their most fertile terrains in that upper-middle-class stronghold, far from the rabble that had landed in the heart of Vedado. Indeed, wondered the Count, who might have originally owned that mansion?

The policemen explained the reason for their visit and the execrated Gómez de la Peña replied that he already knew about Miguel Forcade's death and invited them to come into what he called the reception-cum-living room. A sofa and four whitewashed, welcoming willow chairs were arranged around a similarly coloured table made of the same material, and on the wall where the sofa rested, the Count was struck by the magnificent reproduction of a work possibly by Cézanne that, apart from the plants, was the room's only adornment: a street spread over the canvas – that didn't seem Parisian but from a small coastal or provincial town – lined with trees caressed by an insistent wind, bowing their heads, their leaves dissolving into a round palette of autumnal greens and twilight ochres, which, thanks to a recondite magic, spread their own light, cleverly extracted from the blend of invisible breeze and leaves about to be swept away by the wind into a blue surround of sky, striped by brushstrokes of magenta.

"Do you like it, Lieutenant?" Gómez de la Peña whispered, when he saw the attention the policeman was devoting to the painting.

"I generally like Cézanne and the impressionists, although I didn't know this work. Is it a Cézanne?"

"No, it isn't a Cézanne . . . It's an early Matisse, but very few people know it because it's not in a single catalogue in the world."

"And where's the original?"

Gómez de la Peña passed his hand through the long strands of hair covering his head.

"Everybody asks the same question . . ." and he smiled, as the pause lengthened and he moved his arm as if looking for the direction in which the canvas lay. "This *is* the original," he declared emphatically, pointing at the painting.

Now it was Mario Conde's turn to smile: that stigmatized old sinner had also preserved his sense of humour.

"Don't laugh, Lieutenant. That is the original," insisted Gómez de la Peña. "Take a closer look if you like . . . but if you're not a specialist, you must take my word . . . It is a Matisse."

The Count looked at his host, gnawed by doubt. Could it be a real Matisse? As far as he knew, there wasn't a single picture on the island by that painter, one of the most highly valued in the world, and he thought it absurd to find a work of his, an impressionist one into the bargain, on the wall of a private house. If it were original, it must be worth a real fortune: one million, two million, three . . .? he wondered, as he closed in on the painting and enjoyed its thick pasted texture, the flat, vigorous colours, able to create that magic effect of generating light, while in one corner he found the master's clumsy, valuable signature, discreet and disturbing, with no date, and unable to restrain the policeman within he told himself it would be good to find out how that wonder had come to rest in the reception-cum-living room of fallen angel Gerardo Gómez de la Peña.

"I can see you like the painting, Lieutenant, but you still doubt it's genuine. And if you know something about art, it makes sense you should be suspicious, because this is the only Matisse that exists in Cuba. Everyone who knows something about art reacts similarly when seeing it for the first time: and that's precisely why I decided to put it there, so people would see it, be suspicious, then be convinced and finally astonished I am the owner of such beauty . . . But first let me tell you that the painting is rather unique. As far as I've been able to find out, Matisse painted it around 1904, before his famous fauve period, which one can already glimpse here: can you not see the freedom of colour, those pure tones, the strong line that gives such expressive power . . .? In a word, it is an alarming clarion call from a genius's bugle, hanging on that humble wall. Of course, the fact that I have the canvas there makes me feel important, and I'm not ashamed to say so. Although I'm nothing now and no one publishes or reads my books on political economy, lots of people still remember me and I've kept a few friends in high places. Consequently, whenever someone visits I bring them in here, and if they know something about art, they'll ask the same question as you, and I always respond the same way: yes, that *is* the original . . . and I enjoy seeing them water at the mouth. For almost twenty years I kept it in my bedroom, and almost no one saw it, because I thought it would be showing off to exhibit a Matisse in the living room of a leader like me, with a historical mission, you know? And besides I wanted to avoid tempting thieves and ideological purists, two equally appalling breeds. Do you how much money's hanging on my wall? Certainly at least three and a half million dollars . . . But I prefer to see the looks of astonishment than to hide the painting in my bedroom or to sell it and keep the money in a Swiss bank, because it would also be a crime, according to the laws of this country, to have such money, isn't that so? Of course, it is a bother to have the work exhibited there: every day you have to unhook it and put it away and one is always scared some madman will come in broad daylight with a pistol and do his utmost to get hold of it. Though I decided to assume that risk, so others could feel what you feel . . . It is a minor, aesthetic revenge on oblivion and the ingratitude of society. But what will be of most interest to you is that Miguel Forcade is the man responsible for the oil painting being there. Yes, you heard me correctly. The problem is that Miguel was always a fairly uncultured man, even more so when he was twenty-five and worked in the Department for Expropriated Property. I remember how he only valued the paintings that looked antique and had classical landscapes or characters. Just imagine, one day he almost went mad because he found *Las Meninas* in a house in Vedado . . . Poor fellow. Well, at the time I was working for the National Institute for Urban Reform and was responsible for allocating the houses abandoned by the *gusanos* heading north. My institute would get involved after Miguel's department had done its duty. They confiscated any things of any value, sent them to a variety of destinations, and afterwards we would decide what to do with the houses: whether they should be offices, student residences, or for a specific individual, or if they should be given to several families to divide up. But the day that Matisse and I met up, they'd fallen behind with their work and when I arrived the people working for Expropriated Property were still there. I can remember how it was barely a month after the Bay of Pigs in May '61, and those wretched bourgeois were fleeing the Red Peril in droves, and abandoning riches accumulated over several lifetimes . . . But it was a big coincidence, I can tell you, for I almost never participated in the selection of houses. The problem was we urgently needed several places for scholarship students from Oriente who were going to be concentrated in Miramar. That's why I was in the area and arrived unannounced in that house containing real artistic treasures. You know, as far as I can remember, there was a Goya, a Murillo, several minor impressionist works and this Matisse. But the people working with Miguel, who were even less cultured than he, decided this work had no artistic merit and had most certainly been painted by the son of the household, for the lad was a late-developing tropical landscape artist who imitated the Masters with the perfectionist candour of all eternal imitators. And as I told them I liked the painting they registered it there and then as confiscated property and sold it to me for five hundred pesos . . . Inside I've got the ownership documents, if you want to see them, as well as the certificates of authenticity signed by specialists from New York and Paris, which were pinned to the back of the painting. That was how three million dollars came to rest in this humble abode. What do you make of that . . .? Now I'll tell you how it was that very same Miguel Forcade who did me a favour that day in 1961, who got me the flat when he stayed in Spain in '78. Because after he left the Expropriated Property department, they sent him to study economics in the Soviet Union, and he returned in '68 with brilliant grades. He was then connected to the Department for Planning and the Economy, and when they appointed me as head, in '75 I asked him to work for me and he became my right-hand man. I can tell you that if he was a complete ignoramus as regards modern French painting, he was almost a genius as an economist, so much so I was often afraid that he might usurp my place. But one fine day, totally unexpectedly, Miguel Forcade defected and disappeared in Spain before finally making the leap to the United States. That led to a round of investigations, as you can imagine, and although they never found anything to incriminate him or cause for his defection, various irregularities came to light in the department that forced me to give the fullest explanations I've ever given in my life . . . The hornets' nest was disturbed and when economic plans started to fail because of the cadres' lack of discipline and the country's lack of a work culture, it was decided a head should roll and none better than mine . . . thus was I left without a single hair."

"What do you think of my story?" asked Gómez de la Peña when his wife left the room, after she'd poured their coffees.

"More of the usual," responded the Count, looking for the precise, meaningful adjective that would seem inoffensive to the man who might lead him to Miguel Forcade's past, which is where he tried to move him on to. "And why did Miguel come to see you after what he had done to you?"

"As far as was possible, Miguel and I were friends. Perhaps you know that friendship doesn't prosper when power is at stake: anyone could be a regicide and Miguel had all the qualifications to become my successor. But even so I trusted him, in as much as you could trust anyone, obviously. And now we were both nobodies he came to see how I was and apologize to me for what he'd done."

"Is that all?" persisted Manolo, making himself comfortable on the edge of his chair.

"I think so . . . Unless he wanted to see what the life of a deposed leader was like . . . That's possible, isn't it?"

"Did he by any chance tell you why he'd stayed in Spain?"

Gómez de la Peña smiled wanly and shook his head.

"I didn't ask him directly, but we did have a good chat . . . And he said nothing in particular: only that he'd anticipated what would happen three years later, and knew the development programmes weren't going to work . . . In short, a display of prophetic gifts I found unconvincing."

"And didn't he say why he'd returned to Cuba?" continued the sergeant, not deigning to look at his boss.

"He just told me his father was ill. He was very old. I even thought he'd died."

"And you believed him?"

"Was there any reason not to, Sergeant?"

"Perhaps, as you knew him well . . . And didn't he say where he was heading once he left here?"

"He left at about seven, or just after, because it was already dusk. He said he wanted to see a relative of his, but didn't mention who. But he did say it was very important to him."

"He said it was important to him?"

"Yes, I'm sure he did."

"Did he say he was afraid of returning to Cuba?"

"He said something of the sort. But I tried to reassure him. After all, a thousand others have done what he did . . . Lately it's almost become a fashion, hasn't it? And he had no cases pending or anything similar. As far as I know, he didn't take anything with him."

"Not even one of those objects he expropriated in the '60s and which could fetch as many dollars as that painting?"

"Not as far as I'm aware. But I didn't check his suitcase at the airport, though chance would have me accompany him that day."

"And do you remember if anyone in Customs checked it?"

Gómez de la Peña looked at the ceiling before answering.

"Forgive me, Sergeant, but I'm moved by your naïveté . . . As a leader, Miguel Forcade left through the diplomatic channel."

Manolo elegantly assumed his moving innocence

53

and continued. "So no one checked anything and he could have taken out whatever he wanted."

"Forgive me, Manolo," interjected the Count, troubled by his subordinate's naïveté and by his own for thinking a mere copy of a Matisse could be on that privileged wall in that equally privileged residence, permanently enjoyed by a logically privileged civil servant, who in some safe spot in the house must also possess, in his own name, the documents crediting him as the owner of the building. "Tell me, Gerardo, but please tell me the truth: did you give Miguel Forcade the house where he used to live?"

The old dethroned minister restrained his smile, but didn't banish it from his face entirely: "That's what you'd expect, I suppose?"

"Yes, in the same way you assigned yourself this house."

"True enough," admitted Gómez de la Peña. "Just as it's true I assigned all the houses abandoned by the *gusanos* for several years, in Miramar, in Siboney, in Vedado, in the Casino Deportivo, and so on and so forth . . . It was our turn, after all. The judgement of history, a reward for our sacrifice and struggle, the time of the dispossessed, you remember?"

The Count took a deep breath to relieve the tension. He felt a desire to twist the neck of that expert in cynicism who had enjoyed the socio-historico-politico-material privilege of giving, granting, conceding, deciding, administering, distributing favours from his position as a trusted leader, and in the name of the whole country. He felt his arrogant confession of the way he wielded power to be an insult: he created networks of compromise and debt, corrupted all the byways where he left his slimy tracks. It was no doubt because of people like Gómez de la Peña that he'd been in the police for more than ten years, deferring his own life, to try to dent their overbearing complacency and, if possible, make them pay for some of the crimes that could never be paid for. But this bastard's slipping from my grasp, he thought, as he observed the pyjamas that represented the comfortable sentence he was seeing out: a remoteness from power that, nevertheless, didn't deprive him of a house in the best part of Havana, of the Soviet car he kept in the garage nor even a Matisse worth three and a half million dollars, which he'd legally acquired – and no one would ever know if that was true – for five hundred Cuban pesos, for personal enjoyment and the morbid game he could play with his visitors. If only I could catch you out some way, you son of a bitch, he told himself, trying to smile as he spoke: "If you can bear to be frank yet again, please answer a further question: don't you think it's really shameful that you've got a painting worth millions hanging on your wall, one you bought using your position, when down in the city there are people who spend their week eating rice and beans after working an eight- or ten-hour day and sometimes without even a wall on which to hang a calendar?"

Yet again Gerardo Gómez de la Peña smoothed the pathetic camouflage over his embarrassing bald pate and looked the detective lieutenant straight in the eye: "Why should I personally feel ashamed, a retired old man who likes to look at that painting? From what I gather, Lieutenant, you don't know this neighbourhood very well; there are houses just as comfortable as mine, with other equally beautiful paintings and heaps of beautiful African wood and ivory sculptures, acquired by more or less similar means, where Nicaraguan furniture is all the rage, where they call their servants 'comrade' and breed exotic dogs that enjoy a better diet than sixty per cent of the world's population and eighty-five per cent of the nation's ... No, of course I'm not ashamed. Because life is as the old conga ditty says: if you hit the jackpot, go for it ... And too bad for the fellow who doesn't, but that fellow got well and truly fucked, didn't he?"

Night cloaked the city in two minutes, but the dark sky was still empty, completely indifferent to the flurry of clouds on its predestined path towards the island. His mouth lined by the sour aftertaste left by interviews with characters of that ilk, the Count asked Manolo to drive back to Headquarters so he could fulfil one of the agreements he made: to give the first of his daily reports to Colonel Molina.

"What are you going to say, Conde?"

"That I'm beginning to be grateful to him for giving me this case. Because I'm sure I'll break one of these bastards' legs."

"I hope it's this fellow's. Calling me naïve ..."

"But he really got under your skin."

Manolo forced a smile and asked his boss for a cigarette. He sustained his habit of smoking a little without ever making prior investments.

"And do you think he's connected to Forcade's death?"

"I don't know, I'm not convinced. What do you think?"

"I'd rather not say as yet, because if Forcade did come to reclaim the painting or anything else of value he might have given Gómez de la Peña, this guy would be capable of anything, wouldn't he? But what we really need to find out is who the relative was Forcade had to see in order to resolve important business. I mean, if it's true what de la Peña says and that relative exists . . ."

Mario Conde lit his own cigarette as the sergeant turned into the parking lot at Headquarters.

"Perhaps Miriam knows . . ." he said.

Manolo's violent braking spoke for itself. "Conde, Conde, you want to burn in that fire?"

"What fire are you on about, Manolo? I need to speak to her, right now . . ."

"I know you only too well," he muttered, parking the car in its space. "You couldn't keep your eyes off that blonde."

"Well, she was worth some attention, wasn't she?"

Mario Conde wasn't surprised by the news that Colonel Molina had left at five p.m. The new boss was too much of a novice to know there were no fixed hours and that Major Rangel would be at Headquarters every day, including Sundays and the First of May. But perhaps if they'd have given him the chance, he might have been a good spy . . .

Back in his cubicle, the Count wrote his report, in which he told the Colonel he'd started the investigation, that he'd called in at Headquarters at half past six and that he'd try to carry out another interview that night. He took a breath, picked up the telephone and dialled the number of Miguel Forcade's old house.

"Is that you, Miriam?"

To go up or go down: that had always been the question. Because going down and up, going up and down the Rampa was the Count and his friends' first experience beyond their barrio. Catching the bus in the barrio and going on the long journey to Vedado, with the single purpose of going up and down, or down and up that luminous slope that was born – or died – in the sea, signalled the end of childhood and the onset of adolescence just as their older brothers' had been marked by the Literacy Campaign and that of their parents' generation by sexual initiation in the Pajarito or Colón neighbourhoods: it was tantamount to signing a Declaration of Independence, to feeling your own wings had grown, to knowing yourself physically and spiritually adult, although it really was not the case: now or ever. But they came to believe that all frontiers to adulthood were marked by that alluring avenue, which belonged to the sinful side in their adolescent lore, a slope they were to go up and down – or down and up – in droves, always aiming for an ice-cream at the top and the prize of the sea – always the sea, accursed and inevitable – at the bottom, though their only real obsession was to walk up and down the Rampa, unaccompanied by parents, hoping to find love on one of its street corners. It was almost a second baptism to ascend and descend that street that was like life itself, the only avenue in the city with pavements carpeted in polished granite, where you trod, aesthetically unaware, on unique mosaics fashioned by Wifredo Lam, Amelia Peláez, René Portocarrero, Mariano Rodríguez and Martínez Pedro, because your eyes were glued to the captivating neon signs of night clubs that were banned till the hurdle of a sixteenth birthday was cleared – The Vixen and the Crow, Club 23, The Grotto Cocktail Club – to the mysteries of the Cuba Pavilion and May Salon, exhibiting the last cry of the avant-garde, flanked by the two best cinemas in Havana, showing strange films with titles like *Pierrot le Fou, Citizen Kane, Stolen Kisses* or *Ashes and Diamonds*, which you struggled to see though they were impossible to enjoy. And you also practised urban mountaineering to catch a fleeting glimpse of a few underfed tropical hippies, fake and already damned, or else take a mocking glance at those pansies who insisted on showing what they were, and conduct a drooling survey of the mini-skirts that had only just hit the island, first worn on that incline where all the rivers of the new times seemed to flow: including the first rapids of intolerance, whose rigours they had to flee, though they were still such young, correct and dewy-eyed students, when the politically and ideologically correct hordes started to persecute youths, armed with scissors ready to snip any hair that fell beneath the ear or widen trousers whose thighs couldn't encompass a small lemon: sad recollections of scissors and armoured cars exorcising pernicious cultural penetration, led by four long-haired English lads who repeated such reactionary, pernicious slogans as All You Need Is Love ... Politics and hair, consciousness and fashion, ideology and arse, the Beatles and bourgeois decadence, and at the end of the road the Military Units to Aid Production with their prison-like rigours as a corrective to shape the New Man.

The Count was surprised by the exaggerated innocence of his own youthful initiation as he made that unexpected autumnal ascent, on the cusp of thirty-six, more than twenty years after he'd made his first ascent – or was it descent? – with Rabbit, Dwarf, Andrés, perhaps Pello as well, each armed with a cigarette, chewing a rubber band as if it were enemy chewing gum, with a dream in their hearts – or perhaps a bit lower down. (*All you need is love*, right?) The Count rediscovered on that very same Rampa, which Heraclitus of Ephesus would have dialectically described as different, his hunting ground from the old days, now all in darkness, closed clubs, a dingy Pavilion, the boarded-up pizzeria and the absence of that long-gone girlfriend he would wait for on the corner by the Indo-China shop, where they now sold what must be the last watches sent from a Moscow that was every day more distant and impervious to tears. It was all far too pathetic, but at once moving and squalid, as he replayed that innocent snapshot of his awakening to life, and the policeman on active service thought he could see some remote causes of later disappointments and frustrations: reality had turned out not to be a question of capricious, wilful ascents and descents, unconsciously alternated, with the sea or an ice-cream as a goal, but a struggle to go up and not down, to keep on up, to go up and stay up, for ever and ever, pursuing a philosophy of finding a room at the top from which they had been excluded and definitively locked out – Andrés was right again – and sentenced – almost to a man – to the eternal labour of Sisyphus: to go up only to go down, to go down only to go back up, knowing you'd never stay at the top, getting older and more exhausted, as when he climbed up that night, after walking down, looking for the blonde now waving at him from the corner of Coppelia and who enquired of the Count as he walked up to her: "What's up, Lieutenant? Anyone would think you're about to burst into tears."

"I am, but I won't . . . The fact is I've just found out that some nice kids I knew have just died. But nothing to worry about . . . Anyway, where shall we go and talk?"

The woman stroked her hair and looked to the heavens for an answer. "The Coppelia is impossible, though I do fancy an ice-cream. Shall we go down to the Malecón?"

"Well, back we go down again," said the Count, as he set off in search of the sea.

"I think I made a bad choice, don't you? They only fished the corpse of my dead husband out of this very same sea two days ago and we still haven't been able to bury him. They say tomorrow . . . It's complete madness . . . Do you know something? The worst aspect of Miguel's death was that they threw him into the sea: he had some complex or other and didn't like bathing on the beach. But I like the sea, any sea . . ."

The Count also looked towards the coast, on the other side of the wall, and saw the waves gently lapping against the rocks.

"The hurricane's heading this way," he said, looking at the woman.

"You think it will get this far?"

"Sure it will."

"Well I'm off as soon as he's buried. I mean, if you'll let me."

"I have no objections," acknowledged the Count almost without thinking what he was saying.

In fact he'd have preferred for Miriam to stay: something about her strength – and thighs, and face, and hair and those eyes protected by eyelashes like twisted bars, which made him wonder, poetical as the Count was, whether she would ever go deaf, and that was why God gave her those eyes – attracted him as if it were fated: the blonde, presumably fake, reeked of bed, like roses smell of roses. It was something that seemed natural and endemic and it made him imagine he might breathe that scent in fact in a bed, with its four legs weakening, when she commented: "After all, there's

61

nothing for me here," and she looked at her feet, prey to a persistent pendulum.

Rising from the floor where he'd been lying on the now-shattered dream bed, the policeman searched for an exit: "What about your family?"

Miriam's sigh was long, possibly theatrical.

"My brother Fermin's the only member of my family I care about. The rest got upset when I started with Miguel, and later, when I went to Miami, they practically excommunicated me . . . The assholes," she said, almost unable to contain her rage. "But now I've come with dollars, they don't know which altar to put me on . . . All for a few jeans, designer T-shirts and a couple of Chinese fans."

"And why do you care about your brother?"

"It was through him I met Miguel . . . they worked together. And always got on well. He was the only one who didn't condemn me . . . He's also been the unluckiest in the family. He was in jail for ten years."

"What did he do?"

"Money problems in the firm he worked for."

"Fraud?"

"Are we talking about Miguel or Fermín?"

"Miguel, of course . . . But I need to know more. Who is Adrian, for example?"

"What's he got to do with any of this?"

The Count effortlessly allowed patience to come to his aid. He had to wave his cape at the bull in each confrontation and, without goading, try to guide it to the right pen.

"Nothing as far as I can see. But as he was with you today . . ."

"Adrian used to be my boyfriend, thousands of years ago. My first boyfriend," and something seemed to loosen the moorings of millennial woman.

"You've carried on being friends?"

She almost smiled as she said: "Friends . . .? We haven't seen each other for ten years. I have nothing here, and nothing there either. But I like talking to him: Adrian is a calm man who reminds me of what I once was and makes me think of what I might have been. That's all."

"I understand the car your husband was driving belonged to your brother, Fermín?"

"Yes," she replied, looking at the Count. "A '56 Chevrolet Fermín inherited from an uncle of mine, one of my mother's brothers. They confiscated the one the government gave him when he was jailed, in order to set an example . . . Is that the kind of thing you wanted to know?"

He lit a cigarette. It was pleasant being there, your back to the sea, opposite the Rampa, the night still young, in the company of that edible blonde. But a dead man floated on that still-becalmed ocean, like a dark, infinite mantle.

"That and much more . . . For example, do you think your husband's death was prompted by another husband's jealousy or something of the sort?"

"Are you mad? That was no jealous husband, more like a savage who –"

"It is a possibility though, isn't it?"

"No, of course not. That wasn't Miguel's style. He was more the romantic sort and besides . . . Well, recently he couldn't . . . if you get me?"

"Perhaps it was something that happened a long time ago and that he resurrected . . ." the Count continued, warming to Miriam's confiding tone.

"I've already told you it wasn't, but you can think whatever you want. That's why you're a policeman, even why they pay you to be one."

"True, but not enough," confessed the Count trying to relieve the tension before heading off in another direction. "And what other reason did Miguel have, apart from his sick father, to risk returning to Cuba after leaving the way he did?"

She looked him in the eye and the policeman saw such a profound gaze he could have lost himself in its pursuit.

"I don't understand you."

He was now the one to sigh, looking for the least stony path. "I mean did he return to resolve something he'd left hanging when he defected . . . Or perhaps to salvage something very important that he'd left behind . . ."

"I see where you're coming from. What sign are you?"

The Count breathed out before replying: "Libra . . . Is that what you wanted to hear?"

"Almost. You seem more a Sagittarian."

"But I'm a classic Libra, I swear to you . . . Was he after something?"

"Like what?"

"A very peculiar Matisse, for example. Or perhaps even a Goya. I don't know, something worth much more than a few Tiffany lamps . . ."

She turned her head to look at the sea for a moment. The sea was still there, she seemed to be confirming, before saying: "If that was why he came, he'd have told me . . . And do you think I'd tell you?"

"I've no idea, it all depends . . . Let's say it depends what's more valuable: what he was after, or seeing justice done."

"Forgive me, but you're talking rubbish . . . I still think they killed Miguel, I mean, the people who intended killing him . . . So, anything else?"

"Yes, there's something you perhaps know ... I spoke to Gómez de la Peña today and he says Miguel left his house claiming he had to see a relative of his about very important business. Can you throw any light on that?"

Down came her eyelids and her carnivorous eyelashes almost swallowed Mario Conde.

"No, he never mentioned that to me. I can't think which relative it was, even less what important business he might –"

"And why did Miguel go to see Gómez de la Peña?"

"They'd known each other for years, hadn't they? But I don't think they were friends. I don't know why he insisted on seeing him. Didn't Gómez tell you?"

"He told me but I wasn't convinced and I think he's a great liar. And if that's so, the truth might be somewhere there."

"So you want to find out the truth ..."

The Count threw his cigarette butt into the sea and expelled all the smoke from his lungs: "I'd also like to know how old you were when you married Miguel."

"Eighteen. And Miguel was forty. Anything else?"

The Count smiled again. "Miriam, why do you take everything as an insult?"

She was the one who then attempted a smile, but the smile never reached her lips: the grimace, brought on by tears, pulled her lips down. Down and down, like a waterfall that seemed unstoppable. But the large, shiny tears welling in her eyes seemed unreal: as if they came from another face, or another person, or other feelings, which were very far from that place, perhaps on the other side of the sea. Hollow pearls, concluded the Count.

"But don't you understand anything? Don't you

realize I don't know what the hell I'll do with myself when I get back to Miami?"

"Calle 8 was what I wanted to see first. Before getting to his house, before going to bed with him. I'd created Calle 8 in my head, and it was like a fiesta and a museum. I couldn't imagine it any other way: a place of entertainment, full of bright lights and bustle, where the music played at full volume and people walked along the pavements, happy and carefree, enjoying that Little Havana where the good and the bad survived that had died out in this other Havana. That's why it also had to be a place that had stayed still in time, where I would find a country I didn't know and had always wanted to discover: like this country was before 1959, a café on every street corner, a juke-box playing boleros in every bar, a game of dominoes in every arcade, a street where you could get anything without queuing or finding out whether it was your turn or not according to the ration book. Like every-body else I'd heard the stories here in Havana and turned that blissful Calle 8 into a myth, and trans-formed it mentally into something like the heart of Cuban Miami . . . I remember how it was already dark when we left the airport and after three years without seeing each other I told Miguel my first wish and he asked me what it was I wanted to see on Calle 8 that was so pressing, and I told him: 'That's it, Calle 8, Little Havana . . .' And to do something as simple and straightforward as eating a steak sandwich on a street corner.

"But that is all Calle 8 is: a street manufactured by the nostalgia of those who live in Miami and the dreams of those of us who want to go there. It is like

66

the fake ruins of a country that doesn't exist and never existed, and what remains is sick from an overdose of agonizing and prosperity, of hatred and oblivion. And consequently what I found, in the Calle 8 I'd been fabricating while waiting for my exit visa, was an ugly, lifeless, spiritless avenue, where almost nobody walked on pavements, where I heard no music I wanted to hear, found no carefree entertainment, or fry-up stalls selling the steak sandwich I wanted. Not even arcades with lots of columns, because there are no arcades in Miami . . . Three drunks cursed cars driving by. 'They came out from Mariel,' said Miguel almost contemptuously, and two old people like my grandparents drinking coffee by a restaurant . . . The rest was silence. The silence of death.

" 'Miami is a strange place; not at all like you imagine it, is it?' commented Miguel as we turned at the end of Little Havana and went off towards Flager and his house. 'Take a good look: Miami is nothing. Because it's got everything but lacks the vital element: it has no heart."

"He had a bad time of it in those early years. In Madrid he'd depended on the charity of nuns and when he finally made it to the United States and to Miami, he'd worked as a hotel porter, a toll-collector on the freeway, on a supermarket till, until he got a job in a firm that imported and exported produce from Santo Domingo, and then things improved. But he never got involved in politics, though he had several visits from people who tried to involve him. You know, with the position he held in Cuba, it might have smoothed his way if he'd made a few declarations and ingratiated himself with some of the local political grandees, but he'd already written to me in a letter how he was afraid someone would find out he'd been in charge of expropriating properties owned by many people who now lived in Miami. And people in Miami are not the kind to forgive and forget, I can tell you, although they like to turn a blind eye to the renegades who jump ship: it's mathematics really, a simple matter of addition, you know?

"That night, in his house, Miguel and I could at last talk about why he'd stayed in Spain without telling me anything beforehand and without any proper preparations. I'd never wanted to reproach him for his decision, for I knew there must be an important reason behind such an unexpected exit, living as we did in Cuba, with almost everything that one could wish for. Finally he told me his situation at work wasn't what it had been, and that any day it might have all collapsed, as it did not long after, and he also told me my brother Fermín was getting money together to buy a boat and would leave with me for Miami while he'd defect in Spain because he didn't want to leave by sea. You remember, his trauma about the sea? Well, not long after, they found Fermín had been embezzling, put him in jail and the whole plan collapsed . . . though I never knew anything about it.

"And so there we were, in Miami, a city Miguel couldn't stand, living on a wage and trying to relaunch his life, and I can tell you it wasn't easy. Calle 8 was like a premonition of everything I was and wasn't going to find in Miami and immediately I understood why Miguel said it wasn't how you thought it should be. Although it's full of Cubans, people don't live like they lived in Cuba anymore or behave as they behaved in Cuba. Those who don't work here can only think about working over there and possessing things: every day a new purchase, even though they are working themselves to death. Those who were atheist over here become religious and never miss a mass. Those who were militant communists become even more militant anti-communists, and when they can't hide what they were, they shout it from the rooftops, parade their renunciation like a trophy, fully aware of the consequences, you know? There are even people who left here cursing the place, and who are even more fucked in Miami and so they decide it's their business to say dialogue would be best and that it should all be sorted through talk. Besides, something similar is happening there to what happened here with the image of Miami: the people there are beginning to turn Cuba into a myth, to imagine it as a desire, rather than remembering it as it was, and they live in a half-way house, going nowhere: they can't decide whether to forget Cuba or be new people in a new country, and finally they're neither one thing nor the other, like me, because after living there for eight years I don't know where I want to be or what I want to be ... It's a national tragedy. Miami is nothing and Cuba is a dream that never existed ... The truth is I don't know why I'm telling you about my life, about Miguel and Fermín. Perhaps because I think I can trust you. Or probably because I'm afraid and know that the worst of all this is that I must go back and Miguel won't be there to help me to live that peculiar life he forced on me. Do you still think it's strange that I curse the day we decided to return to this blessed isle for ten days?"

After seven failed attempts, the dialling tone offered by the eighth public telephone he tried was like heavenly music to the Count's ears. At his wits' end he put his last coin in the slot and dialled Manolo's number and the ringing reaching him from infinity seemed a just reward for his labours.

"It's me, Manolo. Listen carefully, let's hope the line doesn't go dead."

"Sing on, Conde."

"Something very strange happened . . ."

"You've seen a ghost?"

"Shut up and listen, I've used my last coin: I spoke to Miriam and she told me half her life-story. I need you to get weaving as early as possible tomorrow and sort two things as quickly as possible: get the Immigration people to act so she can't leave for three or four days for whatever reason, but not let on that we're keeping her here. Get the people on the airline she travelled with to say there are no seats, no flights, that there's no petrol for the planes, whatever, but give her no inkling we're the ones forcing her to stay, get it? Because I need her to keep talking . . . The other thing you should do is look out information on her brother, Fermín Bodes Alvarez. From what Miriam told me, I reckon the man may know what Miguel Forcade was after in Cuba, because I'm now sure he was after something he couldn't take with him in '78 and that's why they killed him. Got all that?"

"Fuck, Conde, I'm not some retard. What should I do then?"

"Pick me up at the Boss's. I'm off to talk to him. I'll wait there."

And Mario Conde hung up, with a sigh of relief, as the cannon fire signalling it was nine p.m. reached him from far off. Time to close the gates to protect the city from pirates, and the policeman looked at his watch, which was slow, as if he were one to worry about precision, and his eyes returned to the figure of Miriam retreating up the Rampa, for the first time freely contemplating her from the rear, buttocks so perfect from the new perspective, compelling, firm, abundant flesh, like a magnet trailing in its wake the premonitions and desires of the Count, abandoned on the shore, a declaration full of doubt ringing in his ears: "I don't know what I'll do with my life," she'd said before taking off and now he thought he should have said: "Walk up the Rampa to heaven, and I'll go with you," but he hadn't and what he now saw at his feet was the dirty Calzada de Infanta, along which his bus was approaching, like a dark, rabid animal, impregnated with all the smells, anger and desires stirring in the city. "All aboard," he shouted at himself, as he ran to hang off a door.

"Just as well you got here."

"Why? You in need of a policeman?"

"Are you in a bloody mood?"

"I don't know yet."

Skinny Carlos smiled from his wheelchair and lit the cigarette between his lips.

"And how should I take that, wild man?"

"With all the shit, like I do . . . I feel fucked, hungry, sleepy, I've got to go on being a policeman and I have no luck with women. I mean, I don't have anything I should have, what more do you want?"

"For you to stop acting tragic and remember that the day after tomorrow is your birthday and that we must organize something."

"You sure, Skinny?"

"About what, Conde?"

"That we have to do something."

"You don't want to?"

"I don't know."

"Well, I do . . . You only hit thirty-six once in your life, you know."

"And eighteen, forty-nine and sixty-two. But hardly ever eighty-two."

"That's what I say. That's why I spoke to the gang and everybody'll be here on Wednesday. Andrés, Rabbit, even Miki . . . and I just have to let Red Candito know, though he'll probably not come."

"How come?"

"What do you mean, wild man? Didn't you know Candito's turned Adventist, Baptist or some such balls?"

Mario Conde was shocked beyond belief.

"You're kidding. Since when?"

"That was what I was told. That he's left the clandestine beer shop, that he's no longer doing the business and spends his days proclaiming Jehovah as his saviour."

"I don't believe it," retorted the Count. "He was always half a mystic, but to go Adventist, or Pentecostal . . .? Hey, but I've got to see this and anyway I need to talk to him. Ring Andrés and see whether he'll take us to Red's place and I'll eat what Jose kept for me."

When the Count entered the kitchen, the last strains of the final theme tune of the nine o'clock soap reached him from the living room. He found the meal Josefina had left for him just in case, under a plate on top of the cooker. She'd poured black beans on a mound of white rice and tucked a fried chicken leg away in one corner.

"The salad's in the refrigerator," he heard behind him, and the Count took a moment to turn round.

The loyalty shown by Skinny and his mother always disarmed him; it was so simple, elemental yet rock-solid. He had a place in that house he'd never had anywhere else, not even in his own home when his parents were alive, and the experience of belonging there softened him to the point that, on nights like tonight, when he felt heartily exhausted, disillusioned, rancorous, worried, destitute and full of angst, he was on the verge of tears, so when he turned round he opted to say: "So that animal in there scoffed all the chips as usual?"

"I told him to keep some for you, but he said he was sure you wouldn't come . . ."

"If you weren't here, I'd say he was a son of a . . . but better not, I suppose."

"That's up to you two," said Josefina, smiling her usual smile.

The Count put his plates on the table and looked at her.

"Sit down for a minute, Jose."

She obeyed and sighed plaintively.

"What's the matter? You tired?"

"Yes, I get more tired by the day."

"Hey, Jose, let me tell you something: your son's had the idea of celebrating my birthday here."

Josefina smiled again, now really enjoying herself.

"Is that what he told you? I'll soon start thinking he's that son of an individual you were about to mention. Because the idea was mine."

"But are you crazy, sweetheart? Don't you know what it will be like with all your son's drunken friends here?"

"Yours as well . . . It will be all right. I've already got the things I need for the meal."

"And where did you find the money?"

"Don't worry about that, it's all sorted."

"And what are you going to cook?"

"It's a surprise."

"You're just like your son," nodded the Count,

abandoning a chicken bone stripped of meat on the edge of his plate.

"Are you hungry?"

"When isn't he?" asked Skinny as he came into the kitchen.

"You ate my chips, you animal."

"Forget the chips and wash your hands, because Andrés is on his way."

"And where are you off to? If one might be so bold," asked Josefina, clearing the dishes from the table.

"To Red's place," said Mario, lighting up. "Your son says he's turned Baptist. Or Mormon? But I swear on my life I don't believe a word of it."

On the slippery slope to his fortieth year Red Candito was sure he was destined to die in the same place he'd been born: a rundown, promiscuous rooming house in Santos Suárez, walls falling apart, electric cables dangling from the eaves like poisonous tentacles. Being born and growing up there had moulded his way of life with an irremediable domestic fatalism: from early on he'd learned that you have to defend even your minimal playing space, with fists if necessary, and when he grew up he also learned how fists opened up other doors in life: respect between men, for example. That is perhaps why he befriended the Count and had remained a friend even when Mario entered the prickly clan of the police: he'd once seen him defend with his fists a dignity that had been hurt by the theft of a tin of milk, when they had gone together to a school in the countryside, and Candito had come to his defence then and ever since. Because loyalty also formed part of the code of his turf, and he practised it, whenever it was called for.

When they met, Candito had already twice repeated the first year of high school and was one of the first to let his hair grow long, to create from red, rebellious ringlets a saffron afro that earned him the nickname he still bore: he was Red and would always be so, even when he was active in a Protestant, Lutheran or Calvinist sect. At the time they got to know each other, Candito expressed himself with a peculiar level of violence that also had its own morality: nobody ever saw him abuse anyone smaller or weaker than himself and the respect his friends felt for him grew till it became a harmonious friendship. Then, when the Count and his other friends went to university, fate or destiny placed Red at the edges of a marginal existence bordering on illegality where he earned his living in the chinks left by state shortages and inefficiency: and the Count, as a policeman, had taken advantage of that situation. In exchange for the street wisdom Red brought him and for information useful in solving some of his cases, the lieutenant offered him, alongside friendship, the pledge of unconditional protection if it were ever necessary in his conflicts with the law. It was an agreement between gentlemen, backed by a single guarantee, the sense of honour and friendship they'd learned in the barrios and meeting-places of Havana, when such words still rang true.

Recently, however, Candito must have experienced a kind of mystical revelation. Contrary to what happened in his usual circles, where African religions ruled firm, promising pragmatically and comprehensively all kinds of protection and help in the material world (as well as in questions of love and justice, hatred and revenge), Red had begun to gravitate towards the Catholic Church, where, so he claimed, he was searching for a peace denied to him by the hostile, aggressive outside world. So, from time to time, he would go to mass or spend time in church, never taking confession, but praying his way, which meant asking God to grant peace and good health to him and his loved ones, including the three men who invaded his home well after ten o'clock at night.

Cuqui, the sinewy, obedient little mulatta now living with Red, opened the door and smiled when she recognized the new arrivals, who greeted her with a kiss.

"And where's your husband?" Carlos asked, looking into the small room where someone was monologuing on television about the excellent forecasts for the next sugar cane harvest.

"He's in church."

"At this time of night?"

"Yes, he sometimes gets back at eleven . . ."

"He's got a bad case," interrupted the Count, and Cuqui nodded.

She knew Candito's friends had a right to certain confidences that were denied her.

"If you want to go and look for him, it's just around the corner."

"What do you reckon, Conde?" hesitated Carlos. "He might not like that."

"I spend my life dragging Candito out of churches. Come on . . . Cuqui, get the coffee on, we'll have him here in no time," the policeman assured her, as he started pushing Carlos's chair again.

You could never have identified the Christian temple from its architectural appearance; it looked more like a warehouse, with a high tiled roof and double door, which when open hid the cross set there to indicate its function. Nevertheless, religious ecstasy spilled out of the place: the shouting and clapping of the faithful, intoning a rhythmic hymn of love to Jehovah, came down the street, impelled irrepressibly by a faith too vehement by half, and strong enough to halt the three friends in their tracks.

"That has to be it," commented Skinny Carlos.

"You really think we should go in, Conde?" asked Andrés, always on the reticent side, as Carlos and Mario exchanged glances. The chorus now sounded a couple of decibels louder, and the clapping quickened, as if the Jehovah they invoked was nigh.

"No, better not go in. I'll just take a peek to see if Red can see me."

Without thinking why he did so, the policeman pulled down his shirt, as if trying to tidy his unkempt appearance, and crossed the small doorway to put his head inside the sacred precinct. And he was moved by what he saw: that church had nothing in common with the concepts of church stored in the Count's Catholically trained brain. To begin with, there was no altar, always dominated by the image of the church's patron saint; all there was on the clean, whitewashed wall was a simple wooden cross that bore no crucified Christ. The walls, also unadorned by saints and decorations, had large windows open to the night. Nonetheless, there wasn't enough ventilation, and the Count's face hit a hot, sweaty atmosphere exuded by the heaving mass of faithful gathered there, clapping like the possessed, while they sang in chorus with the short, thin black man who, without dog-collar or soutane, acted as the leader of that communion with the divinity, shouting periodically: "Yeah, you are, Jehovah!" enthusing the flock, which bellowed "Yeah, hallelujah!" The Count finally spotted Candito's red head in the front rows and took a first step inside the church, when he was struck by a shocking disparity: he realized he was surrounded by people who knew of

God's existence and praised Him with an apparently inextinguishable physical and spiritual vehemence, and he was forced back to the door, driven by his evident inability to belong to that crowd of redeemed believers. Tidying his shirt yet again, beneath which he carried a gun, the Count returned to the street, racked by doubt: who was mistaken: he or all those people gathered in that church without altars or Christ? Those people who believed in something that could save them or he, a man who could hardly think of a couple of things worth saving?

"Fucking hell," he said to himself, as he reached his friends, and Carlos looked at him in alarm.

"What happened, Conde, did they throw you out?"

"No ... Yes ... Listen, I think we'd better wait outside."

"Hey, Candito, what the fuck are you doing as an Adventist, you, a half-Catholic who take your problems to an African high priest?" asked the Count, when they were finally able to rearrange the furniture in the small room to make space for Skinny Carlos's wheelchair.

The smell of the coffee Cuqui was preparing wafted their way from the kitchen, and, still marked by the evidence of faith he'd just observed, the Count's mind was now filled with the image of a rampant Candito clad in white castigating the evil one before a legion of the faithful.

"Don't fuck around, Conde, don't start interfering in people's lives," interrupted Carlos, and turned to Candito: "Hey, Red, so now you can't have a little drink, smoke or swear, or ..." and lowering his voice to a whisper, "or have a fling with a bit of skirt that offers itself?"

Candito shook his head: there was no hope for these guys.

"It's not like you think. I've not been baptized yet. I don't think I'm ready. I just go to the church every now and then and sit there."

"Singing and clapping?" asked the Count incredulously.

"Yes, and listening to people speak of love, peace, goodness, cleanliness of spirit, hopes of salvation, quiet and forgiveness . . . Hearing things people don't say elsewhere, spoken by people who believe in what they say. It's better than selling beer or buying stolen leather to make shoes, isn't it?"

"Yes, it's true. You're doing right," affirmed Andrés.

"What? And will you take the same righteous path?" the Count demanded, and immediately regretted his sarcastic tone.

"What the fuck is eating you, Conde? I said Red was doing right. That's all. Isn't it, Candito?"

Their host smiled. The Count searched him for visible physical changes and thought Red's smile seemed different: perhaps more peaceful, more accepting: strengthened and able to withstand jibes. A smile expressing a hope in belief.

"It makes sense for the Count to get like this, Andrés. Well, you know him better than I do . . . I once told him to watch out, because he was turning cynical, you remember, Conde?"

"Sorry, Red, it isn't what Andrés is thinking, but the fact is even after I've seen you in action I can't imagine you're really into that," replied the Count, trying to salvage something.

"And why can't you imagine me into that? Isn't it better than being a petty criminal for the rest of my life worrying every day in case the policeman knocking on

79

my door isn't you? Or downing a bottle of rum morning and night to forget how fucked I am, which is what you do? Isn't it better to pray and sing a bit, Conde, and think someone somewhere only wants you to have faith and be good? You know, Mario, I'm sick of all the shit out there . . ."

"You said 'shit', Candito," quipped Skinny, and Candito smiled. His inner peace is already becoming evident, thought the Count.

"Yes, of the shit everywhere. You know what my life's been like. But I think you can change if you make it in time, although I've got to forget a lot of the things I've been for a long time. And besides, I don't feel empty anymore, like I used to, and I'm learning you can't live a life of emptiness. You get me?"

"I get you, Candito," replied Andrés. "I know what it's like to feel empty . . ."

As if he'd not heard the doctor, the Count looked Candito in the eye and took out a cigarette. He made a gesture to ascertain whether he could light up and the other nodded. The Count thought his friend had said something that could convince him and he now envied that possibility of change and fulfilment Red had glimpsed by way of his religious faith. Were all those in the church better than he was? The certainty that that might be so alarmed Mario Conde's incredulous spirit even more.

"And how do you feel the change, Red?"

"You don't feel it, Conde. You search it out. The first step is to want it. For example, to want to change, or love one's neighbour, or want to live free of anger and bitterness."

"And forgive everyone?" asked the Count, out of interest.

"Yes, forgive. Nobody must stand in judgement . . ."

"Well, I am fucked. Well and truly. Do you want people to forget everything? No, my brother, there are things one can't forgive, and you know that's so . . ."

"You can, Conde, you can."

"In which case I'm happy for your sake. If only I could change and want to believe and even love all my neighbours, including the two million bastards I know only too well. The truth is sometimes I don't even believe in myself. I'm not in the running. I don't want to forgive: not fucking likely. The fact is I don't want –"

"I'm not going to say you should go to the church, because I respect you as a friend and I don't like to tell anyone what he must or must not do in this kind of thing. Not even my wife . . . But if only you could."

"Forget it, there's no cure for my state, but if you feel good then I'm pleased, because I'm not the cynic you sometimes think, and I love you more than you can imagine . . . But tell me just one thing: can people of your religion go to a friend's birthday party?"

Candito nodded again and smiled on. If the grace of God has really touched him, it seems to have done so at nerve points that generate laughter, thought the heretical, anatomical Count.

"Of course they can. And if he's a real close friend, I can even have a couple of drinks. You know I'll never be a fanatic. What I want to change are other things that are in here," and he touched his head, now a grey-flecked red, "because I can't change some things that are out there . . ."

"Great, the day after tomorrow, at Skinny's place. It's my birthday and this guy says you only get to be thirty-six once."

"Of course I'll be there. And don't worry. I know what I have to bring, right, Conde?"

"May God keep you this wise, Red . . . But I also came because I wanted to ask you something, to sound you out, because you might be able to help me in the bit of bother I'm investigating now. Listen, a fellow comes from Miami to see his family. He comes with his wife, who is twenty years younger than he is. The fellow was a high rider in the seventies and then defected in Spain, but they let him back in, to see if he'd come looking for something, even though he appeared to be clean. But one day the fellow throws his tail and disappears, immediately after he'd seen a horrible individual who had once been his boss . . . And he turns up two days later on Goat Beach, half eaten by fish. A blow with a bat to the head killed him, but as well as that, and here's what I want you to mull over, they cut off his cock and balls with a knife . . . Does it sound to you like jealousy or something else? Do you think it could be the *abakúas*, or something similar?"

Red Candito shifted in his armchair, trying to protect the area of his genitals with his legs. His smile had gone and he seemed like the Candito of old, the owner of that feline mistrust with which he now looked at his friends and replied: "It wasn't jealousy, and you know the *abakúas* don't do that, Conde . . . It's something else, something really fucked . . ."

"I quite agree."

"It reeks of revenge."

"But a bastard form of revenge . . ."

"There you are, Conde, and still you reckon you shouldn't forgive . . . It's terrible what they did to that fellow."

"Well, I need you to find out what it might mean without making too much fuss. Just see whether there's any gossip going the rounds."

Candito looked at his hands with great concentration.

"I've totally left that scene, Conde, but I'll see what I can turn up. What we really need to know is what the fellow was after . . ."

The Count glanced at Red and thought that, despite the respect and envy he now felt towards him, he couldn't let such an opportunity go by.

"The only ones in the know are the dead man, his killer and Jehovah. Hey, Red, why not have a word with your man who knows all and see if he can't help me get to the bottom of this mess."

From now on everything should become much clearer: obviously, a tropical cyclone is not a rebellion of all nature's forces against man, nor a curse from on high, nor even an act of vengeance wrought by the atmosphere against its predators. "At this time of year it is simply a common meteorological phenomenon in the Atlantic Ocean and Caribbean, created by a system of low pressure, near the centre of which the wind gyrates at great speed, in an anti-clockwise direction when it develops in the northern hemisphere," stated the commentator on Radio Reloj before adding: "Six minutes past eight the correct time." The Count noted that his watch was slow as usual, perhaps it was going backwards like a northern cyclone, but he left it to its own devices and turned up the volume on the radio: "The central area, called the eye of the hurricane, reaches a diameter of between six and thirty-five miles, and at the perimeter the sky is clear, with no currents of air, only a kind of ring forming around the eye where the strongest winds blow . . . Tropical cyclones are almost always formed out to sea, from clusters of clouds associated with different meteorological systems, such as tropical waves, sudden drops in temperatures and, in the southern section, cold fronts." And added: "Radio Reloj, seven minutes past eight the correct time," and didn't say anything about fear. Because, like the Count, the announcer must have recalled as he spoke that in the island's historical memory, even

84

before it had any notion of history, the hurricane was the god most feared by the first men to live there, who considered it to be the Father of All Winds and bestowed upon it strength of intellect and will, power and perversity. Its possible image, perpetuated in small mud and stone figures by the imagination of these peaceful, nudist barbarians, smokers of tobacco and other more cheerful herbs, splayed unmistakable arms that grew from its belly, and a face stricken with terror: it was engendered by fear of what had been experienced and suffered in the past, that most tangible of fears, later inherited and assumed by other men who came in other centuries and stayed on those coasts that dazzled them with their beauty, despite the terrible autumnal scourge that, in diffuse reminiscences, was said to have provoked downpours of blood, fire, sand, fish, trees, fruit and even of strange anthropomorphic beings, unlike any other of this Earth's inhabitants, transported from unknown climes by the hurricane's fury. And fear followed its course, because the new islanders also became familiar with the hurricane's treacherous ability to deceive, which Mario Conde himself now recognized, as he observed the patch of sky, visible from his kitchen window, that was still blue, an intense blue, as if it were in the eye of the hurricane, even as the man on the radio was declaring that Felix, with winds of a maximum speed of 130 miles an hour and a minimum pressure of 910 hectopascals – and what the fuck were hectopascals? – could be seen, according to the six a.m. report on that day, 8 October 1989, between 81.6 degrees latitude north and 18.1 degrees latitude west, some seventy-five miles south of Georgetown, Grand Cayman, and two hundred and eighty miles south of Cienfuegos, in central Cuba, and that its estimated route over the next twelve to twenty-four hours would take it north-north-west, at a rate of speed that had reduced to some seven miles an hour, perhaps so the phenomenon could recharge its zone of intensity, like a cunning long-distance runner conserving his greatest burst of energy for the final strait. That is why they said it might gather speed in the evening, and the island's western provinces should be alert to this shifting meteorological organism, particularly the province of Havana, Radio Reloj added yet again, and the Count didn't hear the time announced because he proclaimed loudly: "I knew it. The bastard's heading here."

And he calculated, with an arithmetical effort worthy of Hector Pascal: at a rate of seven an hour, that's seventy in ten hours, one hundred and forty in twenty hours and a hundred and fifty-four in a day. No, that's one hundred and sixty-eight a day and three hundred and thirty-six in two, so that possibly on the 10th the Count would be watching cyclone Felix walking round his house, crossing the road through the barrio and finishing off everything and everybody, as if the destructive forces of nature were rebelling against man, like a curse from on high, like an act of righteous revenge wrought by the atmosphere against its predators, despite all the wretched newscaster might say, who read what had been written by an equally wretched weatherman, who must know nothing of curses, punishments, or the debts and sins that could only be atoned for in that terrible, awesome way: by hurricane, for example. An earthquake was another such. Armageddon or the Apocalypse as prologue to a Final Judgement?

The Count lit his cigarette after he'd finished his huge cup of coffee, the only magical potion able to take him out of his beetle-like state and turn him back into a person after he woke each morning, and he remembered that, officially, this might be his penultimate day as a policeman and, certainly, his final day as an inhabitant of his thirty-fifth year, and what he saw around and within him didn't seem particularly pleasant.

"My wife wants me to clean up the garden today, what do you reckon?"

"That you'd be mad to buckle down ... It's the beginning of the end: she'll want you painting the house, cleaning the cess-pit and even washing that ugly dog of yours. Then you'll be fucked for good, because she'll hand you a bag and the ration book and I'll be seeing you in the queue at the grocers, collecting the bread every day and finding out whether they've got chicken or fish at the butchers. And there's no salvation: you'll be what is universally known as a crusty old man."

"You're right," agreed Major Rangel, after he'd finished listening unusually attentively to the oh-so-predictable array of concrete dangers outlined by the Count. "Do you know what I've found out now I'm always at home? That Ana Luisa always keeps a plate of cooked yucca for a week. You know, she puts it on a plate in the fridge and you've got to move the bastard plate and its four hard yuccas to get at the jug of water ... And yesterday I'd had enough of the wretched yuccas and asked her why she was keeping them and she said she wanted to fry the yuccas but the store hadn't got any oil yet. They'll stay put till some oil turns up ... Don't you think that's taking it too far?"

"That's what I'm telling you: you've got to fight back," the lieutenant continued, sinking his hand, if not his arm, into the sore where he'd just stuck a finger. "Tell her you're not a crusty old man and that if you aren't a policeman anymore you're going to be, let's say, a cigar taster."

"Now you *are* talking nonsense, Mario Conde."

"Well, I might be talking nonsense, but can you imagine what a good job it would be. You know, you'll be in an office in a Montecristos, H. Upmanns or Cohibas factory, or whichever turns you on most, and they'll bring you cigars made that day, all lying in their boxes. And you'll pick them up one at a time, light them, take two or three puffs, not too many, so you don't die within the week, and if the cigar's good, you put it out and give your approval, and place it back in its box. And you go on like that with the ones they've been twisting that day. The boxes will get a bit smelly from all the cigars you put out, but any buyer has a guarantee, unique in the world, that an expert smoker has tested his cigars."

The Boss smiled as broadly as he knew how. "I don't know if I can let you in the house. If Ana Luisa hears you, she'll stop me seeing you."

"Women don't understand these niceties."

"But there are others they do . . . Now she's cottoned on to the fact I'm off work and she's taking the opportunity to order me around all day."

"It's a bugger," agreed the lieutenant. "You spent your life giving other people orders and now . . . Don't you miss that power, Boss?"

Rangel looked at his clean desktop and coughed before answering.

"That ordering thing is like an illness. After you get used to it you almost prefer life with it, though you know it will take you to the grave. I think it's a terrible vice, and one that isn't so easy to give up."

'But you liked it?'

"In a way yes, I used to enjoy it, though you know I was never unfair towards others. I demanded of them what I demanded of myself. Do you want to know something else, now I'm confessing all this? I haven't been to bed with a woman who wasn't Ana Luisa for twenty-eight years. And not because I was never pro-positioned, believe me. It was because I didn't have the time, because I didn't want to complicate my life, to be at risk, I wanted to carry on as chief . . . It was as if I'd picked up all the other things life has and put them in a bag and thrown it into the back of a cupboard; and only kept what I needed in order to be a good boss . . . And look where it's got me. They're kicking me out because I wasn't a good boss and now I'm like a snuffed-out cigar nobody wants to smoke."

"You feel empty inside?"

The Boss tried to smile, but laughter must have been one of the things consigned to the bag he'd hidden: the good intentions aborted on his lips and his last routine as a boss came to his rescue.

"Hey, that's enough tomfoolery. How's the case going?"

The Count looked at the garden opposite and saw it needed a good clean-out, just as the walls of the house needed a good lick of paint and his sense of smell indicated that the Major's psychotic dog, a long-legged poodle that ran at the sight of a stranger, could do with a good deep bath: and he felt mildly sorry for the Boss and his empty life. Not even Candito's Jehovah had the power to revamp those historical sources of satisfac-tion truncated by other concrete historical necessities: a sorry final destiny for a monogamist like Antonio Rangel, now condemned to live among yuccas shelved for want of cooking oil.

"Yesterday I spoke to the dead man's family, in particular his wife, and she told me some pretty interesting things. The strangest was that she almost told me to investigate her brother, one Fermín Bodes. And I also interviewed his former boss in Cuba, Gerardo Gómez de la Peña, you remember him?"

The Boss nodded and the Count related details of his meetings with those characters and the story of the escape planned by Fermín Bodes and Miguel Forcade, twelve years back.

"I reckon I should forget the possibility of revenge prompted by jealousy."

"Forget it right away," bellowed the major, as if back at the helm of the Headquarters for Criminal Investigations. "Concentrate on Fermín Bodes: he could be the thread to unravel the skein."

"And the owner of the Matisse?"

"You'd like to nail him, wouldn't you?"

"You know I'd be delighted to."

"But don't get carried away. Don't take your eye off him, because he knows something too, but he's a hard nut to crack. Damn me, a picture worth three million. Well, get one thing straight, Mario Conde: you've got two days to solve this one and you'll solve it in two days: show the spies' colonel I wasn't wrong when I said you were the worst disaster in my working life but the best policeman I'd ever worked with. Do it for my sake, right?"

"What if I fail this time?"

"Forget it. You can't fail."

"What if I do, Boss?"

Major Antonio Rangel looked the Count in the eye.

"You'll have disappointed me . . ."

"Hey, it's not that bad."

"It is as far as I'm concerned. Get on with it, Manolo's just arrived: and ring me if need be."

The Count stood up and the pistol in his belt clattered to the floor. He picked it up, blew the dust off and returned it to its place.

"If I get any skinnier I'll have to tie it to me like a dog. OK, let's see if I sort it between today and tomorrow."

"Off you go, Mario, before I boot you out. Hey, and listen to this: watch it with Miriam. Don't complicate life, right?"

"Whatever you say, Chief," and he saluted him in an almost perfect military style that would have delighted the sweet-scented Colonel Molina.

In 1979 Rolando Fermín Bodes Alvarez was sentenced to fifteen years imprisonment for prolonged embezzlement, trafficking in perks from his position in an important state body and for forging documents. The one crime the Count liked best was embezzling: he remembered the joke told by Baby-Face Miki, his old friend and bad writer, about a once well-known Cuban scribbler who'd even been given prizes for his occasional verse, a homage, salutes, celebrations and favourable opportunities, who'd been sentenced to have his hands chopped off for cooking the books and, when accused of being a poet, had been let him off because of lack of proof . . . Fermín had spent ten years inside – two thirds of his sentence, for good behaviour – and was barely three months out of prison. Only three months? thought the Count and it seemed too much of a coincidence: one left prison and the other came to Cuba. At the time of his arrest, Fermín Bodes had defrauded his company to the tune of one hundred and fifty thousand pesos, of which eighty thousand were confiscated from him, and he'd spent the rest, among other luxuries, on building his house (also confiscated), in distributing favours and buying an out-board motor (confiscated as well), which had never been linked to a clandestine departure from the country. Why would he want to? The trading in favours wasn't investigated in any depth either, or at least wasn't written up in the file Sergeant Manuel Palacios had got hold of that morning. The most extraordinary aspect of the whole case was that Fermín had quietly stashed away one hundred and fifty thousand pesos without anyone noticing. Just fucking incredible, thought the policeman as he closed the folder.

From his small office at Headquarters, the Count observed yet again the almost becalmed landscape he could see through the window. That sea of treetops, punctured by the domes of the nearby church, had always helped him think and he now needed to think as on few occasions in his career: his next step would be to question Fermín, but he foresaw how that con-versation might just confirm him in the knowledge and prejudices he already possessed. Miriam's brother would be wily enough not to disclose facts that could lead to his being implicated if it were true Miguel had returned to Cuba for something only his brother-in-law could give him or help him achieve. Of course, pondered the Count: perhaps Miguel had preferred to avoid taking any risks at the airport, despite his diplo-matic and customs privileges in 1978, because what he wanted to take out of the country was possibly too big, obvious or dangerous. But what could it be? A man whose hands had touched a Matisse worth three million, exchanged for a house in Vedado, must have encountered in serial expropriations things able to change the lives of one person, if not several. The frantic flight of the Cuban bourgeoisie, forced to fulfil its wish or need to depart with just a few personal belongings, had led to the abandoning of real treasures, often hidden inside false-bottomed wardrobes or mattresses, with the hope they'd be recovered in the course of a speedy return to their lost privileges. Diamonds? Pearls? Gold and jewels? No, Miguel could have taken all that if he'd been sure he could go through a diplomat's bureaucratically privileged channels. Something more voluminous? He couldn't get the strange Matisse on Gerardo Gómez de la Peña's wall out of his mind as he sought out a possible object. Yes, it could be a particularly valuable, large canvas. But where the fuck was it? The ones the Count had seen in his house didn't rate that highly, but how could he know for sure? What if it wasn't a canvas? Or if it were, in fact, the Matisse belonging to Gerardo Gómez de la Peña? Yes, of course it might be, thought the Count, and he thanked Candito for his new mystic fervour, which even stopped him from drinking alcohol: if they had done the usual the previous night (drink at least two pints each) his head would have exploded by now, with that plethora of possibilities lurking behind a castrated man cast out to sea – a sea he feared so much – after his head had been smashed in a drunken rage . . . Yes, the sea was part of the story: the sea across which Miguel could have fled with his probable booty almost safe, if he hadn't had an irrational fear of that same ocean where he'd been flung, like a posthumous metaphor for a phobia that almost ruined him and placed him at the mercy of charitable nuns in the cold Madrid winter of 1978. The ocean that also opened its abyss between Miriam and Fermín, on the island, and Miguel, on the Florida peninsula: a sea that had claimed so many lives over thirty years and that had sicked up, perhaps in revulsion, the corpse of Miguel Forcade, the brother-in-law of ex-jailbird and former leader Rolando Fermín Bodes Alvarez, who just then stepped into his cubicle, through a door kindly opened by Sergeant Manuel Palacios, who said: "Do go in."

Fermín was forty and showed no visible trace of having spent a quarter of his life in the prison he'd left only a few months before. His skin was still smooth, tinged with pink that reddened towards the neck, and his body was finely toned, his broad chest and muscular arms revealing an evident fondness for physical training. To the Count's mind, his hands and manicured fingers were too exquisite, and his eyes were like his sister's: a vague grey veering to green or blue, the same thick, curly eyelashes. He had surely been a very successful womanizer in his heyday as a wealthy man of influence, and the policeman felt his rancour and frustration rise at the sight of a man who could have done whatever he most desired in the world: go wherever, choose a really pretty, sexy woman, and say: 'jump on board' . . . hoisting her on his shoulder without further ado. Besides, that pair of arms was certainly able to thwack a ball right out of the ground . . .

"You like playing baseball?" the Count began, staring at Fermín's arms.

"When I was a kid, I used to play like anybody else, why?"

"Nothing in particular," retorted the policeman, sighing wearily. "I saw on your file that you got out of jail three months ago. What were you doing in prison?"

"What do you mean?"

"I mean did you work at all."

"I'm an architect and I worked at that almost all the time."

"I see," said the Count, and though he tried hard he couldn't restrain himself. "And did you do weights in prison?"

"No, I've never done weights. I do circuits . . . You brought me in to ask that kind of question?"

The Count ignored him, as if he wasn't concerned by Fermín's question that was almost a carbon copy of his sister's. He looked back out of the window and spoke from there to the gymnast architect who played baseball as a kid: he was undoubtedly a man apprenticed by the hard knocks of life now displaying the acquired skills of a porcupine: the smell of danger made him turn in upon himself, and show only his aggressive spikes.

"You know why I called you in and I hope you can help me . . . Your brother-in-law's death remains a mystery to us, particularly because of one thing we can't fathom. What did Miguel come to Cuba for? Did he come to see someone, or to reclaim something he left when he stayed over in Madrid?"

"I still don't get you," said Fermín, after staring at the Count for a few moments.

"I never imagined you'd find it so difficult, Fermín. I've no choice but to spell it out . . . I mean, don't you think this murder seems quite random, far too random, if there weren't some powerful motive from Miguel Forcade's past. Don't you think Miguel came looking to reclaim something, something of great value that fell into his hands when he worked as an expropriator and which he couldn't take out when he left Cuba in '78?"

"To be frank, I hadn't really given it a moment's thought," Fermín replied, after a longer pause.

The Count felt his nerves tensing. That bastard was trying to wriggle out of it, but he wouldn't let him. Miriam and Fermín were still his only visible paths to the truth, and truth, not that criminal's arrogance, should be his only concern.

"When was the last time you saw Miguel?"

"The day before he was killed. I went to his place and left him my car in case he needed it."

"And you didn't arrange to see each other the following night?"

"No."

"He was going to see a relative of his that night?"

"I don't know who it might have been."

"So I should conclude you don't have the slightest idea why Forcade was murdered?"

The architect smiled. A smile that assumed he was probably holding all the trump cards.

"I'd say it was a case of assault and robbery, wouldn't you?"

"And then they cut his balls off? And left his car intact without taking even a tyre? Nobody's going to believe that, Fermín . . . And of course you didn't bring up your clandestine departure again, the one you were planning when he defected to Spain?"

The Count expected a visible reaction to this awkward question, but Fermín didn't flinch. Ten years in prison must have taught him something about life.

"I don't know what departure you can be referring to."

"Yours and your sister's. Miriam told me the whole story."

"I don't know why she told you about something that never happened."

"And why would you want the out-board motor they found in your house when you were arrested in '79?"

"To install on my boat, of course. I like fishing, like lots of people in this country who have boats and lots of other things and do legal and sometimes even untoward things with them ... The newspaper is still talking about that and they were all leaders or military; some were even policemen, like yourself ... Or even more police than you," he sounded off, as he put two fingers up to one of his shoulders.

"Yes, you're right," allowed the Count, his muscles stiff with mounting anger. That fellow had just uttered the only verifiable truth in the whole conversation and had touched a very raw nerve: he saw his friend the Major again, forlorn and forgotten, and felt the dam break, so his anger could flood out: fuck the lot of them, he thought, though he spoke in more measured tones: "Well, now we've reached this juncture, you give me no choice but to tell you: make sure you aren't mixed up in Miguel Forcade's death, because if you are I'll do everything in my power to ensure you spend the rest of your life doing press-ups in prison. I'm not a policeman for nothing, as you reminded me. You may go."

Fermín Bodes stood up and looked at Sergeant Manuel Palacios, who had stayed obediently silent, and then at Lieutenant Mario Conde.

"Thanks for your advice," he said, and left, gently closing the door behind him.

The Count listened to Fermín's footsteps move towards the lifts, and snorted, as he pressed the tips of his thumbs against his temples.

"What do you make of the fellow, Manolo?"

"That guy knows more than a roach and is in shit up to his elbows, Conde. But he got your goat. I've never heard you say anything like that to anyone ..."

"Bah, Manolo, I just wanted to see if he got jittery..."

"Well, what should we do, put a tail on him?"

The Count paused a moment.

"No, it doesn't make sense ... You know, nothing makes sense in this business."

"So where do we go from here?"

"To find out what Miguel Forcade was after ... Just phone this person," and he jotted a name and a number on a piece of paper. "Ask if we can see him in an hour's time. I'll go and see if Colonel Molina has finally made it to his office and tell him to sit tight until the case is solved ..."

"No, stop, my boy, don't tell me more. Let's see if I know which one it is: a fairly impressionist Matisse, where you can see trees swayed by the wind in a deserted street, and in the background there's a small yellow patch that could be a dog?"

"I didn't see any dog, but I think that's the picture."

"It's *Autumn Landscape*. Fancy finding it there! And how come I never found out that fellow had it? What do you say his name is?"

"Gerardo Gómez de la Peña, ex-head of Planning and the Economy. Do you remember him now?"

"Vaguely," replied the old man, Juan Emilio Friguens, who smiled, with that characteristic gesture of his, hiding his mouth and irony behind a hand, cupped like a closed umbrella: his fingers were so long they must have had more bones than were necessary, and they moved as if belonging to an animal skeleton powered by St Vitus. Despite their length, the digits barely hid the wolfish teeth of an old man ever ready to laugh at his own jokes. "The fact is I have to conserve my memory for more important things, you know? Every day my brain cells are less active ..." and he covered his laughing mouth again.

The Count smiled as well: he felt nothing but admiration for that quiet, sarcastic man. He'd got to know him on an investigation of a theft of various paintings from the National Museum, when the deputy director of Fine Arts recommended he consult him: Friguens was the best informed person in Cuba in the matter of works of art and possible markets for them and his mind held the most reliable catalogue of all the important items that had at some time crossed the island's coasts, in one direction or the other.

"Rumour has it that the Matisse in question is worth a toast. I've got white or vintage rum, which is best on the road to perdition?"

"White and no ice," the Count replied.

"Vintage, but only a drop," demurred Manolo.

"I too prefer vintage, but I don't place any restrictions like that young man. After all . . ." said Friguens, who receded into the house repeating: "After all, after all."

Seeing him walk was also a spectacle: he had kept an erect posture into his eighties, perhaps helped by the scant flesh covering him, and splayed out his feet as he walked, at a rate of knots as vital as the light-coloured *guayaberas* he wore in summer and the dark suits he sported in winter: Friguens was the last representative of the species of the elegant gentleman and had even welcomed them into his home wearing that grey long-sleeved *guayabera*, suited to the autumn.

Now an almost dessicated old man, he'd been art critic for the *Diario de la Marina* for thirty years, a role that had given him real power in Cuban art circles: Friguens functioned at that time as a kind of guru and an unfavourable opinion from him, trumpeted from the pages of that age-old, Catholic, conservative newspaper, could be the ruination of a joint exhibition, even of Picasso and El Greco. However, his prestige went beyond the platform from which he launched his eulogies or anathemas: it was well known that Friguens behaved like a true incorruptible: spurning the usual practice of his colleagues, he never accepted cash handouts or goods in kind from any of the painters, gallery-owners or dealers he came into contact with and the walls of his house were evidence of his true asceticism: the only drawings visible were those idyllically commercial copies of *The Last Supper* and *The Sacred Heart of Jesus* that could be found in the living rooms of any Catholic Cuban of the old school.

When the newspaper was definitively shut down soon after the victory of the Revolution, almost all of Friguens's colleagues took the road of political exile. He, on the contrary, decided to stay on, wedded to the island's cultural offerings: life in Cuba (at least while rum is manufactured and there are still such good painters, he once told the Count) was the only possible cornerstone to his existence, even when he'd been delivered an emasculating "loss of by-line" and buried alive on a radio programme where his name disappeared in a farrago of words flung into the ethereal ether. His Christian resignation must have helped him in that calvary, thought the Count, for, after enjoying years as a real influence in the land, to see oneself suddenly thrust into the mediocre world of news bulletins could have been one punishment too many for someone used to seeing his signature printed daily in a large-circulation newspaper of real substance. But Juan Emilio had accepted the challenge, also without being corrupted: he wasn't a hostage to bitterness or hatred and retained his pride in being the encyclopedia freely consulted on anything anybody wanted to know about artistic and commercial movements in the Cuban fine arts between 1930 and 1960.

"Here's your rum," he announced, returning to the living room, and giving each of them a glass. His and the Count's were at the upper limit.

"Maestro, do your doctors know you're still taking this medicine?"

Friguens smiled, hiding his mouth as usual, and said: "My dear boy, I haven't been to the doctor for twenty years. The last time I went was when my bunions started playing up . . ."

"Here's to my health and his, you're already far too healthy," said the Count, raising his glass, and the three sipped their rums.

Juan Emilio took a second sip before speaking.

"My dear boy, I'm so glad you came to see me. Because that Matisse has been intriguing me for more than thirty years. Well, not just me . . . You realize that right now it's easily worth four or five million dollars? Yes, because it's a rare work, one of the last from Matisse's post-impressionist period, before he became one of the fauves when he had that exhibition in the Paris Autumn Salon in 1905 with Derain, Rouault and Vlaminck. I don't know if you realize it was there that the fauvist movement was invented? That's when they started to make paintings in which the drawing and composition were the most important ingredients and pure colours were rediscovered, and quite aggressively at times. Though the fact is Matisse always paid tribute to working with that light he had learned from his master Cézanne . . . You know, according to the information I have, that painting must have been created in 1903, at a time when the poor fellow was always up to his eyeballs, grabbing help from wherever, one hand behind him and the other God knows where, and he sold very, very cheaply. Just imagine, he was working as a decorator's assistant and was one of the painters of

101

the friezes in the Grand Palais. And Marianito Sánchez Menocal, a nephew of General García Menocal who was strutting his dandy stuff in Paris, took full advantage of that bad patch, and, bought the picture for a rock-bottom price. Marianito then brought it to Cuba when his uncle was President and the 1914 war was starting in Europe, and the family kept it here till the 1929 crash, when they also sank in it up to their eyeballs and decided to sell it to the Acostas de Arriba, owners of sugar refineries in Matanzas who didn't know too much about art, but had too much money by half and a son who was half, well, half pansy, a gay, as they say nowadays," and he emphasized the nowadays, as an evil thought went through his head. "In short, the little queer decided he wanted to buy the picture, because Matisse was now famous and he imagined the work must be rather important. When the Acostas de Arriba left the country, lots of people said the painting had already been lost, because they didn't take it with them, but nobody knew where it had gone. I remember it being said the family no longer had it because one of Batista's ministers had bought it around 1954, but the truth was nobody knew where the Matisse had ended up. You follow me? What we do know is that when the little queer who bought it from the Sánchez Menocals arrived in Miami, he can't have had the picture, because a few months later one of his lovers shot and killed him with two bullets to the chest and nobody mentioned finding a Matisse in that shakeout . . . The fact is a haze descended over the painting and whoever bought it didn't want people to see it or talk about it again. They must have had good reason. So, what's the verdict, my Count of Transylvania?"

The policeman took a long draught and two drags on his cigarette. "Devious."

"A synonym for trickery, as well as for cunning," the old man riposted, performing his entire smiling routine.

"Now one would need to know how it reached that house where it was expropriated as property reclaimed by the State that never reached the hands of State."

"Oh, my dear boy, if I start telling you those tales . . ."

"So I'll have to find out who owned the house and see if we can conclude the story of that painting . . . Because there were other impressionist paintings in the place and even, I was told, a Goya and other things as well."

"Did they tell you what the Goya was like?" jumped in the old man, goaded by professional curiosity and deep pride.

"No, they didn't."

"Because there were three Goyas in Cuba, and if that one was in Miramar it must have been the one the García Abreus owned . . . So were they the ones who bought the Matisse?"

The Count attacked his glass of rum once more.

"And, Juan Emilio, are you sure the Matisse had a yellow patch like a dog in the middle of the street?"

"Yes, in the background. You almost can't see it, but it is there, as God is in Heaven. Most definitely."

"Did or didn't you see it?"

"I didn't see God, and don't need to. Or the dog."

"So how do you know the damned dog was there?"

"Because I was told about the painting and committed it to memory," he responded, smiling, dental occlusion included. "Remember it was my livelihood . . ."

"And how come I never saw the damned dog, if I see every stray dog going? Tell me something else, Juan Emilio, are there more of these famous paintings, worth millions, that went missing around that time?"

"You know, my dear boy, as far as I am aware there are three that could submerge in pesos whoever owns them. But I don't think they exist any longer, because some people who left, rather than abandon their possessions, preferred to hide or set fire to them. That was what Serafín Alderete did, the man who owned half Varadero, when he set fire to guess what: to a Titian . . . You know, just the thought gives me the shakes," and to exorcize his trembles he downed his rum in one gulp. "Poor imbecile. Well, as I was saying, apart from that Matisse I still have to see to believe, there are three other works on which silence descended and that must now be worth several millions, with the added bonus of the mystery of their disappearance thirty years ago. These eyes of mine saw one when it was still a sketch, a table by Lam. You're familiar with *The Chair*, I expect? Well, Lam was working on a diptych, which was that chair and a table, on which he was going to paint a kind of 'active' still life, as he put it to me. But as Chinese Lam was always hungrier than a church mouse, when he finished *The Chair* he sold it to the Escarpentiers, I think for three hundred pesos. We never knew the exact sum, because the Escarpentiers never let on and Lam forgot within the week, after eating away half the money and drinking the other half with his friends, and owing another half to several individuals . . . And that was when he began to work on the sketch of the table, which was going to be better than the famous chair. I know he finished it, but Lam never said where that painting went. Nobody saw it in a finished state, but I can assure you it exists, although Lou Lam, his widow, told me the last time she was in Cuba that he never finished it. But, believe me, for I know more than that French girl: *The Table* exists . . . The other is a Cézanne owned by the family of the marquesses of Jaruco. I never saw it, but María Zambrano did when she once went to their house and she told me about it: Mariita said it was a Normandy landscape, with a lake reflecting the surrounding trees. In '51 they announced the theft of the painting and no more was ever heard of it, and the fact is it's not in any known museum or private collection anywhere in the world. Can you imagine, my dear boy, a Cézanne gone missing? And the third is a blue-period Picasso owned by a family in Cerro because Alfonso Hernández Catá gave it to them. The gossip is that when Picasso still gave drawings away as presents, he gave it to Hernández Catá in Paris and that Alfonso, on one of his trips to Cuba, had an old man's affair with the daughter of the household and to show them he was a true gentleman, he gave her the Picasso. Then, when those people left, a fake Picasso was found in their house, a dreadful copy of the supposed original: the strange thing is that those people, who still live in Miami, never sold the picture and have never exhibited it. My brother, the one who lives over there, knows them, and he's asked after their Picasso and they always say it was a fake, which is why they left it in Havana, but I don't believe a word. Hernández Catá wasn't a poor fool who'd go giving bad fake Picassos as presents to a woman who had sent him crazy, now was he?"

"No, that doesn't sound right, though you can expect lecherous old men to get up to all manner of tricks, can't you? One final thing: what size were those canvases?"

Juan Emilio shut his eyes and the Count thought he was looking at a dead man. But he knew the brain of the apparently deceased man was working overtime. "I'm no lecherous old man, you know . . . Well, the

Lam must be about two and a half yards by two. Yes, more or less. And the Cézanne, from what Mariita Zambrano told me, must be around a yard square. And the Picasso was smaller: forty-five by thirty inches . . ."

The Count calculated the sizes as Friguens gave out the measurements and concluded: "The Picasso and Cézanne can be carried pretty easily. But the Lam is too big."

"Yes, my dear boy, it's large even when rolled up," the old journalist agreed and he asked: "Another little tot?"

The Count stood up and looked at his bereft glass. He felt like filling the void, but opted to fly the white flag of alcoholic truce.

"No, Juan Emilio, thanks. I've got to keep a clear head because the plot's still thickening . . . but you're the one who can help me clear a way through . . . But we must go now," he said, though his last wish was a lament that Friguens hadn't repeated his alcoholic invitation.

Ever since he'd been promoted to detective, Mario Conde had always avoided that kind of labour: reviewing legal documents, probing archives, checking though papers. Although he often had recourse to investigative routine, his approach was more and more based on hunches, prejudices and intuitions rather than assembling statistics or proceeding to logical conclusions, and that was why he preferred to leave the scientific side of the investigation to his aides. But the rush imposed by the day and a half deadline meant he had to shut himself up with Sergeant Manuel Palacios in that oppressive study in the National Archive and dive in to locate two remote facts: the address of the

García Abreus in Miramar and the existence of the inventory of objects made in that house by the functionaries working for Expropriated Property, who must have included Miguel Forcade. The Cuban itinerary of that Matisse brought by Sánchez Menocal, later purchased by the Acostas de Arriba, and supposedly sold to a Batista minister in 1954, could perhaps be plotted further if it could be proved the work had been in that house in Miramar that Friguens assured him had belonged to the García Abreus, who must have had a good reason not to make their million-dollar acquisition public. Moreover, the Count's inability to visualize the yellow patch the old critic identified as a dog had started to gnaw at him as irritatingly as a nagging suspicion.

"Did you take a good look at the painting, Manolo?"

The Sergeant marked the file he was examining and looked at his boss.

"Fuck, Conde, I looked at it. And I really don't think I like it very much. You can hardly see anything, man."

"You're an ignorant savage, and insensitive to boot. It's post-impressionist . . . But did you see the dog?"

"The yellow dog?"

"Uh-huh."

Manolo closed his eyes for a moment, like old Friguens. The Count supposed he must be reviewing the picture mentally, and when he raised his eyelids he said: "No, to be honest, I can't remember."

The Count sighed and accepted defeat.

"All right, get on, keep looking."

And they turned to the bundles of documents. It was only at moments like that that the Count longed for the efficiency of computers, which could digest a name – "García Abreu" perhaps – and tell the whole story with photos included. Otherwise, his cybernetic

107

inadequacies made him think of those machines as an aberration of human intelligence, which had perhaps created in them one of the monsters of its own self-destruction. The infinite trust placed by people in the electronic reasoning of those insensate gadgets scared him in the end: it was inevitable that if man transferred all his wisdom and analytical ability to those soulless creations such an unnatural act would wreak devastation. Luckily for the Count, the island's chronic under-development and pre-post-modern intellectual stance had vaccinated it against that unstoppable world pandemic. Although, at the end of the day, he thought it wouldn't be a bad idea if the archive did possess a little engine of salvation, which could tell the whole story (canvases included) in response to a single name: Henri Matisse, for example.

"We've got three days' work here," he declared desperately and lit a cigarette as he stood up. A physical need to flee had hit his stomach, and threatened to drill through.

"You've given up so soon?" Manolo asked with a smile. "You almost lasted an hour . . ."

"The fact is I can't stand it."

"But I have to . . .?"

The Count took a drag, looked at the bundles, and said: "You shouldn't have to. Nobody should have to . . . but if somebody has to do this shit, I think it's your turn today . . ."

"It always is . . ."

"Don't start, Manolo, I let you off when I can," he replied, searching his repertory for an excuse that rang with elegant conviction. "Look, while you try and find something, I'll go and see somebody who can help us. I'm not sure how but I think they can. It's ten past eleven? Well, let's meet back at Headquarters at two.

108

If you don't find anything, I'll tell Colonel Molina to send some people . . . Because I can't get into this, even if they turn me back into an ordinary policeman . . . I just can't: look, I've already got a rash . . ."

The old avenue down to the port, between the area around the National Archive and the church in Paula, must be the eyesore of Havana, thought the Count, as he always had: it's not even ugly, dirty, disgusting or disagreeable, he listed some adjectives, discarding others: it's alien, he concluded, contemplating it beneath the harsh light of a midday that was summery rather than autumnal, as he walked up the street lined by anti-aesthetic stores on the sea side and unfriendly blocks on the city side: brick and concrete blocks built to the single criterion of utility with no concession to beauty, forming an impenetrable, ochre wall on both sides of the street, covered in rubbish that had fallen from the overflowing bins where a few dogs sniffed, hoping against any real hope. What was terrible was that people, probably too many, inhabited those build-ings without balconies, arches or visible columns: their tiny flats designed in function of the rapid pleasures bestowed by prostitutes on passing sailors, port-workers and city dwellers who dared to descend to the last fron-tier of the old district of San Isidro, in the heart of Apache territory: the "quays", that place permeated with the whole history of modern pirating, vice and perdition, those dark annals through which the Count felt a longing for the unknown, inherited by way of stories he'd heard from old men who'd swum in those lagoons of bottomless evil. Later, many of those practitioners of sex, morally redeemed and socially recycled, had stayed on to live in rooming-houses, thus transformed into family residencies by ex-whores who now had children that couldn't always be dubbed sons of whores for reasons of timing: because, in fact, the correct classification depended on the moment they were born: before or after maternal rehabilitation ... The Count had occasionally visited those sad apartments, marked by a sordid past, which, after one fine morning, thirty years ago, were no longer reached by running water, and now he thought of the additional daily sadness of those people, trapped by the cruel fatalism of town-planners, people who went into the street only to see that same dark, desolate panorama, so far removed from a possible landscape by Matisse or Cézanne, or by chairs and tables tropicalized by Chinese mulatto Wifredo Lam. No, it couldn't be pleasant to spend your life in that area, a bucket of water in each hand and congenital ugliness behind you, he told himself as he walked by the old church of Paula, now marooned in the middle of the street by utilitarian modernity, and turned his prow towards the Alameda in search of a tree able to give shade and a bench from which he could contemplate the sea. Nor was that really the sea he was looking for, since he judged that corner of the bay to be equally sordid, its waters polluted by oil and gases spilled there, a sea without life or waves, but he reaped the reward of a patch of freedom he so desperately needed: an open space to pitch against archival claustrophobia and streets bordered by peeling walls and whorish anecdote.

As he breathed in the putrid stench of the bay, the Count realized why he had fled the Archive where the legal memory of his country rested: he really couldn't care less whether he found anything. An unhealthy apathy had invaded him at the revelation of so much dead past, so much existence reduced to certificates, declarations, forms, extracts, protocols, registers, in duplicate and even triplicate, emptied of passion and blood: the whole devalued detritus of history without which it wasn't possible to live but with which it was impossible to co-exist. The violent revelation that all was reduced to a piece of paper, numbered and filed according to entries of birth, marriage, divorce and death had been far too apocalyptic an illumination for his spirit on the eve of a birthday and liberation from work: the arid wake of nothingness left by being thirty-six less one day exposed to him the alarming futility of his efforts, as man, as human being, as supposedly intelligent animal. What could he do to hold off that pathetic, dismal destiny, as someone who considered his memory and memory itself to be a most precious gift? Perhaps art, as the unashamedly queer dramatist Alberto Marqués had reminded him recently, might be the remedy most within his grasp in order to escape oblivion. But his art, he knew already, would never enjoy the transcendence able to save him (art and myself, as Martí had cried on a day of despair; either we save each other or go down together). Or perhaps it would? he wondered, remembering that other genius who had committed suicide sure he'd failed artistically and whose novel then won prizes and recognition that were well and truly deserved. No. He'd never write anything like that, he shouldn't delude himself, he concluded, and depressed himself a little bit more before standing up and walking along the old Alameda de Paula, Havana's elegant eighteenth-century prom-enade, equally devalued by age and neglect, with its leonine fountain distressingly dry, before heading to the still distant mouth of the bay. It was inevitable his steps would take him past that mythical bar in the port,

The Two Brothers, where Andrés had once lived his most memorable bout of drinking, and had learned – then communicated the experience to his friends – that having a whore as a mother doesn't turn the offspring (necessarily) into the son of a whore, despite being born (as he had been) while his progenitor was still on the job ... There were then more than temporal or labour issues that determined whether you were to be (or not to be) a son of a whore. The Count, on the other hand, had downed so much alcohol on binges others would find unforgettable and that he'd forgotten and blurred in terms of quantity and incident, cause and effect. And something similar happened with the sons of whores: he knew such a quantity that to classify them according to maternal trade and time of birth would have required a real investment in cybernetics. But the bar's façade managed to activate the magnet: Lieutenant Mario Conde looked at the swing doors and found the bar semi-abandoned at high noon, occupied by a few drinkers beyond salvation. Yes, he did like that place. But it was the deep, rancid smell of a place dedicated for over fifty years to the sale of alcohol that propelled him remorselessly into the cool, welcoming inner reaches – or at least so he thought – of that dirty, irresistible bar.

"What rum you got?" he asked the mulatto bartender as if it were important or as if it were at all likely he would be able to choose brands and quality in a down-at-heel bar where the only matter of true significance was the availability (or not) of any distilled liquid to drink.

"White Legendario, Padre," the mulatto replied, flashing a golden gleam of his teeth his way.

"And what's the damage?"

"A peso a tot, Padre . . ."

The Count sunk a hand deep into his pockets and extracted all the notes and coins he could find. Placed them on the shiny wood of the bar and managed to assemble three pesos ten cents. Put away the useless surfeit and looked at the mulatto.

"I'll have a triple and don't call me Padre again, I never even made it to altar boy."

The mulatto looked him in the eye. Took the bottle of rum and poured four tots into his glass.

"I asked for a triple . . ."

"But the fourth is on the house. Padre . . . Reckon you're in need, don't you?"

The Count looked at the liquid filling his glass to the brim, its fake pearl colour and scent of perdition, and told himself that that mulatto, expert in handling alcoholics and melancholics, both depressed and desperate, was quite right: more right than lots of people in this world, and duly acquiesced: "Yes, you're right, Padre . . . I think that's what I need," and downed a first gulp before he heard a voice approach from behind, and from an evil corner of his memory.

"Give me the same as this guy."

Leaning on the bar, the Count felt a nasty shudder as the sound of the voice turned into a mental image. And thought: It can't be, before turning round and concluding that yes, it could be and was.

"Don't I get a salute, Lieutenant Mario Conde?"

Ex-Lieutenant Fabricio's ruddy face tried to conjure up its usual sardonic laugh but the Count refused to give him the pleasure of the sight of his teeth. The last conversation they'd had, six months ago, had led to mutual recall of their respective mothers, before giving way to the liberation of violence: they'd set to punching each other in the middle of the street and even now the Count could feel the lacerating pain from the leathering Fabricio had dealt to his face.

"What's up? You still sore?" Fabricio asked, leaning back on the bar and almost touching Mario Conde's shoulder.

"Ask yourself the same question. You look as if you've got the mange."

Fabricio reeked of cheap liquors that had fermented each other. He smiled drowsily and the Count, who knew a thing about such things, surmised he was drunk.

"You don't change, do you, Mario Conde?"

"Nor do you apparently," retorted the latter, making it clear he didn't like that conversation, which could sour the pleasure of his beverage.

"I'm well and truly fucked, Mario Conde, I'm done for . . . I don't even have a pistol, like you," and, saying that, he pointed to the Count's belt, where a weapon's presence made itself felt.

Clearly he was well and truly fucked: the ex-policeman looked as if he was in the phase prior to delirium tremens. The Count could imagine the rest. Lieutenant Fabricio, one of the detectives at Head-quarters, had always been one of those guys who liked to be a policeman because of the social distinction and everyday power the job conferred. He usually wore his uniform and stripes, and had more than once used the pistol that was now a requisitioned subject for nostal-gia. In the end he'd discovered his police status brought him other advantages: more money than his monthly wage packet contained, among other things.

"It was of your own making . . ." the Count finally said, trying to concentrate on his rum.

"I was stitched up. I didn't do anything. They're sons of bitches."

"So why did they kick you out?"

"I don't know, you know what they're like. Those guys are like hunting dogs: once they bite, they won't let go, until they pull your guts out."

"But did you or didn't you?"

"That's neither here nor there. Once you fall into their clutches, watch out."

"Thanks for the advice," said the Count, and he tried to down his last swig.

Something in his throat prevented him. The sacred ritual of swigging rum, at the knowing, grimy bar of a dive like The Two Brothers, while listening to a toothless, alcoholic black man, with the face of a boxer defeated in a thousand fights, who had begun to sing in crystalline tones a beautiful bolero written at least a hundred years ago, bore no relation to the bad vibrations and worse memories triggered by Fabricio.

"I heard they did for your buddy Rangel . . ."

The Count put his glass on the bar, and in the same slow, subdued key he'd used thus far addressed the other fellow, staring him in the eyes: "Hey, I don't want to hear Rangel's name in your filthy mouth . . . He got fucked because he trusted shitty types like you . . ."

And he tensed his muscles, ready to enter the fray. It was only his basic ethics as a drinker of alcohol that stopped him going on the offensive: the Count would never have begun a fight with a drunk and, if it weren't filthy petulant Fabricio, with whom he had accounts to settle, he'd even have taken a first blow without reacting. But Fabricio smiled, with that sour distinctive twitch of his.

"So you're still buddies . . ."

"Don't push me any further, Fabricio."

"No, I won't mention your mate again . . . After all, he's as fucked as I am. Did they take his pistol away too?"

He couldn't stop himself now: the Count smiled. Fabricio felt mutilated by the absence of a weapon that fulfilled him as a man and his drunkenness was truly pathetic. He realized the guy was as dead and castrated as Miguel Forcade. Relieved by this thought, his throat opened up again and he downed the last swig of warming rum.

"You know, Fabricio, at the end of the day it has been a real pleasure talking to you. I am delighted you're so fucked and I couldn't care a fuck and I can't and won't forgive you. I'm glad to see how you bastard police end up . . . So stew in your own juice and don't raise a fist, because I'll do you in . . ." he concluded, letting go of his glass, moving away from the bar, and shouting from the swing door: "Hey, Padre, thanks for the liquor and keep an eye on that fellow, he's a nark and an evil bastard, and when he was police he liked to blackmail people like you," then went into the street, feeling he'd swept the soot from a hidden corner of his consciousness.

He watched him come in, clutching a plastic cup and spoon of calamine in his left hand and nervous indecision in his right. It was as if he didn't know what to do with that second arm, which should be doing something and, in its enforced leisure, felt ill at ease and superfluous, as if it was in fact a third, unexpected extremity. Conversely, his face revealed a degree of satisfaction the Count attributed to the lunch he'd just downed in the canteen of the nearby factory. Adrian Riverón was finally back in his office in the Municipal Offi-Record, the hub for organizing the system of ration cards and lists of consumers that lots of people, perhaps possessed by sharp poetic imaginations, used

116

to call Offi-Queue, packing into a desperate neologism everything engendered there: that office being the mother-begetter of all queues, a national institution forged by a demand that always overwhelmed the strict offers ruled by a ration book that had become eternal, and through which everything was distributed from cigarettes to shoes, from sugar and salt to underpants (one or two pairs a year? wondered the Count. Or none at all?).

When Adrian spotted him, all the contentment in his belly visible on his face began to evaporate, and his right arm searched for something in his shirt pocket that it didn't find despite a thorough check.

"Something wrong, Lieutenant?"

Mario Conde muttered good afternoon, as he placed a cigarette between his lips and returned the packet to its place. He lit up, displayed deep pleasure, dragging and exhaling smoke, and said: "No, don't worry, Adrian, nothing's wrong," adding, as if regretting his lack of forethought, "Sorry, I didn't offer you one," and taking the packet out again.

"No, thanks all the same, I don't smoke," said the other, with a hollow cough.

"Well, I'd like to talk to you. Can we do so in your office?"

"Of course."

As a result of his post as the municipal director of Offi-Record, Adrian Riverón enjoyed the privilege of a small private corner in that place that once must have been a shop, bar or liquor store. It was just one of so many businesses shut down by the Revolutionary Offensive in the Sixties and then transformed into houses, offices or warehouses. Consequently, even

117

with the fluorescent light switched on, the spot exuded a sense of claustrophobia and misery. Adrian offered him a seat opposite his desk and the Count contemplated on the wall the map of the municipality, divided into commercial districts, with little stickers registering the number of the region and quantity of consumers.

"I suppose you're very busy?"

"We always have work: every day someone dies or is born or is divorced or has their seventh or sixty-fifth birthday and that all means we have to introduce changes on the register and add or subtract names. As you can see, very creative work."

The Count nodded understandingly, and put out his cigarette in an earthenware ashtray.

"Adrian, I came to see you on two counts. Miriam told me you were her boyfriend thousands of years ago, as she puts it," and he noticed how, in spite of his skin's reddish hue, Adrian turned even more blood red. "And, from what I've seen, you are still good friends."

"Yes, we are friends. Have been for thousands of years . . ." and he coughed.

"Then perhaps you can help me, because I expect you are only too aware that Miriam and her brother, Fermín Bodes, are two difficult characters. I at least am sure they know things that can shed light on Miguel's death and for some reason they're keeping quiet. Get my drift?"

Adrian Riverón had recovered his usual colour and, filling his lungs with air, leaned back on his swivel-chair.

"I'm not sure what exactly I can tell you, but you're right in one thing: Miriam and Fermin are two very complicated people. Miriam's marriage to Miguel would make a good subject for a bad novel . . . She was practically forced to marry him and I was removed from circulation. Miriam's father is one of those people who make you want to throw up. He must have twelve or thirteen children, with seven or eight wives and whenever he divorces he leaves his house to his previous wife, because he knows they'll give him another house for the next in line. He is one of those men they like to call a historic leader, and he really is that because he's been leading whatever for thirty years, always badly, but never gets the chop."

"I'm acquainted with such men of history."

"Well, this fellow, who'd never done a thing for Miriam, turned up one day in that house with Miguel Forcade and apparently Miguel fancied the girl: she was seventeen and if everybody's mad about her now, imagine her then."

"Yes, I am," and the Count really was imagining her.

"And old Panchín Bodes, as his friends call him, decided there and then it would be a good marriage and practically forced his daughter to marry Miguel."

"Family agreements."

"More like disagreements," Adrian corrected him, coughing. "But they married Miriam off to the old man and got a good position for Fermín, who had miraculously managed to finish his degree in architecture. You know what happened after that."

"More or less. How did you get to know them?"

"Through Fermín. He's two years older than me, but we were in the same scholarship year and we rowed in the same team. One day I went home with him and I met Miriam there."

"So you were a rower?"

"And still am, though I don't compete anymore. I love being in the water."

"So I see from the colour of your skin."

"That's right."

"There's another important aspect to Miguel's death ... he was castrated. What do you make of something like that?"

Adrian Riverón coughed again, a more prolonged salvo this time. The blood red hue of his skin deepened again and a smile came to his lips.

"What do I know about such things, Lieutenant? I reckon they have to do with *abakúa* blacks and *santería* priests? Religious business, I expect."

"No, I don't think so, that's not their way, because *abakúas* and *santeros* don't do that kind of thing ... And what was Miguel Forcade after in Cuba? Did Miriam tell you?"

The municipal director of Offi-Record smiled even more expansively.

"Lieutenant, rather than investigating Miriam, who's been a plaything of others, and Fermín, who's a wretched son of his father, I think you should get to know Miguel Forcade a bit better. Because if he did come back for something, not even his mother would be in on the secret. You can't imagine what kind of person Miguel Forcade was."

"I do have some kind of an idea ..."

"A rather distant one. As the youth of today say: that guy was a tricky shit. Miguel Forcade was never straight with anyone ... He always deceived half of humanity and I can tell you there's a lot of rubbish you still have to dig up about his past."

"From what I see, you didn't like him very much, true?"

Adrian Riverón's cheeks turned bright red again, while his right hand, definitely at a loss, landed on the earthenware ashtray, which it placed in the middle of the table.

"No, I didn't like him at all, but that's not saying

much, lots of people had accounts to settle with him. Lieutenant . . ."

"Mario Conde."

"Of course, Mario Conde. Miguel Forcade was one of the biggest bastards on the planet and, though I don't like to say it, the way he was killed he got his just desserts."

Sergeant Manuel Palacios was collecting up the last grains of rice from his tray when Mario Conde entered the canteen at Headquarters. As ever, the lieutenant was astonished by his subordinate's appetite and skill at salvaging scattered morsels of food: he squashed them with the back of his fork and lifted them to his mouth, and chewed them conscientiously.

"I told them to keep food for you," Manolo announced when he saw him walking in.

"What's on the menu?"

"Rice, peas and sweet potato."

"How low we've sunk, comrade! You eat that sort of thing, so eat mine if you want . . ."

"Really, Conde?"

"Really, I make a present to you of today's grub. And how come you got here so quickly?"

Manolo smiled, pleased by the fruits of his labour and by the thought of another trayful. "Because I found what I was looking for."

"You're kidding!" exclaimed the Count, even more astonished than by the four rums he'd got for the price of three."

"No, siree. I found the deeds for the García Abreu household on Twenty-Second Street, number fifty-eight, between Fifth and Seventh."

"And everything else?"

121

"That was much easier once I'd got the address in my mitt. The García Abreus left Cuba in March 1961 and the inventory of Expropriated Property is signed by Miguel Forcade in May of the same year, but there was something that surprised me: they didn't list any paintings. So I spoke to a girl who works in the Archive, a skinny mulatta, with pert little breasts, and asked her if the document was legal and she said it was. So I explained how important paintings weren't listed and she told me that came in an appendix, because important paintings were a Patrimony issue. So she helped me look for the appendix and we couldn't find it anywhere . . . What do you make of the story so far?"

"That I'll kill you, if you don't get to the end quickly . . . And no more 'sos', if you don't mind."

"OK, so, with the inventory number she called Patrimony, to see if they had the copy of the other appendix in the archives . . . You know what they told her?"

"That they didn't have it either, that it never existed, that they never saw one, that there was no appendix."

"Elementary, my dear Conde."

"And if there is no appendix it's because they never filled one in and just as they sold the Matisse painting to Gómez de la Peña, they sold the rest to other people . . . It's called a straight favour on the side."

"You really think so, Conde?"

"I think that and something else, Manolo: that Miguel Forcade knew more about painting than Gómez de la Peña imagined and if that's true, the dead man screwed the one living twenty-eight years ago."

"But how, if he sold him a painting worth almost four million for five hundred pesos?"

"Because he sold him a painting not worth ten for well over five hundred . . . I bet you anything that no appendix ever existed because all the paintings found in that house were fakes and that's why Patrimony didn't want them. Somehow or other the García Abreus got their paintings out of Cuba and left only copies in the house that could deceive any impromptu inspector. But Miguel didn't swallow that pill; he took advantage of the situation and sold those copies as originals. The most likely scenario is that he quoted a price to the State for a painting he registered as fake, sold like any other object, and pocketed the difference for a painting that was handed over as very valuable, which even came with the certificate of authenticity the García Abreus certainly left behind, but with the proviso it wasn't shown for some time. Miguel Forcade wasn't crazy about selling that Matisse on the free market, let alone the Goya and Murillo that everybody knew were in the house. Unless he had a good reason . . . Do you remember how the young García Abreu was an imitator of famous painters? Well if things are as I think they are, what Gómez de la Peña has in his house is by García Abreu junior and if Gómez de la Peña found out, I don't doubt he'd cut off all Miguel Forcade had dangling. Go on, eat the other trayful, we're leaving in half an hour . . ."

Manolo's eyes, momentarily squinting with admiration, followed his boss as he left.

"Hey, Conde, how did you figure out all that?"

"Helped by Bacchus, a Padre and the ration book. All for three pesos," he responded, not mentioning how the cleansing of his rage at the memory of ex-lieutenant Fabricio had also played its part.

He didn't even look at the lifts but climbed the stairs after a telephone in the hope of finding his old friend Juan Emilio Friguens at the radio station: they'd go together and check out the sick joke about the yellow dog García Abreu junior stole from Henri Matisse.

Clad in the pyjamas of his relaxed life-sentence, Gerardo Gómez de la Peña smiled at his new crop of visitors. His hairstyle that afternoon appeared a little less than perfect – short on Vaseline, thought the Count – but his self-confidence remained intact, even riding high, when the lieutenant explained the reason for his visit: "It's just that we would like our friend Friguens, who is an art critic, to take a look at your Matisse."

The former potentate's smile broadened.

"That painting set you thinking, didn't it, Lieutenant?"

"A Matisse is a Matisse . . ."

"And even more so in Havana," Gómez de la Peña added suggestively, as he invited them into his living room, where he spoke to Friguens. "It's right there."

The Count saw Juan Emilio's meagre body shake all over: three yards from Matisse's final offering to impressionism and Cézanne's mastery, the old journalist kept a respectful silence, tongue-tied perhaps by the wonder of seeing before him, after several decades, the masterpiece he had thought lost for ever. When he'd asked him to accompany him to see Gómez de la Peña's picture, the Count hadn't mentioned his suspicions and anxiously awaited the specialist's final verdict: let it be fake, he prayed mentally, so he would have a motive to find Gómez de la Peña guilty or, at least, to see his cockiness diminished by a twenty-eight year-old fraud . . .

"Please be seated," said their host, and the policemen obeyed.

124

Meanwhile, old Friguens took two steps towards the canvas, like a prowling tiger closing in on its prey. He didn't speak, almost didn't breathe, when he took a third step, and reduced to inches the distance between him and the Matisse.

"Have you got anywhere with Miguel's death?" asked Gómez, unimpressed by Friguens's wonderment, as if he were used to that kind of spectacle.

"Maybe," replied the Count, keeping his eyes on Friguens.

"It's hot, isn't it?" interjected the former minister, refusing to accept the silence.

"It's the calm before the hurricane," nodded the Count.

"Yes, that must be it."

"That's it," he said, when Friguens took another step nearer, as if he wanted to walk down the street on the canvas and enjoy the breeze rustling the trees in that French village.

The Count's interest forced Gómez de la Peña to look at the painting, into which that emaciated old man was now sinking his face, as if about to swallow it whole.

"What do you think, maestro?" came the sarcastic question from the Matisse's accidental owner, and Friguens turned round.

"And have you got the certificates of authenticity?" asked the critic, coughing a couple of times, hiding his mouth behind the hand that formed a closed umbrella.

"And endorsements from Paris and New York."

"Could I see them?"

"Naturally," agreed Gómez de la Peña, standing up, after putting his misshapen toes in his slippers.

When the men left the room, the Count lit a cigarette, wishing to defer the moment before he put his question.

"Well, what do you reckon, Juan Emilio?"

The old critic looked at the Matisse again, as he moved away and settled into one of the willow armchairs.

"Let me sit down. It's incredible . . ."

"And what do you mean by that?"

"Precisely that: that it is incredible," Friguens reaffirmed. "Oh, I didn't tell you, but I think I found out why the García Abreus bought the Matisse secretly. The problem was that in 1952 Fernando García Abreu got into a bank fraud up to his neck, and got out unscathed because of his friendship with President Batista. That's was why he didn't want it to be known he'd bought such an expensive picture, you see." He trailed off as Gómez de la Peña came back, extracting papers from a brown envelope.

"Here they are," he said, handing Friguens a few attached sheets of paper.

Juan Emilio lifted the certificates up to his eyes, and read them a smile briefly hovering on his lips, until he said: "Now this really is incredible," as if his flowery vocabulary had been dried up by the aesthetic impact of the Matisse.

"What is incredible?" queried Gómez de la Peña, smiling more confidently.

"The fact that the certificates are genuine but the painting is more fake than a twenty peso bill bearing the Count's face. Now what could be more incredible than that?"

In the sparse space of that tiny office on the third floor of Police Headquarters, far from the futurist flourishes of the house he'd assigned himself, Gerardo Gómez de la Peña, in ordinary shoes, incapable of inspiring envy

126

in anyone, seemed a man who had aged instant-aneously. In fact, the process began the moment Juan Emilio Friguens made the credible incredible, declaring with a triumphant smile that it was a fake Matisse painted in Havana, many years after the French original had been created. The absence of the yellow dog was the most obvious hint from the forger, who'd left other mischievous traces of his labours as a copier, so many crumbs thrown to whoever wanted to travel the road of truth. After shouting that none of it was true, Gómez de la Peña had begun to crumble before the Count's evidence: "If it's genuine, perhaps there'll be no problem. But we must be sure, so we'll take the picture to the National Museum, where two specialists are expecting us. But if they say it's a fake, I think you did have a good motive for killing Miguel Forcade, don't you?"

Gómez de la Peña looked at his toes and didn't reply. The Count was delighted by the vacillations of the petulant ex-minister and gave him an option: "Will you accompany me now to Headquarters or wait for me to come back with an arrest warrant when they submit that the Matisse is a fake?"

Gerardo Gómez de la Peña preferred to accompany the lieutenant, who led him to his third-floor office, where all the heat of that pre-hurricane evening seemed to have gathered. They could now see a grey, grey sky through the window, palpably threatening rain, although the tops of the trees kept perfectly still, as if warning of the evil latent in that excessive calm, before a most destructive storm.

"Hurricane, hurricane, I feel you coming/and on your hot breath/I await gleefully/the lord of the winds," the Count recited to himself, thinking of the physical and spiritual cyclone that filled the island's first great poet with despair, almost one hundred and sixty years earlier, when nothing was known of hecto-pascals or predictable paths, though they knew every-thing about the harsh lessons of the vertiginous horrors that lay behind the word hurricane. And Heredia, in his poet's voice, called on the cyclone to come, his cyclone, the one he wanted and awaited with baited breath. Why do we need the same things, poet? wondered the Count as he grew more on edge because Manolo was taking too long to appear with the definitive response on the other whirlwind, imagined in oils on canvas. So he turned round, sat down in the chair behind his desk and looked Gerardo Gómez de la Peña in the eye.

"And did you really believe all that time that the painting was genuine?"

The man breathed sonorously, expelling all the hot air accumulated in his lungs.

"What do you think? That I was going to say I had a real Matisse when I knew it was fake?"

"The will of men, like the hurricane's, is unfathomable . . . Who can say . . .? Because one would like to know whether you have a Swiss bank account, engorged by a real Matisse . . ."

"But don't you understand that son of a bitch deceived me like an idiot? I can't believe it even now . . ."

"Nor can I. Because even now I still believe the real Matisse existed or exists, and the painting was the reason why Miguel Forcade dared to return to Cuba. And I also think they could have killed and castrated him for that real Matisse, which is worth five million and not the three and a half you estimated, or am I wrong?"

"I don't know what you are getting at."

"That perhaps you both hid the real work twenty-eight years ago . . ."

128

"Don't be naïve . . ."

The Count smiled but pointed an index finger at his man: "If there's anyone naïve here, it's you. And that may be your sole salvation: that you could have been such a fucking fool you thought you'd bought a Matisse worth a million for little more than five hundred pesos and the assignment of a house in Vedado, though at the end of day, the house wasn't yours either, was it, and could be given to Miguel or to Jacinto, if Jacinto could repay in kind . . . But if you're not naïve and an idiot whom Miguel Forcade fooled over all these years, you may be a criminal on various charges, including perhaps homicide. Which label do you prefer, naïve or idiot . . .? I highly recommend one or the other, because all other paths now point to prison."

Gómez de la Peña shook his head, still in denial. It was still incredible apparently – Friguens had said so – the disastrous fakery of a painting he used to unfurl as his victory standard over the way he'd been punished for his failed economic management, when the door finally opened and, as the Count had been hoping, Manolo's fingers signalled a V for victory.

"Faker than a nurse's virginity . . ."

Gerardo Gómez de la Peña heard the sentence and slumped further into his chair, before saying: "I'm glad they killed him. For being such a bastard."

"Well, now tell me something new about Miguel Forcade," requested the Count, eager to digest more novel or revealing information.

Colonel Alberto Molina remained tight-lipped as he listened to the whole story as recounted by Lieutenant Mario Conde: the long haul after a fake *Autumn*

Landscape that existed because another real one existed whose whereabouts were still unknown, and that might be – one or the other, or perhaps both – the cause of Miguel Forcade's death. Standing up, smoking his second cigarette since the Count had put in an appearance, the new boss at Headquarters scrutinized the certificates of authenticity and the proof of sale of that Matisse, signed by Miguel Forcade and Gerardo Gómez de la Peña.

"And I suppose these García Abreus took the picture out of Cuba?"

"Apparently. But when Forcade found out this one was a fake, he realized he had a good deal on his hands and thought on his feet."

"He was a real devil," he added finally, returning to his seat. "I'm not surprised by the way he was killed."

"There are various kinds of demons," commented the lieutenant and thought of Major Rangel: "The country's mad," the Boss would have said as if there were still something that could shock him.

"And do you think Gómez is the murderer?"

The Count yet again weighed up the possibilities in the light of his prejudices and decided not to take any risks.

"We can't be sure, though I would be delighted if he were, because I don't like his sort. But he says he never knew it was a fake and he doesn't seem to be lying. And that leaves him without any apparent motive. At any rate I'll let him spend another night sleeping inside, in the same cell as the rapists, the black guy and the little white one. That usually helps, I can tell you . . ."

The Colonel stood up again. He was clearly fazed by the riddles cast in his direction by a story of serial lies and deception, sustained over almost thirty years.

"I don't know what to say . . . this is all new to me. What is undeniable is that you've upturned a cartload of shit . . . But if it wasn't Gómez, who the fuck did it?"

"You know, I've got Fermín Bodes in reserve, Miguel's brother-in-law. I am convinced he knew why the dead man came to Cuba, and if he knows why he may also know why they killed him. And quite likely may even have killed him himself. But I've got no way to bring him in. He's another livewire and he's got guts."

"And Miguel's wife?"

"She's really tasty . . . And she also knows things she's not letting on and lets on about things she's not been asked. She's the one I really can't get my head round . . . Besides, I don't believe she's a natural blonde . . . But what I'm more and more certain of is that Forcade's murderer knew what he had come here for, and that was why he killed him. Though the castration business is a spanner in the works. What do you reckon?"

The Colonel put his cigarette out and looked at his subordinate.

"I don't know why I let myself get dragged into this madness, when I was so quiet and peaceful in my office . . ."

"Now you can see how difficult this is to solve in three days. But I'll promise you something . . . What's the time now?"

"Ten past five, why?"

"Because tomorrow at this exact same time I will answer your question: I'll tell you who murdered Miguel Forcade . . . I hope you'll have my release papers ready by then. All right?"

"All right . . . to the good health of us both," and he half turned, not even remembering to give his military salute.

Mario Conde would only sing boleros in two precise states of mind: when he foresaw he might fall in love or when he was already madly and desperately in love – which was the only way he ever fell in love. Although his fortune in love had not been particularly favourable for nurturing his gift with boleros, several of those lyrics, made from words that could sing equally of love or disappointment, of hatred or the purest of passions, had lodged in his mind during vehement spates of amorous frenzy, during which he'd sung them, even outside the shower. And he preferred one in particular to any other bolero on the face of this earth and on his tongue:

> *More than a thousand years, many more, will pass,*
> *I don't know if love enjoys eternity*
> *But here or there your mouth will carry*
> *A taste of me . . .*

The feeling of febrile possession expressed by that song communicated, more than any other poem, more than many other words he sought and feverishly rehearsed, his longing for permanence: he always wanted his women to carry the trace of his love eternally, like a pleasurable taste on the lips. Unfortunately, it was usually soon forgotten, while the Count suffered and abandoned his boleros until another bacterial process of chronic, fatal infatuation began.

That afternoon, treacherously, the policeman felt a desire to sing a bolero, even though he knew any possibility of falling in love was remote. Miriam could never have been the woman to provoke the sensation of helplessness that love inspired in him, though he wouldn't have hesitated a second before bedding her anywhere the blonde showed the slightest sign of

132

letting him or wanting it. He liked her thighs, liked her guile and latent fears, but above all he liked her eyes, the eyes of a predatory animal conjured up by another old bolero – ". . . that's why on beaches/they say there are sirens/with grey eyes/deep as the ocean" – in a situation where, if he remembered it clearly, line by line, note by note, he, the Count, could never have sung it: because he was not and would not be in love with Miguel Forcade's widow, fluttering her eyelashes as she spoke, in apparent disenchantment: "I never imagined Miguel could have done such things. Did he really sell a fake picture?" she asked, fanning herself with her hand, as if the intense heat had caught her by surprise.

Two Tiffany lamps lit the room, making Miriam's grey eyes glint even more. At her side, on the sofa, her inseparable companion Adrian Riverón also listened to the litany of falsehoods listed by the Count, because Miriam insisted he should stay there: Adrian was like a brother to her and she trusted him entirely.

"So you knew nothing of the fake picture either?"

"No, I told you. Nor did I know Miguel wanted to come back to Cuba to get something."

"This is wonderful: nobody knows anything, but *somebody* must have had a reason to kill Miguel, don't you think?"

She nodded and Adrian Riverón started to speak, after coughing twice to clear his throat.

"If you'll allow me, Lieutenant . . . As I think I said to you this afternoon: why don't you take your investigations elsewhere and let Miriam be? You've already seen what Miguel was capable of, haven't you? She had to bury Miguel today, who was her husband, after all. Don't you think she's already told you as much as she can?"

The Count smiled. Miriam's eternal suitor had ridden forth, shield aloft, to save his maiden's honour. Another naïve soul?

"No, I don't think she's told me everything she could and I don't believe the half of what she has said ... But I'd like you to realize I'm not harassing her: I only want her to help me find out who killed the man she buried today, and who was her husband, after all. Does that reassure you?"

"Must I sit here listening to myself being called a liar?" protested Miriam, her eyes and lashes begging her friend to come and rescue her.

Adrian shook his head and coughed, as if accepting the inevitable.

"Look, for her sake, would you like me to tell you some things that might help?"

The Count thought for a moment. He'd have preferred a better focused image of Adrian Riverón in order to anticipate his likely hunting ground but resigned himself to listening to him.

"Of course," he acquiesced, looked for a cigarette for himself, and offering Adrian another.

"Thanks, but I don't smoke, remember?" he said with an exaggerated gesture of refusal the Count could not fathom: how come he had such a tar and nicotine cough then? Without more ado he lit his cigarette and concentrated on what Adrian Riverón had to say for himself.

"Look, I know – or rather knew – Miguel Forcade, even before he married Miriam, because I had the misfortune to work with him. And I told her once: only once, but I did tell her: he was not a good man. He was an unscrupulous social climber and when he saw the ladder was rocking he stayed in Spain, for a reason I can't explain, though it can't have been an honest one. You've seen a fellow who sold fake paintings

134

that weren't even his . . . Miguel Forcade left lots of accounts pending in Cuba apart from that one, and that was why he was afraid to go into the street, now he was powerless here. You follow me?"

"I follow you and I'm grateful for your help, because you're telling me I'm right: I must look everywhere, because any of the people he harmed could be the murderer. And if Miriam wanted to, as she said she did yesterday, it would be best for her to help me a bit more now."

She hadn't taken her eyes off Adrian while he stripped Miguel Forcade in public, exposing what seemed to be his real flesh, and now she looked at the policeman, who saw a new glint in her eye. Was she going to cry again? But she didn't, she only let rip her full fury: "You two are as bad as each other. Feeding on a dead man. All of this disgusts me . . . When can I leave Cuba, Lieutenant?"

The Count transferred his gaze from Miriam's eyes to the floor.

"Give me just two days more."

"But only two. I've finished here. I want out and I don't think I'll ever tread this soil again . . . Poor Miguel."

"One night, some six or seven years ago, Miguel confessed that leaving Cuba was the biggest mistake he ever made. I remember it was the end of December and unbearably cold in Miami, especially for a man who always started to wear an overcoat at the first sign of a north wind. On such a night he'd never have gone out, but the owner of the firm he worked for had organized a party in his new house in Coral Gables, and he'd invited a group of his employees, including

Miguel. It was like a New Year's Eve party the owner gave his closest workers because business had gone so well and, according to Miguel, so we would all die of envy at the sight of the house he'd bought a few months earlier, about which he boasted endlessly.

"You know, dying of envy was a very real possibility: the house was in the most exclusive part of the neighbourhood, in a spot you could only reach along a street where there was a sentry-box and private security guard you had to show the printed, embossed invitation to in order to be let in. Then the side road went through a wood, where there were several houses, including Mr Montiel's, which was one of those mansions that, if you haven't seen one, you can't imagine even in your dreams: according to Miguel the house had cost going on for two million dollars and the decorator had been paid more than a hundred thousand for following the new owner's every whim. When I went inside and saw that wonder, full of mirrors, lights, marble and carpets, I thought it was the best spent money in the whole world, especially if you have several million to spend and can permit yourself the luxury of a life-size Saint Barbara, complete with sword, crown and horse surrounded by baskets of dark red roses and ruddy apples . . . The party was in the patio, by the swimming-pool, and although Miguel downed several whiskies and we sat under an awning, as near as we could to the barbecues where the meat was roasting, he kept shivering and I said to him: 'You know, we can go if you like,' but he told me no way, we should last at least until midnight, so as not to insult that Cuban magnate who was his boss and who'd made his millions by stamping on whatever heads tried to push in front of him. That was why he smiled at Montiel and congratulated him when the guy came over to ask us what we thought of his hovel, and, beaming, Miguel told him his house was fabulous and Montiel replied: 'Well, you know, Miguel, not half as pretty as your wife,' and he burst out laughing and slapped Miguel on the back. Still smiling, Miguel watched as Montiel walked off to joke with other employees and there and then he began to shake more violently and after drinking another glass of whisky he told me: 'The biggest mistake I ever made was to leave Cuba,' and I thought he meant because he was cold, but later I realized it was envy.

"We lived in a rented house in South West district that would have satisfied the wildest aspirations of anyone here: it was fine for us, we had a patio with a lawn and barbecue, air-conditioning and a Florida-room, a sun-room that looked over a garden with flowers and trees. We both had a car and at the weekends we'd go to Tampa, Naples, Sarasota, St Petersburg or Key West and could afford the luxury of a Friday night dinner in a restaurant on Calle Ocho or in Coconut Grove or Bayside. But all that was only the first step up a slope that could rise much higher to where Mr Montiel had climbed, with his house in Coral Gables worth more than two million. Besides, Miguel knew time was against such an ascent: he was pushing fifty and, as he said, he had yet to meet a person who'd made it through honest toil . . . Consequently, Montiel's house was like the epitome of everything we would never have, unless a miracle occurred. But what most upset Miguel was his employee status: here in Cuba he'd always operated at a high level and could feel the real power his hands wielded. Now, though he had a house and a car and money in the bank, Miguel had no power and that was the most difficult part for a man like him to accept. You understand?

"Consequently, when we stayed at home at night or went for a drive round Florida, he would often tell me what he'd do if he had eight or ten million dollars. I can remember that first on the list, whenever he broached the subject, was starting his own business and having his own office, where sometimes I'd be his secretary or it would be a woman dressed in proper English style, according to his mood on the day . . . Then he'd be Mister Forcade and would demand his employees address him as such, because those imaginary millions put a distance between him and the rest of us mortals. Poor Miguel.

"In recent years, though we moved to a better house in Coral Gables, which we've only half paid for, and Miguel was promoted within Montiel's enterprise and had his own office and a secretary he shared with another head of department, he'd always talk of the possibility of changing everything and living as he deserved to live. He'd tell me about a big business deal he might conclude at any moment and when I asked him what that might be, he'd always reply: 'You'll find out when you swim in the pool in the house I'm going to buy, Mistress Forcade,' and he'd laugh to himself. I felt his spirits rising and over recent months, when he decided we'd come to Cuba despite what he had done, Miguel was almost the confident, self-assured man I knew here and that I'd fallen in love with when I was a young girl. He investigated and found out that the best way to return to Havana was via negotiations with the Red Cross, by showing his father's medical certificates, and he started to phone Fermín, who was out of prison by then, to get him to do the necessary paperwork here. That's why, two or three days before our trip, I asked him if he didn't now regret leaving Cuba, and he replied: 'What I regret is putting off my return for so long,' and he laughed, just like Cuban magnate Montiel might have laughed at one of his own jokes."

"Do you like fallen flowers, Lieutenant?"

The voice came from behind a shrub and caught the Count in the act of plucking a tiny white flower, asleep on the path to the street.

"Yes, you may smell it: it's from the white weeping-willow to your right. Its real name is *Sambucus Canadensis* and it belongs to the family of *Caprifoliaceae*. If you look around you'll see it's very common in gardens, because it has strong medicinal properties ... Did you realize that? Go on, smell it. It's very distinctive, isn't it?"

The Count took a few steps and then glimpsed the shrivelled, desiccated figure of the old man, resting on a wrought-iron bench, by the side of which two wooden crutches were resting. In the midst of that solitude, surrounded by so many trees, flowers and silence, he was like a prophet tarnished by memory and time.

"Are you Señor Forcade?"

"Doctor Alfonso Forcade, at your service," he replied and initiated the deferred gesture of presenting a hand to shake, declaring, "And you, beyond any shadow of doubt, are Lieutenant Mario Conde."

"And how come there are no doubts?" the Count decided to ask, as he felt an unexpected pressure issue from the old man's hand.

"Because Caruca, my wife, is the best physiognomist I have ever known and she told me what you were like."

"Your garden is very pretty. That's what I told your wife as well."

"Yes, it is pretty, that's why I try to come every day, to

139

look at my plants and watch them grow . . . It's one of the few pleasures left to me in life. But there are days I cannot even do this. I don't know what will come of them after my death, an event concerning which there are also few doubts but that it will be very soon . . . Look, except for the laurel tree, the silk-cotton tree, the *mamey* and the *picuala*, which is on the back fence, I sowed all the other trees in this garden with my own hands or watched them grow, after they'd been sown by the hand of God. Do you know what the tree is over there, the one like a paunchy silk-cotton tree? I expect you don't. Well it is a baobab, or, rather, one of three baobabs that exist in Cuba, and I sowed it . . . When I entered this house this whole terrain was a bare lawn, which I took up myself in order to plant the wonders of nature you now see."

"For business or pleasure?"

Old Forcade's face started to move in a strange way. His wonderfully false teeth gleamed in a one-dimensional, gloomy smile that pursued only a vertical path. His face muscles, worn by the years or by a wasting illness, sagged as if in need of instant lubrication, then lingered before regaining their position of repose. That facial play seemed beyond the grasp of the man's physical possibilities, as he remained static, waiting for the grimace to disappear.

"Both," he said finally, "both. Beauty and business can go hand in hand in some walks of life, and botany has this advantage. Policemen aren't so fortunate, if I am not mistaken. I've got a real catalogue of Cuban plants here and each has a double function: the ability to be beautiful and useful to the people who know its secrets."

The Count lit his cigarette and looked at the hanging flowers.

140

"And have you written about those secrets?"

"I've published some things, and upstairs I have several unfinished catalogues that the university will inherit when what has to come comes . . . It's terrible how life never gives us enough time, although sometimes one has it in excess, as is my case. But that's not the problem worrying me: it is that the plants will be all alone and abandoned. Though you probably won't believe me, each of these trees knows I am its creator, or at least its guardian, and that my hands have nourished, cleaned, looked after and watered them for thirty years. That my voice has talked to them and my presence has accompanied them from the instant they sprouted their first shoots. My absence will create a void for them and you can be sure many of these plants will get sick when I die and several will die soon after, for they will be the first to discover I am dead . . ."

"I'd never heard about such things happening to trees. To dogs but . . ." and to some people, he was about to say, but he bit his tongue.

"Well, I can assure you, each plant has a life of its own and consequently a spirit where the centre of its consciousness resides: soul and matter, you see? Don't look at me like that: they are living beings, Lieutenant, and life begets spirituality, you know. It is not a sensibility like ours, but it would be cruel and stupid not to admit it or respect it from a simple perspective of blinkered anthropocentrism . . . Do you have the time for me to tell you some things about plants? If so, listen to this: it has been demonstrated scientifically that when plants are on the same wavelength as a particular individual, they can establish a permanent relationship with them, wherever that person goes and even though they are surrounded by millions of people. But that isn't what is most surprising: plants can also feel

141

fear or happiness and are equipped to perceive the thoughts and wishes of men, even to detect their lies . . . But we also know they can have intentions, because they possess the ability to perceive and react to what is happening around them. I'll give you an example you might find interesting: the Indian liquorice tree, of which regrettably I've not managed to rear a single specimen, is so sensitive to all forms of electric and magnetic pressures that it's used as an indicator of the weather, because it has mechanisms that can forecast hurricanes, electric storms, earthquakes and volcanic eruptions. That is something only very sensitive spirits and intellects can achieve, surely?"

The Count nodded at that panoply of scientific animism proposed by old Forcade. There was something about the old man that recalled the final days of grandfather Rufino, when Mario would sit next to his bed and ask him to tell him those few stories he knew so well, which grandfather used to retell to grandson like the only recordings saved from the fires of time: the one about the day he'd managed the feat of stealing the home run in a game of baseball, which they won thanks to that act of desperation; the one about the night when he had to flee a jealous husband, leaving three strips of his flesh on the spikes of a fence; the one about the death of that many-coloured rooster with which he won the incredible tally of thirty-two fights and about whom he spoke as of a beloved son he should have given a better chance in life, but no doubt Grandad Rufino also thought his rooster was particularly intelligent.

"Do you know anything about spirits?"

"Depends what you mean by spirits, Lieutenant. If what you mean by spirit is a manifestation of matter organized by an inscrutable higher power or force, then I do believe. Because it's not only what is visible and obvious that exists, as you know . . ."

"Marxist manuals would have slotted you into the category of a materialist idealist . . . But, do you know why I ask?"

"I think so, because you're very transparent," suggested old Forcade. "Or didn't you notice that I guessed you intended to smell the flower from the willow that you saw on the ground? It was too predictable . . . But not your desire to put it in your shirt pocket. Or your anxiety at the approaching hurricane."

The Count smiled again, surprised by the old man's powers of intuition.

"How do you do that?"

"Nothing could be simpler, if one is well prepared and, naturally, if the right conditions exist. Equally, there must be two people able to communicate limpidly."

"Do you mean telepathy and thought-transmission?"

"That's right."

"At university they also told us telepathy was a pseudo-scientific lie . . ."

Old Forcade made a gesture to cut dead the Count's materialist diatribe, but he fell into a deep silence, and remained completely still, his hands in his lap. The closeness of his death was in this case one of those evident, visible circumstances, even before it had happened.

"I usually respect the most diverse opinions, but I like to confront them with my own . . . I think we must agree that nerve impulses carry their own charge of electricity, mustn't we? And that these impulses have a transmission centre, which is the cortex of the brain, agreed? Why not allow that that matter is able to emit from its mass an electromagnetic charge and that

143

another similar charge can capture the specific waves from that spectrum and decode them? Obviously, the right conditions must exist for this to happen ... Would you like me to tell you what you're thinking right now?"

"Yes, I would."

"That I'm an old windbag, isn't that so?"

"Almost: I was thinking you are a good conversationalist ... and a bit of a windbag. How did you know?"

Forcade's smile escalated higher this time and the Count had to wait for the curtain of his lips to descend slowly before he heard his reply.

"Because lots of people think that about me. Heh-heh," he said laughing, as if he were coughing, not bothering to loosen his facial muscles. "Speaking to you has done me a power of good. I even almost forgot you'd come because of the death of my son Miguel."

"I'm very sorry, Doctor," said the Count, who couldn't think of a more worthy reply.

"So am I. I loved my son more than these plants, as you can imagine. That's why I should like you to find out who killed him in a worse way than if he were a rabid animal."

"I'm doing my best."

"My son played dangerous games and at times that costs dear ... When I saw him come back to Cuba I had a feeling something bad might happen."

"Did telepathy let you in on something that can help me?"

Old Forcade stayed silent, as if he hadn't heard the question. But his hands wandered from his legs to his head and his fingers ran through his wisps of white hair.

"Telepathy has told me nothing but experience tells me he was murdered by someone close to him."

144

"That's what I think. But who do you suspect?"

"It wouldn't be right for me to answer your question and influence you, because I've seen you are a man who is easily prejudiced . . . But let us agree the following: get as far as you can and if you feel all the paths are being blocked, then come and see me and we shall exchange opinions, what do you think?"

"I don't think it is the best approach, but if it is what you prefer . . ."

"I think so. You are in a hurry to solve this case and your intellect is clearly up to the task, that much is obvious. And I want you to solve it, because it was my son who lost his life in this tragedy. But I prefer to remain a spectator until I have no choice. You understand? A man who is about to die and loses his son after not seeing him for ten years usually has unreliable prejudices: passion can dominate everything, and it would be regrettable were I to influence you in the wrong direction. That's why it's better your mind worries at it alone, till it has exhausted all possibilities."

"Well, my reading of your brain tells me you can help me. I need to know what Miguel came for and at best you might know something that –"

"So now you do believe in telepathy?" the old man interrupted.

"Slightly more than I did . . . but I want more proof. I will think of something very concrete and try to communicate it to you. Shall we begin?"

Alfonso Forcade smiled and nodded agreement. The Count, for his part, concentrated on one thought, and on propelling it out of his mind.

"Done?" the policeman asked.

"Wait a minute . . . Done," said the old man.

"What is it?"

"Very easy, Lieutenant. It's astonishing, but your

145

thoughts are totally transparent: you are thinking about a painting, a painting where you can see a few trees. Although everything is slightly blurred, isn't it?"

"Of course, it's an impressionist landscape," the Count confirmed, surprised by his capacity to communicate.

"It must be a pretty landscape. A pity I didn't see it."

"I didn't either," the policeman lamented, and reached out to shake the old man's right hand, which had gone back to sleep on his exhausted legs. "Thanks for this conversation," he said, letting go of the old man's hand: he hoped Forcade hadn't guessed that he shivered at the idea of touching a dead man's bones.

"Don't be embarrassed, Lieutenant," said the old man, and the Count forced a smile.

"Forcade, what are your plants telling you about hurricane Felix?"

The old man swung his face round towards the garden, and contemplated his plants for a few minutes.

"The sage is afraid. I can tell that from its leaves. And the garlic flower, if you look, seems to be clinging tighter to the trunk of the *mamey* . . . The cyclone is on its way, and, Lieutenant, will hit here for sure."

"Just as well," said the Count and he moved off, not daring to think of anything. So he was transparent, was he?, and he salvaged the flower so he could smell its scent once more.

Sergeant Manuel Palacios drove the car along Rancho Boyeros at a speed faster than the Count could tolerate, but this time he let him flirt with death: after all, that outcome – sometimes visible and very real – tended to be capricious and elusive. Mario Conde wanted to reach home as soon as possible and that's

146

what he told Manolo when he asked him if he wanted to stop and look up his friend Carlos.

"No, what I want is to sleep and not to think about Miguel Forcade for twenty-four hours."

"I can't think why you told the new boss that we'd solve this case by tomorrow. It's going to be difficult."

"God will provide, as my grandad used to say," the Count retorted with a sigh, by the time the car was progressing along Santa Catalina and approaching the house of his oldest, most sustained love: the twin Tamara.

Several months had passed since their last encounter, which had finally materialized in the depths of a soft bed of gentle gullies created by their bodies: his on Tamara, Tamara's on him, and the Count could still feel in his arms and on his skin the round densities of that female form he'd longed for over some fifteen years, in the course of which she'd been the focus for his best masturbations. Then his fevered brain always had to supply the detail, for apart from the twin's face and the reality of her smooth compact thighs, which his eyes devoured in the recreation ground at secondary school, the rest was pure poetic-pornographic imaginings, developed on the basis that what was unknown must be in line with what he'd imagined: and the margin of error had been minimal: Tamara's backside was as tight, her pubic hair as curly, her nipples as lively as he'd ever imagined, and the mere idea he might kiss that flesh again stopped the policeman's breath whenever he went past her house. But they left Tamara's spell behind and the Count wondered whether he should take the offensive and try once more to sink his lance into that pliant Flanders field. Indeed: would that beautiful, superficial woman, used to an easy, carefree life, always be the sexual obsession

147

of a guy as fucked and useless as himself, unable to guarantee the slightest security to anything or anybody, even himself?

When he was finally back home, the Count thought it better to forget Tamara so as to avoid yet another of his solitary exercises. In the undesirable silence of that empty house, he felt the accumulated hunger, doubts, depression and exhaustion he'd been dragging around all day weigh down on his shoulders. A physical sluggishness spread to his legs, releasing muscles, nerves and joints that fell to the floor like useless scrap metal, but the desire to flop on his bed was subdued by uncomfortable tremors in the intestine, urgent to the point of cannibalism. The possibility of finding nourishing relief at Skinny's place had been dashed by inertia: the physical need to be alone with his hunger and solitude had forced him back to a deserted home, where a disastrous gastronomic drought reigned: not even a fighting fish stirred. His friend surely would want to speak of parties and saint's days, when all he felt was rancour and frustration, and it wasn't fair: Carlos was already fucked up enough without downing him further with his sado-maso-police depressions . . . In short, the outlook was bleak until, on opening his refrigerator, he had a pleasant surprise: he saw entwined there, like friendly worms, spaghetti he'd left in a dish several days ago, red-flecked by tomato and dotted with dark specks of a mince presumably of animal origin.

While the pasta was heating up in the bain-marie, the Count got under the shower and let the cold water run over his head, cleansing him of his outer filth. He soaped himself thoroughly and as he vigorously washed his penis felt a temptation called Tamara that he repressed with a policeman's rage. "If I jerk off, I'll die", was his rational conclusion, and he allowed the

148

cold water to dampen the rising motion triggered unawares by the physical needs he'd postponed too long. The painful memory of his adventure with the twin always provoked a similar effect. But now that Skinny had summoned her to his birthday party, the imminence of the encounter meant the woman was enthroned as the unchallenged queen of the Count's erotic memory, and he wondered rhetorically how long he would remain in love with her.

Body still wet and towel wrapped round his waist, he went into the kitchen and turned off the flame. As he finished drying his hair, he switched on the television, which was broadcasting the late-night news. The expansive impact upwards and downwards of the investigations against police corruption was repeated and given scope in the report, gravely intoned by the newscaster, who spoke of necessary punishments, exemplary measures, unacceptable attitudes and moral, historical and ideological purity. But what nobody knew was how such radical surgery, now extending into high ministerial reaches, would end, although the prospect of escaping unharmed the necessary purge, announced in the report, relieved the lieutenant's contrite soul, and he pondered hopefully on the short time left to him before his final liberation: a mere twenty hours ... As the Count had decided, he refused to continue assessing the possible reasons for Miguel Forcade's death and concentrated on the special weather report the Official Weatherman was solemnly reading:

"At eight o'clock, only a few minutes ago, satellite reports located Felix here –" and he pointed his marker at a crazy white whirl in the middle of the Caribbean – "at eighty-two degrees longitude north and twenty-one point four latitude west, that is, some fifty miles north of Grand Cayman and almost one hundred and fifty miles south of the eastern tip of Juventud Island. It is estimated that this strong tropical hurricane, the most violent in recent years, will continue to progress in a northerly direction, at some ten miles an hour, meaning it represents an immediate threat to the island's western provinces, in particular to Havana and Matanzas, where it might hit between early and late Thursday morning, bringing torrential rain and winds of more than one hundred and ten miles an hour, and occasional gusts of one hundred and fifty an hour, which may even be stronger in areas close to the centre of the hurricane," he added before handing over to the Colonel from Civil Defence, who enumerated the precautions to take before the seemingly inevitable arrival of cyclone Felix, which, as the Count had predicted and concluded, had to come. And he felt scared.

Just as the country was preparing to resist the onslaught of this meteorological phenomenon, a harassed Count downed his dish of spaghetti resurrected by the sudden change in temperature to which they had been subjected at the ripe age of six days after they'd first been cooked. But the fuckers taste good, he thought, chewing the pasta and merely regretting that the island's hellish, cyclonic climate didn't allow vines to grow and wines to be manufactured: because a red wine, unrefrigerated, would have lifted heavenwards those juicy mouthfuls fit for a Neapolitan cardinal, promoted up the culinary-church hierarchy by a policeman's hunger on the eve of his retirement. A pity he couldn't add fried yucca, and he smiled mischievously at the dilemma confronting Major Rangel, a wretchedly monogamous, dethroned king reduced to imbibing infusions.

150

The empty plate went to sleep it off in the sink next to the other plates, glasses and dishes piled there, betwixt grease and apathy. Without wetting his fingers, the Count rescued from the summit of deferred filth the container for grinding coffee and, after cleaning his teeth, he placed his Italian coffee pot on the stove and waited for it to percolate. His melancholy gaze reviewed the selection of dead bottles demonstrating in one corner of the kitchen, and when he heard the first gasps from the coffee pot he had his brightest idea of the night: he poured into one glass the residues of various rums – all cheap – sloshing around in the remote bottoms of those bottles, and managed to gather almost a tot of rum in a glass that welcomed the remains thus milked. Palpably happy, the Count ground the coffee and returned it to the pot, then poured a long measure on to the combination of rums, thus creating, in a unique solution, the communion of two tastes so necessary to his life: and took with him the honey dew that even tasted good as he went to dial Skinny Carlos.

"It's me, you dog," he said, when he heard his friend's voice.

"So, wild man," came the reply. "What are you up to?"

"Nothing at all."

"Cracked the case yet?"

"Yes and no, it's going both ways . . . Come to think of it, today I found out my thoughts are transparent and communicable."

"Well I'm happy for your thoughts. Now tell them to remember tomorrow."

"Course I remember . . . The bastard is I'm broke and can't buy anything."

"Forget it: it's your birthday . . . So come by early on.

The old girl says better not eat during the day, because she's going to cook a lot."

"She's mad, she'll get put away . . . Hey, I called you for two reasons . . . Don't know about you but I'm really worried about Andrés. There's something up with that bastard, I've never seen him so aggressive."

"Yeah, he's as queer as a coot. I spoke to his mother and she says he's odd with her as well. Something not quite right with our prince of Denmark. What was the other thing?"

"Oh, I'd like your opinion; you're an intelligent man, would you believe anything from a woman who dyes her hair?"

"What colour?"

"Blonde."

"Not a word."

"Why?"

"Because blondes who aren't blondes are whores or liars. Or both at once, which is when they're best . . ."

"Yes, you're right. Hey, thanks for the advice. Tell your mother I'll fast in her honour."

"I'll tell her. But don't get caught up, and come early, my friend."

"You bet . . . See you tomorrow, my friend."

The Count gulped down his mélange of coffee and rum and felt that, although he was tired and sleepy, he should strike a few keys on his decrepit Underwood: he needed to lance a painful boil and say something he didn't dare to express verbally to Skinny Carlos and perhaps the story of friendship, pain and war he'd been concocting in his head for several weeks was finally ready to see the light, tonight of all nights. His spirit now carried a high enough dose of love and squalor to commit it to paper and, without more ado, he put the typewriter on the dining table and read the last of the pages he'd left on the platen on the distant morning of the previous day.

The youth slumped to the ground, as if pushed, and rather than pain he felt the millenary stench of rotten fish issue forth from that grey, sterile land. The dust irritated his eyes and blocked his nose, making it difficult to breathe, if not almost impossible when the pain finally came: it began mid-waist and started to extend its feelers towards his legs and over his chest, barely dampened by the blood devoured by the infirm, pestilent earth.

Almost without thinking the Count put his fingers on the worn keys and felt as if his hands were thinking for him, while the letters etched themselves on the fresh paper in the platen.

Before losing consciousness he realized he was wounded, that he couldn't move and soon perhaps everything would be over: he thought the idea strange but logical, for although he was only twenty-two and was not used to thinking of death, the fact he was in a war put that hitherto remote possibility on the wheel of fortune.

He woke up to hear the noise of engines and a voice said: Keep calm, we're going to the hospital, and from his position, flat on his face, he saw the tops of fleeting trees, made small by the height of the helicopter, but the dead sea stench from the ground still lingered in his nostrils, as insistent as the pain that made him faint again.

In fact the young man never found out where the bullet came from that broke two vertebrae and destroyed his spinal cord. Then he remembered how, before falling to the ground, he'd been thinking about the things he had

153

to do when he got back home. They were simple plans, full of everyday simplicity, supported, as ever, on two feet: dreams of love, the future, life projects postponed by the decision to participate in that distant war. Consequently, when he regained his lucidity and felt an empty numbness towards the south of his body, he asked the nurse whether they'd cut his legs off and she smiled, assuring him they hadn't, and when he asked her if he'd walk again, she just shook her head and tugged his hair, in a gesture of possible consolation for the inconsolable.

Why had that particular bullet chosen to hit him of all people and change his whole life in less than a second? He knew that was one of the risks of war but it seemed to him too cruel for everything to come to an end like that. He, who'd never thought of wars, who'd detested the cold weight of guns, and who'd said yes ever since he had use of his reason, thinking obedience would take him to a very different place from the bed where he now lay, an invalid for the rest of his days: a bullet with no return to sender had hit him of all people, aimed by a faceless being and shot with a hatred he had never felt or shared.

And the Count wondered: is this the moving story I want to write? No, it was but the prologue to an episode summing up the cruel experience of a generation and the burning reflection of another's guilt assumed as his own, for he always thought his back should have been the one to get "a bullet with no return to sender" and not Skinny Carlos's, the finest man he'd ever known. He struggled with the dilemma of continuing in that vein or tearing up the sheet of paper, when he grasped the real extent of his doubts: was he able to say all, without hiding anything, about what he felt, thought, believed, wanted to write? Could he be honest enough with himself to commit to paper his fears, dissatisfactions and incurable pain. Could he say what others silenced and that someone, some time, should say? The Count lit another cigarette, closed his eyes and accepted that he too was afraid.

He boldly opened his eyes, in the certain knowledge that he had reached the horrendous age of thirty-six and that it would indeed be his last day as a policeman, and what he saw no longer shocked him: an empty goldfish bowl, a bed only slept in in its most sunken half, a few books burdened by dust, deferred longings and envy, a bottle of Caney rum squeezed as dry as a rag, a murky, threatening future and, framed by the narrow angle the window now offered, a scrap of sky, once again that goddamned persistent blue. But he hardly thought about hurricane Felix, which was probably just round the corner, at an obedient halt, waiting to be invoked by the Count before it took to its preferred route of the Calzada and carried through its general clear-out, but rather he scrutinized his watch, which warned there were still six hours to go to the change of age: as if that were at all important. His mother had told him he was born at one forty-five p.m. on 9 October and each year when they were together she patiently waited for that moment before she went over, hugged him and gave him the third of the four kisses they exchanged in the whole year. The three others corresponded to her birthday, 15 April, Mother's Day, always the second Sunday in May, and the last kiss came on 31 December, just as the bells rang out the final seconds of the year and they swallowed grapes, if there were any: as many as twelve, if they could. When the Count grew up and decided to see the New Year in with his friends, at street parties or at Skinny's house, the annual kisses were reduced to three, and Mario Conde now regretted that irreversible dearth of affection and love he and his mother established in a deep yet timid relationship where they were unable to express physically what they felt within themselves. Because many other events might have deserved the natural congratulation of a kiss: his graduation from high school, perhaps; the publication of his short story 'Sundays' in the bulletin of the school literary workshop; his first communion, when he was so pure and ready to receive Christ's flesh and spirit and she was all in white in that crackling starchy lace dress the Count remembered better than the moment he was unsure whether she had or hadn't kissed him. Nevertheless, his mother showed him other forms of affection he treasured in the holiest sanctuary of his memory: for example, the day he went into the bathroom without knocking and saw her naked. Mario must have been around nine and already thought he knew something of the secrets of female nakedness, and his mother's wet, shiny body, those luscious breasts, crowned by large, brown nipples and her jet-black abundant bush, froze momentarily before he half turned to flee that feminine vision he knew was prohibited, and she called to him and said: "Come, Mario," and he turned round slowly, looking his mother in the face so he didn't see her breasts and dark sex again, and she repeated, "Come, I am your mother," and she took his arm and placed his hand on her wet belly and said to him: "Take a good look at that scar," and he saw an ancient red weal on her skin, which started under the navel and disappeared into her pubic hair, and she said: "You came into the world through that gash," and he engraved on his mind for ever that eternal sign of an unrepeatable oneness that used to bind him to a woman he did not wish to see naked again until the day she died, when, contrary to all he could have predicted, he decided he'd be the one to clean the still body with her favourite cologne, and stroked again the gash from which he originated and gave her the first and only kiss for that year, since she died on 16 January, three months before his birthday. The number of kisses still pending was so great the Count always wondered why the kiss was the highest sign of love: totally Eurocentric and Judaeo-Christian, sexual, labial nonsense, he'd tell himself then, and told himself now, remembering how on his eighth birthday there was an additional kiss, granted after the inevitable one forty-five p.m. kiss, an evening kiss specially permitted for the last birthday photo with cakes and cold drinks, an occasion on which, for the last time, he'd be snapped with so many cousins later lost to remote paths of exile, and with Grandad Rufino, who died a few years after. He preferred not to look at those photos, consigned like stigmas to a box of festering nostalgia, in order to conceal the truth that he'd once been so happy and loved, an active member of that vanished concept of the family, garnering his mother's kiss and a hug from the old patriarch of the Conde clan, on whose vanquished legs he'd already sat, in order to smile at Oliverio's camera, as his arm fell round the neck of the old man who'd given him his first notions of the real world: for example, the one about not playing if you aren't sure you can win. Old Count Rufino, eternal bard of his youthful feats, was still a strong presence on that piece of card, a far cry from the final image of a man corroded by an illness about to waste him entirely, after softening his legs of stone, legs that accepted defeat and decreed the end

158

of his rule as a cock-fighter when mid-flight they told him they were no longer up to helping him escape a police raid on clandestine organizers of cock-fights. In the last memorable photo of that memorable birthday, the Count remembered one by one the relatives gathered there, all smiles behind an eight-candle cake, as if they knew that conjunction of the third, fourth and fifth generations of the family of Teodoro Conde, the Canary Islands escapee who'd reached Cuba a century and a half ago, was to become an alarmingly final image: diaspora, death, distance and memory-loss haunted that family photographed on 9 October 1961 and already predestined never to meet up again, not even at the wake of Grandad Rufino, who saw his greatest desire perish as he lived: to embark on death surrounded by all his children and grandchildren. Destiny's a bastard, thought the Count, and violently repelled that image now captured in his brain in order to recall, with the tiniest grin he could manage, his private celebration of his eleventh birthday, held in the solitude of the bathroom at home. It was an irrefutable axiom for him and his friends at the time that only at the age of eleven, at the exact moment your eleventh year began, did your penis start to be of use for more than shedding urine several times a day: now the peter, knob, thingy, willy was transformed, via the workings and grace of the age attained, into a weapon of struggle called cock – or dong, or tool, or prick, or wick, or meat, anything but the polite member it wasn't – and could shoot out white drops full of new potential, including a harvest of pleasure. And, following wise advice, Mario Conde shut himself in the bathroom with uncle Maximiliano's old magazine, which his cousin José Antonio had requisitioned, in which several women had allowed themselves to be

159

photographed showing their tits, arses and even hairy twats (one shaved). José Antonio, jerker *extraordinaire* if ever there was, skilled practitioner of the phantom jerk, the Capuchin, the two-hander, the soap-sudder, the mongrel and seven other varieties (including the suicidal jerk of the bat, the one you could only achieve by hanging by one arm from the eaves of a house, as you looked through a bathroom window and rubbed away with the other), had advised him that the best way to do it (especially if it was the first time) was by moistening yourself with saliva: saliva's hot and slippery as if you'd put it up a woman or a sow . . . But the Count was worried by the absence of other complementary signs of his sexual debut: not a single wisp of hair had sprouted in his armpits or pubis, his voice was still childish and reedy, and – no doubt worst of all – he preferred baseball to women. But he was eleven years old, eleven on the dot and his time had come: contemplating the steamy photos of naked women, he felt a flicker of current in his genitals and a degree of hardening of his small member, on which he spat a couple of gobs of saliva before beginning a rhythmic rub, back, forward, back, forward, that hardened his ex-peter, now transformed into an adult, masculine cock, which got harder and harder, and grew like a snake charmed by magic pipes, back, forward, more saliva, until something stirred in a spot on his body that he couldn't locate and a few drops of white amber ran along his hand, which reeked of sweat and saliva, leaving him empty and wondering: is this the shit that's supposed to be so wonderful? which he wasn't convinced of on his eleventh birthday, only understanding his extremely serious lack of appreciation when, nigh on a year later, he glimpsed the breasts of his neighbour Caridad, popping out of an indiscreet

160

neckline, which stirred his scrotum and forced him to run home, shut himself up in the bathroom again, where, seized by an urgency he'd never before experienced, and forgetting all about the saliva, began to rub himself with Caridad's breasts in his mind's eye – two hard protuberances, he knew, inflamed at their tips by earth-coloured nipples – and taken almost unawares felt a brutal shudder, heat coming from all his pores, a burning sensation coming from his testicles and shooting up his back, and the white, gleaming spillage, which propelled itself from his penis and splattered the tiles on the wall, and he knew why his cousin José Antonio had earned himself a diploma for jerking-off: that was the life . . . he concluded and, after smoking a cigarette that made him cough, he returned to his saliva and enjoyed a second adult masturbation. From then on he practised two or three times a week, until he discovered, almost on the day of his twentieth birthday, that there was an even better life to be lived: provoking the same spillage on a much better place than bathroom tiles: a woman's vagina.

"A woman's vagina," he called out loud, returning to consciousness as a policeman presumably on his last day of duty: perhaps Miguel Forcade's death had nothing to do with sublime works of art whose fakery he was aware of, but with something much closer, more mundane and sometimes more important, like a woman's vagina. Or, at least, perhaps the truth could be reached along that risky, moist, desired and lethal path. It was an unexpected revelation that came with fatally grey eyes (or were they green? or blue?) half hidden by lashes as wavy as the sea when a cyclone is approaching.

Colonel Molina's order erupted from the intercom and the petty subaltern who was acting as the new office boss and had been critically examining the detective lieutenant's visage stood up to open the door for him. The Count, who'd enjoyed the woman's displeasure at his deplorable mien and get-up, grunted to his feet, and, unbeknown to her, tugged at his old blue jeans so the pistol in his belt clattered to the floor. Nevertheless, the Count continued to walk towards the office door, as if oblivious to his loss, and the woman, whose astonishment had spread geometrically, shouted: "Hey, Lieutenant, you've dropped your pistol."

The Count turned round in front of the Colonel's office door, smiling at her as beatifically as he knew how.

"What pistol?"

"Yours," and she pointed to the abandoned weapon.

"You know, I keep leaving it all over the place," commented the Count and yawned before he picked his gun up and slotted it back into the waistband of his trousers.

And now he walked unsmiling towards his boss's door and whispered, "Thank you," as he sidled past the petty officer, who was undoubtedly thinking of starting on the report she'd file on his negligent attitude towards his regulation firearm.

"Come in, Lieutenant," said the Colonel, sitting behind his desk, a cigarette between his fingers.

"Good day, Colonel. I've come because I need to hear you repeat what you said two days ago."

"What did I say then?"

"That you gave me carte blanche in this case."

"But I also told you to be careful and cautious, and not to go too far. Remember we have to avoid a scandal in the international media . . ."

"That's all very well, but tell me what I asked you . . ."

Colonel Molina stood up and walked round his desk till he was face to face with Mario Conde.

"What is it you want, Lieutenant?"

"To solve the case."

"But what are you going to do that means you need to hear my authorization again?"

"I just want to rough up some people who are lying to me . . ."

The Colonel raised his eyebrows, as if not believing what he'd heard, and turned round a moment to stub out his cigarette.

"Lieutenant, what do you old-school police mean by 'roughing up'?"

The Count steadied himself. He'd alarmed this novice, too, and without having to set up the spectacle of an abandoned pistol.

"I don't know, it depends on . . ." and he halted on the edge of the precipice.

He was perhaps risking too much if he joked, even his retirement letter, and preferred not to: though he was sorry. He would like to have seen Molina's face as he listed medieval instruments of torture used as synonyms for roughing up.

"What does it depend on, Lieutenant?"

"On whatever one wants to find out, Colonel. And in this case I want to find two things out: first, what Miguel Forcade came to Cuba for, something he couldn't take out ten years ago, something that could make him rich in two days . . . and then to know who killed him, and if it was to grab whatever could make a man rich."

"And who do you want to rough up?"

"A blonde who's probably not blonde, a North American citizen who has a Cuban passport, a hitter who can slam hard and a man who stole the shoes from my dreams . . . Will you just repeat the bit about my having carte blanche?"

The Colonel seemed to hesitate. He looked at the Count, studied his hands, thought about what he should do as the lieutenant added: "Colonel, you can't always be orthodox and patient in order to reach the truth: sometimes you have to strike back and dig out the truth from wherever it is hidden. And this blonde, despite all my efforts to keep her here, will return to the States in two days. And if she goes, the fucking truth goes with her. Do you understand? Besides, I only have nine hours left to present you this case gift-wrapped. Now I want to hear you repeat yourself, please."

Molina smiled briefly and lit another cigarette, after offering the Count one.

"Lieutenant, either you are mad or I'm the one who's mad for telling you this: go for it, you've got carte blanche . . . And may God look favourably upon me."

If time had been on his side, the Count would have preferred a different scenario: for example, to keep Miriam in his hot cubicle for a couple of hours, as if he'd forgotten all about her and under the apparent supervision of two uniformed men who wouldn't respond if she asked a question. That would have made things easier, he thought, as he watched Miriam smile calmly, after she'd asked: "So, you're going to put me inside?"

Sergeant Manuel Palacios, who had brought her into Headquarters, looked over the woman to the Count and waved a hand, warning him to prepare himself: he'd certainly already taken more than his fair share when he'd asked Forcade's widow to accompany him there.

"Nobody is going to put you inside," the Count said finally, "unless you've done something that merits your being there, of course."

"And what might I have done?" She returned to the attack, with that sour persistence the Count had met before.

The woman had guts, he told himself, and almost rejoiced he hadn't been pronged on the bars of her eyelashes. Or was that ripe fruit from Paradise still worth tasting? He had time perhaps, he consoled himself, ever a greedy sod.

"The fact is I don't know, Miriam, but I am sure of one thing: you know much more than you've let on."

"And what do you reckon I know?"

"I told you: what your husband was looking for in Cuba . . ."

"And I've told you more than once: he came to see his father. Or did they make a mistake when they allowed him in?"

The Count again regretted he didn't have time to soften her up, although he also thought such gentle techniques wouldn't have produced the goods with this hard-bitten woman. Worst thing of all was that if Miriam blocked all routes in, he'd have no paths along which to progress the case: Fermín still hadn't said anything to incriminate himself and Gómez de la Peña had been sent home blubbering at dawn, after he'd sworn a hundred times he didn't know his extraordinary Matisse was a fake and didn't know where Miguel Forcade went on that fatal night after he'd visited him. To cap it all, the ultra-efficient Candito had called him that morning to confirm what the Count suspected: the Havana underworld was not involved in the death and castration. "So why did they cut his tail off, Red?"

"You find out, Count, that's why you're the policeman on this job, isn't it?"

As a false trail, to hint at revenge, jealousy, or was it another queer affair? Who can tell . . .? Now what did he have left? Perhaps he should try his luck with a loose cannon, like Adrian Riverón, suspected of the heinous crime of being a closet smoker, Miriam's friend and ex-fiancé and now perhaps her confidant; or go back to talk to the dead man's mother, who didn't seem to have the slightest idea of what world she was living in. And old Forcade? he wondered, as his consciousness felt certain all paths had been blocked. After all, everybody insisted Miguel had returned to Cuba to see his father and that apparent lie might be the one and only truth.

"So he came to see his father?"

"I've told you so at least ten times. Why won't you believe me?"

"No, I believe you, Miriam, but tell me just one thing, what's your father-in-law's mental state?"

She seemed surprised by the question that dragged her from the circle of denials and rejections behind which she had fenced herself.

"He's been slightly mad ever since I've known him. And now he's eighty-six I think he's gone even crazier . . ."

"But he's not ga-ga, is he?" he asked tightening the rope, and the rope twanged.

"He is as far as I'm concerned. The poor guy doesn't know which planet he's on . . ." she replied, after hesitating briefly, and the Count knew he'd hit the bull's-eye. Smiling, the policeman seized his moment.

"You must forgive me, Miriam, but I have to ask you

to stay here at Headquarters. Only for an hour or so. I'll soon be back and we can continue our conversation. OK?"

"Do I have any choice in the matter?"

The Count's smile broadened a little: he tried to appear charming, even relaxed and cheerful, as he told her: "I don't think so," and went out into the corridor before she could batter him with appeals to civil, consular and democratic rights that she'd no doubt take to the UN Security Council. Manolo, who'd followed him at a speed accelerated by his fear of being left alone with Miriam, asked him on tenterhooks. "But what are you going to do, Conde?"

"Head with you to the Forcade household. But first of all find two guys to stay and keep a watch on her. Tell them to put her in another office, not to leave her by herself and not to talk to her . . . And get a move on, because El Zorro rides again," he said, taking out the avenging sword of the defender of the poor, and slicing through the air three times, zas, zas, zas, engraving there the indelible Z of the masked righter of wrongs.

Miguel's mother welcomed them with a confused smile and the usual accumulation of magnesia at the corners of her mouth. She was perhaps glad to see them, as they might be bearers of the faintly good tidings of the capture of her son's murderer. Nervously the aged lady asked them in and the Count took advantage of a possible confusion to touch on a matter he'd not yet broached.

"What beautiful lamps, señora," and he walked over to the genuine Tiffanys and trailed his fingers over the lead veins on the standard lamp whose glass panes

167

imitated a fruit tree till he found the authenticating signature: yes, it was. "I'd never seen one of these . . ."

She nodded proudly, and also walked over to the lamp.

"The fact is, that Tiffany is a rare object. They only made five of this model. Can you imagine? I know because we've had several visitors wanting to buy them. My husband knows all about it, but has always refused to sell anything without Miguel's permission, because my son asked him to try to preserve everything . . ."

"Because it all belonged to Miguel, didn't it?"

"Yes, he brought it all here."

"I really don't understand how he could give up so many beautiful pieces . . ." the Count let drop, in case the hare jumped.

The old lady rubbed her hands, perhaps wet with perspiration, and confessed: "I don't either."

The Count gazed on her as benignly as he could, and dived in at the deep end: "Caruca, we still don't know what happened to your son. We have an inkling, and need a little help from you . . ."

"But in what way?"

"We need to speak to your husband right away."

She rubbed her hands again, surprised by the kind of help sought. Her eyes had now moistened, as if irritated by an unexpected cloud of smoke.

"But he's an invalid and hasn't been out of the house for ages. He lives in his own world, what can he know . . .?"

"That doesn't matter. I spoke to him yesterday and it's clear his mind is in good working order, and we want to talk about things that happened some years ago. May we?"

"The fact is he was very influenced by Miguel's . . ." she whispered, trying to erect a final parapet to protect her husband from the interminable shadow produced by her son's death.

"Caruca, it can only be worse if he never knows who the savage was that killed Miguel, and worse still if they go unpunished. Tell Dr Forcade that my mind has exhausted all possibilities and my only option is to exchange opinions with him. Tell him in those words."

The old lady hesitated a few seconds, but the Count knew her defences were vulnerable, like the digestive system that could return that white paste to her lips. The policeman was ready to reopen the wound, but she nodded.

"Wait a minute. I'll get him in a fit state and tell him you want to see him, because your mind has exhausted all possibilities and your only option is to exchange opinions with him."

She didn't wait for a reply but headed for the stairs. She took short, visibly confident steps.

"Hey, Conde, what's a lamp like that worth?" asked Manolo when the old lady had vanished from sight.

The policeman lit a cigarette and lamented, as always, that he couldn't find an earthenware or metal ashtray. He only saw objects that should be on display in a museum: bone china, sculpted glass, rococo style pieces that ran the risk of dying at the clumsy hands of a Mario Conde.

"I don't know, Manolo, but it could run to several thousand . . . What would you do with a lamp like that, you could sell for fifty thousand dollars?"

"Me . . .?" came the surprised response, and he smiled. "Well I'd sell it and and paint the town and nobody'd stop me – not even by tying me up. What about you?"

"I'm an artist, Manolo, remember . . . But I'd also

sell up and they'd have to tie me up with you. I swear on the sliver of liver I've got left . . ."

The two policemen devoted almost ten minutes to improving or destroying their lives with the fifty thousand dollars they had earned so easily, until Caruca peered over the rail to the top floor to say: "You can come up now."

When he was by her side, the Count asked quietly: "How is he today?"

"I don't know, quite tired, but he says it's fine, he wants to speak to you."

Thank you, Caruca, you'll see how important it is," the Count reassured her before going into the bedroom.

The Count found the weary old man seated on a wood and willow armchair, looking more brittle and vulnerable now he was away from his plants. Behind him the Count contemplated an altar built into the wall, where he saw the central dominating image of a crowned Virgen de la Caridad del Cobre, flanked by a bleeding St Lazarus escorted by his dogs and a jet-black Virgin from Regla. That altar, the Count recalled, immediately cursing his memory, was almost a replica of the one that had always been in his parents' house, on the wall where they placed the cradle of the newly born. A Virgen de la Caridad del Cobre like theirs, wearing a blue robe and golden crown, floating on a choppy sea from which three small men in a boat were praying to her, could well be the first image the eyes of the Count and his sister had retained, the same sister who, in order to accede to her red Communist Youth card, persuaded her mother it would be better to dismantle the altar that had always been there, on the finest wall in that room where they were conceived and received their first notions of love.

The Count felt his anger rise and took another look at the Virgen de la Caridad before returning alarmed to real time; old Forcade must have spoken to his wife in the ten minutes she'd taken to come back, because the old man's face, almost always motionless, was now wet with tears streaming from his bright-red bloodshot eyes, as if his weary skin were hurrying them on their way. The pyjamas he wore, elegant and buttoned to the neck, helped emphasize that image of an end as desired as it was nigh, and completely accepted.

"Good day, Dr Forcade," said the Count, daring yet again to grip one of the old man's withered hands.

"A bad day and a bad year," replied the old man, his tears disappearing down the bloody well of his eyes.

"I'm sorry to bother you again, but you know as well as I do how important it is we chat a little more."

"Was every path really blocked?"

The Count let go of the defeated hand.

"You know they were always closed off. And you, who must know what I'm thinking, won't deny me the opportunity to confirm my belief that you alone hold that key."

"Not even if I were St Peter . . . But let's assume that I *do* hold it. Why should you suppose I'm going to help you?"

"That is easier to explain: because you want us to find the person who killed your son. And I'm even surer now, after your wife told me that in all these years you didn't sell a single piece of what he left when he went. I can imagine at some point you needed . . ."

"That's true, more than once. And you're also right in what you assume I must be thinking: I certainly want you to find who did this to Miguel. Do you know something I never told you yesterday? I am a Christian, as you can see, though in my work I'm considered to

171

be a scientist and many people say that science and religion are irreconcilable. But it's not true: I spent almost seventy years studying plants and I think one can only understand the spirituality of those beings if one assumes them to be creatures created by God, because in many ways they are more perfect than humans . . . In many ways. And as a Christian I should believe in forgiveness rather than earthly punishment, but as a man of this world I also think there is guilt people should begin to pay for down here. Don't you agree? And then let God forgive those he chooses to forgive . . ."

The Count shook his head and went to grip the worn-out skin and brittle bones of the hands the old man placed on the arms of his chair. For a second time awareness that death might be a step too near was moving him, he thought, as he looked at the old man who so reminded him of his grandfather Rufino, when Caruca walked over to her husband and put an arm round his shoulders.

"You feeling ill, Alfonso?"

The man looked up, eyes redder than ever, and smiled. When his lips returned to their usual place and he recovered his speech, he said: "What does it matter any more, Caruca?"

"Don't talk like that, dear," she reproached him, caressing his neck, in a gesture that could only express the deepest, truest love.

"And what do you want me to tell you?" the old man asked, in a voice now as clear as a bell, looking at the two policemen.

The Count couldn't stop himself and looked back at the Virgen de la Caridad, while thinking that his question was surely going to be cruel, and he weighed up cruelty against truth. Persuaded of his lack of options, he decided to throw out a question only that oracle, endowed with the gift of speaking to plants and entering the compartments of a policeman's mind, could answer: "Doctor, if you know, tell me and be done with it. What did your son come in search of after so many years?"

"Have any of you heard of the Manila Galleon? Of course not, and I'm not surprised, because that boat is like a dream lost in the memories of historians, although for more than two centuries it made a crossing every year as daring as Christopher Columbus's, the only difference being that this galleon was definitely looking for the East by sailing westwards . . . But the history of journeys by Spaniards to the Philippines doesn't begin until after 1571, when Miguel López de Legazpi founded Manila, and naturally trade began with America, as it was easier to get there from Mexico or Panama than from Spain, by skirting Africa round the Cape of Good Hope. So, immediately lucrative trade from Mexico, Panama, Guatemala and Peru started from those islands, where they brought products from America and Europe, and these sold very well for silver, though the money rarely reached the treasurers of Seville's monopoly on trade. That was why the Spanish crown decided to restrict that semi-clandestine trade and authorization was given only for sailings to Manila from the port of Acapulco, in the Mexican Pacific. From 1590 two ships would leave there taking thirteen or fourteen months for the round trip, and then two more would set out to the same destination, in a constant, well-guarded plying of trade . . . Just imagine, this trade with the Philippines was one of the most profitable in an era when ships sailed with two hundred and fifty thousand pesos worth of goods and returned with more than half a million in silver, because long before the Spanish reached the Philippines those islands were a commercial centre attracting merchants from China, Japan and other Asian countries, and it was one of the richest places in the world . . . But as the Spanish kings didn't like anybody else getting too wealthy, in the seventeenth century the two boats were reduced to a single vessel, with a greater tonnage, and under greater supervision, known from that time as the Manila Galleon: that solitary boat sailed from the Philippines in June, before the typhoon season began, and crossed the Pacific in three months, to return to Manila in December and to Acapulco in June, laden with even more wealth. Imagine that it must have been a roaring trade, for by the end of the seventeenth century the captainship of that vessel was the most coveted position of all those in the gift of the governor of Acapulco, and to get it one had to pay some forty thousand pesos, because whatever deal was done in Manila gave profits of one to two hundred per cent . . . Naturally, items the Western imagination found hard to conceive travelled in the hold of the Manila Galleon: jewels, gold, jade and porcelain and silver galore. Then the cargo unloaded in Acapulco crossed the Chapultepec isthmus on mule-back, and was kept in Veracruz, until the boats from the Spanish fleet in the Gulf arrived to transport it to Havana, just before the beginning of winter . . . What happened in that city between the months of December and March each year must have been something special: all the vessels in the royal fleet, from New Spain and from Southern Terra Firma, returning loaded with gold, silver, jewels, pearls, furs, and all the treasure they could steal, dropped anchor in Havana Bay and the sailors and functionaries of the crown lodged there, and the city was transformed into a veritable playground of luxury, lechery and reckless gambling, prompted by the converging of people of all kinds and rank, enriched in two days and ready to impoverish themselves in a single night. Remember that those men knew the next journey across the Atlantic might be their last, for the treasures they were taking to Europe were a prize target for lurking corsairs and pirates waiting for them to leave the Caribbean, because they knew the fleet only set out for Seville in spring. The treasures, as they waited for the boats to sail, were stored on land, with all appropriate security measures in place. Those in charge were the Overseer General, the Captain General of the Fleet and a person with the very appropriate name of the Royal Keeper, who was designated by none other than the King of Spain to look after his economic interests.

"But the truth of the matter is that the story I am about to tell, and that may be connected to my son's death, did not begin in the time of those fleets, but long before. Because it all started with the T'ang dynasty, the royal household that governed southern China between the seventh and tenth centuries BC and was the great propagator of Buddhism in that region of Asia . . . You know, Buddhism was known in China from the time of the Han dynasty, and contemporary artists had begun to represent the image of Buddha, thanks to influences brought by monks and pilgrims arriving from the west, particularly from the lost city of Gandara, where a concrete image had been given to the creator of that religion for the first time. Because, although we might think it strange now, the image of the Buddha was initially a symbolic not a physical

175

representation, in porcelain and sculptures nearly always made from stone. But with the T'ang dynasty, more than five centuries later, Buddhism reached a religious peak and art flourished in the country, and they say the capital of this southern empire, called Chang-an, became the most cultured metropolis in the world at the time, outstripping Rome or Byzantium, and enjoyed a truly cosmopolitan atmosphere: consequently there was a large number of Buddhist monasteries and all had images, paintings, murals, the most exquisite objects of worship and ornament, some of huge material value . . . But this magnificent display of Buddhist splendour in China begins to decline with the great persecutions of 843 to 845, when thousands of temples are destroyed and Buddhist artefacts are stolen. What happened in those years in Chang-an is still considered one of the greatest catastrophes in the history of human culture, and there has been no shortage of those . . . Temples were devastated, stone and wooden images destroyed and bronze or gold images of the Buddha were melted down and turned into coins and profane accoutrements . . .

"Many years later, at the beginning of the seventeenth century, and via a route that remains unknown, the Spanish came into possession of a gold statue of the Buddha, created during the T'ang dynasty and which had somehow survived the catastrophe in the ninth century. Although the custom at the time was to melt down many works and only transport gold and silver to Spain, that item must have impressed its new owners so much that the governor of Manila decided to send it intact to the King of Spain, to swell his treasures in the most suitable way possible: either as mere metal or as the singular work of art it undoubtedly was, for, though that governor could never have known this, the style of that piece was undoubtedly from the T'ang period, and one of the few representations of the Buddha made in pure gold, because it was much more usual to use wood, stone and even bronze, not gold . . .

"Now, I will try to describe it, so you have some idea: it was a statue of a standing Buddha, wrapped in a cloak that fell in folds around him. The hands of the god were clasped in prayer, and his feet rested on a lotus leaf, as delicately as if he had descended from heaven to settle there. An oblong halo opened out behind him, furrowed by lines creating veritable labyrinths. The Buddha's body was lean, as he was usually represented at the time, his face almost square, fully expressing his power. But he wore the hint of a small smile, which drew out his slightly oriental features. That extraordinary statue, created a thousand years ago by an artist whose name we shall never know, weighed thirty-one pounds in pure gold and stood seventeen inches high, in today's measurements. Can you imagine . . .?

"The item finally crossed the Pacific Ocean, with more careful handling than usual, and was unloaded in Acapulco, crossed Mexico, reached Veracruz and was shipped again, now to Havana, whence it should have gone straight to Seville and then to Madrid, a royal offering to a Philip IV beginning to witness the decline of his empire and like all Spanish kings quite short of funds. That sculpture had great value in its weight in gold alone and its curators took special care, set in train special security measures, convinced his Majesty would appreciate such a piece at a time when great art from the Orient was beginning to be rediscovered and valued in Europe. The only risk the work ran was in what it stood for: in the period of the

Counter-Reformation and Inquisition, an image of the Buddha might perhaps be ill-fated, and the king or one of his economic or spiritual advisers could recommend its destruction by fire and transformation into a still valuable pile of gold . . .

"Here history ends and speculation begins: because the last trustworthy news we have of the journey of the gold Buddha from Manila to Europe is of its arrival in Havana on 3 December 1631, at the height of the war between France and Spain, and it was moved to the Captain General's coffers on the island, where it would be stored with other treasures from Mexico, Peru, Bolivia and Guatemala until its definitive departure for Spain . . . which never happened. The mystery of the Buddha's disappearance provides scope for endless speculation and several characters can be suspected of the theft: from Juan Bitrián de Viamonte, who was Governor of the Island to the Admiral of the Fleet, including the Royal Keeper himself and the General Overseer, who accounted for all riches sent to Spain. The head of the Governor's official guard was also suspected, and several functionaries of the imperial bureaucracy who were privy to the information about that fabulous item's existence, and knew moreover how much it was worth and where it was kept. The investigation of the theft was carried out by a lieutenant from the Royal Guard, one Fernando de Alba, who two years later wrote a memorandum to the king detailing the story, and apologizing for his failure. What we do know is that the gold statue disappeared from where it had been located, and even from people's memories. And when it reappeared, it only brought misfortune, deceit, disappointment and death, as if wreaking revenge on behalf of an Oriental deity . . ."

Dr Alfonso Forcade's stiff smile imposed a long pause, which none of those listening dared break. The old man struggled to breathe, as he waited for his facial muscles to relax. On the edge of his seat, the Count realized he'd forgotten to light up, despite the anxiety that gnawed him. He waved a cigarette and waited for the old man's nod of approval. Only when he lifted his lighter did the policeman feel his hands shake: where would that strange, forgotten story, graced by old Forcade's astonishing erudition, lead? To his son's death, obviously; and the certainty that Miguel Forcade had returned to Cuba solely for the object that could make him a wealthy man showed the Count his suspicions were well founded and revealed to him an immediate danger.

"Doctor, forgive my interrupting you . . . Are you sure nobody else knew this story?"

Finally released from his paralysing smile, old Forcade looked at his wife.

"Please bring me some water."

"Wouldn't you like one of your pills? Or a lime infusion?"

"No, water," he repeated, and as his wife left, the old man at last looked the Count in the eye. "Don't despair, Lieutenant, we will to get to my son Miguel, but there's still some way to go."

"I'm not despairing, I even think I'm enjoying the story, but I don't like the conclusion I'm already imagining."

"The end is indeed quite predictable by this stage . . . But what is surprising are the paths along which everything flows from now on. But don't worry, the end isn't exactly how you imagine it. Some surprising things still await you."

"And do you know where this Buddha is now?"

interjected Manolo, leaning forward. Curiosity had him well and truly hooked.

"I think so, though I'm not sure. But we'll get there soon . . . And as for you, Lieutenant, smoke as much as you want. I love the smell of tobacco. I smoked for forty years, haven't smoked for twenty-five and I still feel the desire to do what you are doing."

The Count nodded sympathetically at that confession from a repentant smoker and looked around for an ashtray. In the corner of the room he spotted a beautiful bureau he'd almost not noticed before, so enthralled had he been by the story of the missing Buddha.

"A beautiful piece of furniture, Doctor," he commented, pointing to the table, ideal for someone devoted to writing.

"Yes, it is beautiful. Does it suggest anything to you?"

The Count deposited the ash in the palm of his hand.

"What should it suggest?" he asked and, almost without thinking, he added: "Is it connected to the Buddha?"

The old man smiled again, cadaverously, and when he'd recovered his speech he held out a hand to Mario Conde.

"Lieutenant, why waste your time on this job? With your intuitions . . ."

The policeman looked back at the magnificent bureau, from which a strange call of destiny seemed to emanate, and swayed his head before saying: "If only I knew, Don Alfonso. And if only I knew how this story really ended . . . one you should have told me by now."

"No, it wasn't the right moment. First I had to know who you were and what you thought and if you really wanted to find out who killed my son and why . . ."

"And do you know who killed him?"

"I don't unfortunately. But I'm breaking a promise by telling you the story of the Buddha. Because I hope that then you will be able to find out ... Thanks, Caruca," he said and drank the water his wife had handed him. "Now where were we?"

"Nothing more was heard of that gold Buddha until two and a half centuries later, in the midst of the War of Independence, when it came back to life to drive more people crazy ... It all started when one of the richest men on the island, the owner of land and sugar refineries in Matanzas, by the name of Antonio Riva de la Nuez, tried to take the statue to New Orleans, perhaps afraid his properties would be confiscated or ransacked by revolutionaries fighting for independence, their ranks thronged by former black slaves: the Haiti syndrome still haunted the minds of many Cuban landowners and several took out part of their wealth in order to be spared the total ruination meted out to the French settlers in Santo Domingo. It's the same old story repeating itself, isn't it, Lieutenant? The eternal fear of predatory barbarians ... But, unluckily for Don Antonio Riva de la Nuez, it was the time when, prompted by the war, a decree went out that all goods entering or leaving Cuban ports should be registered, and when that statue of the Buddha was found, the Royal Customs officer informed the Captain General of the existence and possible departure of a most valuable item to Mexico, and when the latter researched the origins of this singular treasure someone must have discovered it was the same Buddha that had been stolen from the King of Spain in 1631 ... And the statue was impounded, on behalf of the Spanish Crown, which was still its lawful owner, as you must agree? It is a real pity, but nobody ever really discovered how the statue that had been lost for more than two centuries came into the hands of Don Antonio Riva, and how it was extracted from the Captain General's treasure room. Because he always stated in the court cases he initiated against the Crown that he'd inherited it from his father, who in turn had bought it in Santiago de Cuba from a Franco-Haitian landowner, ruined by the war in the former French colony. Did that purchase really happen? Probably not, but nothing was certain in relation to that item . . .

"And thus the gold Buddha returned to the Treasury in the Captain General's new building, while it awaited a favourable opportunity to resume its interrupted journey to Spain. And in August 1870 it was put on board the sailing ship *Las Mercedes*, and surrendered to the tender care of the boat's trustworthy captain, one Nathaniel Chavarría, a Basque what's more, and a retired officer of the Royal Navy, where he'd enjoyed an excellent service record and was valued as one with an expert knowledge of transatlantic shipping.

"On 23 August, in the teeth of several weather forecasts warning of the approach of a hurricane like the one on its way now, Captain Chavarría raised anchor after deciding that if a storm threatened he should seek shelter in the bay of Matanzas, where he would anyway have to put in for two days. *Las Mercedes* set sail in the morning and that same night, when it reached Matanzas, the storm seemed to be lying in wait for her in the mouth of the bay, and despite the Basque's acknowledged seafaring experience, the sailing ship foundered on one of the rocks in the entry to the port. Three new mysteries were then added to the history of the gold Buddha: firstly, why did Chavarría decide not to wait for two or three days, until the cyclone passed, before sailing to Matanzas?; secondly, the divers employed to search the ship's sunken remains in the very shallow area close to the coast never found the famous Buddha that weighed thirty-one pounds; and thirdly, in the shipwreck disaster only two of those travelling in *Las Mercedes* disappeared: an Andalusian sailor called Alberto Guarino, a man with a long criminal record, and Captain Chavarría himself, and their bodies were never given up by the sea.

"And the Buddha disappeared once more, as if that were its cyclical destiny. Nobody heard anything about it for a long time, though in the course of the investigations I carried out over the years into the history of that Buddha I formed a very poor opinion of Captain Nathaniel Chavarría . . . Because it just happened that one day, when conversing about Basque genealogy with a Uruguayan botanist called Basterrechea, who came to Cuba some fifteen years ago, he told me of the existence of a town in Uruguay by the name of San José de Mayo, of rich cattle ranches where he had done soil analyses at the request of the owners, the Chavarría family, of Basque descent, naturally. On hearing that, I asked him to find out the origins of the family and he wrote to me soon after, relating how the present owner's great grandfather had come to Uruguay around 1880 with a substantial amount of money he quickly invested in land, to avoid losing it all on the night-time binges in which he used to indulge in the brothels of Montevideo and Buenos Aires, despite the fact that he was sixty. I suggested he find out if the family was aware of the existence of a gold Buddha from the T'ang dynasty and whether they knew where their great-grandfather's fortune came from and what his line of work was before he emigrated to Uruguay. And the response was surprising and most revealing:

they knew nothing of any Buddha or the source of Nathaniel Chavarría's wealth, although they suspected he'd got it from an inheritance or his own commercial genius, because the old man was a poor second son who had been a military and then merchant sailor, only a few years before reaching that god-forsaken corner of South America, his pockets stuffed with gold and in the company of an Andalusian colleague who went by two names: Alberto Guarino, or Federico del Barrio.

"Chavarría's ruse was thus exposed and anyone not possessing the information I managed to put together could imagine two alternatives: either the Basque had sold the Buddha somewhere in Europe or America, or he'd melted it down, a much safer option for him, and had sold the thirty-one pounds of pure gold and disappeared to a remote town in Uruguay . . . But the second possibility never made any sense, because thirty years after the Matanzas shipwreck the Buddha was known still to exist, as smiling and healthy as ever, and had even returned to the hands of Don Antonio Riva de la Nuez . . .

"Because after Cuban independence, in 1902, when Spanish law ceased to be in effect on the island, a man called Manuel Riva Fernández, son of the Don Antonio who had lost and clearly recovered the gold Buddha, which he must surely have bought for a very goodly sum from Basque Captain Chavarría or his sidekick by the name of Guarino, showed the family relic to some friends and even allowed the press to photograph it. At the time there was talk of the statue costing more than two million dollars, because of its undoubted artistic value, since it was authenticated as a T'ang sculpture that had survived the disastrous banning of Buddhism in the ninth century, and was obviously one of the most extraordinary treasures from that time about which any information existed. And if any doubts remained as to its real origins, they could be forgotten after Manuel Riva was invited to an exhibition in Paris to exhibit his piece by the side of other treasures of ancient Chinese art. And Paris swooned at the feet of that magnificent Buddha, which was remarkable in so many ways.

"Manuel's daughter, Zenaida Riva y Ponce de León, inherited the Buddha upon the death of her father, in 1936. Zenaida, who had married the Cuban banker Alcides Guevara, one of the richest men in Cuba, took the Buddha to their Miramar home, and placed it in a security-locked, unbreakable glass cabinet, specially built in London for the Guevaras. I know of several people who saw the sculpture there and it was undoubtedly the family's pride and joy, which they could indulge the luxury of exhibiting and not selling, for if there was something the Guevara-Riva y Ponce de Leóns had to excess it was money . . . but that was of no use when in 1951 thieves deactivated the alarms, broke the security lock and removed the item from the house in Miramar. It is very easy to trawl this part of the story, because the press at the time printed reams on the case, photos of the Buddha were circulated, and a famous detective was even commissioned to investigate the theft, apparently a semi-specialist in such *chinoiserie*, one Júglar Ares. Neither the police nor the detective could track down the Buddha or its thieves, and people began to forget the case, particularly after the events that started to unfold from 1952: Batista's coup d'état, Fidel and his group's assault on the Moncada barracks, the arrival of *Granma* in Oriente province, the uprising in Santiago de Cuba, the failed regicide of 13 March, the war in the Sierra

Maestra and the victory of the Revolution, which by the way did not take Alcides Guevara and Zenaida Riva by surprise, for in September 1958 they had had the foresight to go to live in Zurich with their whole family, which must still be thereabouts, probably in the banking business.

"But not a word about the Buddha. The theft couldn't have been a put-up job like Chavarría's, because after Cuban independence the Rivas had become the legal owners of the treasure and had no need to hide it, indeed, it was their misfortune that they did quite the opposite.

"Yes, the Revolution triumphed and from January 1959 the Cuban bourgeoisie began to emigrate to the United States, Spain, Mexico, Puerto Rico, taking with them anything they could. Some dallied a little longer and their lingering cost them dear: they could leave Cuba, but the government confiscated everything it considered part of the nation's cultural patrimony and passed it into the hands of the State. Consequently, many people must have left real fortunes behind them: they didn't always surrender them, though, but sought out every possible means to hide them so they could later take them out via an alternative route or recover them, if as they anticipated, the Revolution didn't hold out for very long . . . But what you are imagining, Lieutenant, didn't happen: Miguel didn't steal in that way . . . be patient, the best is yet to come . . . or the worst, you will have to tell me.

"One of those Cuban bourgeois families was the Mena y Carbó family, who by chance lived only three blocks from the former residence of Alcides Guevara and Zenaida Riva . . . They fled Cuba in October 1960, leaving Señor Patricio Mena's spinster aunt in the house. But that aunt, who was only fifty and lived comfortably on the income assigned her as a result of the Urban Reform requisitions, died suddenly in January 1962 leaving no heirs on the island, and consequently the house was also inventoried by the government and the objects of value it contained were expropriated as goods of the State, and my son Miguel was in charge . . . In reality, there weren't many objects in the house of any importance: the mahogany furniture, a few Chinese porcelain vases of little merit, and that beautiful desk that caught your attention, which does have a special worth, though little appreciated by non-connoisseurs: it is the work of a pupil of Boulle, the famous French cabinet-maker who created a whole school for building cupboards and desks, which were particularly noteworthy because they had hidden compartments that could be barely detected if you compared the exterior and interior dimensions of the piece of furniture.

"It was just another bureau as it was for everybody else and Miguel knew I needed one for my papers and decided to buy it and give it to me as a present; we brought it here and found a suitable spot in that corner . . . As you already know I am a scientist, and I told you that I believe in God and the Virgin, didn't I? Well, it was that combination that led me to look for references to the style of my strange bureau and hence I came across Boulle and his practice of constructing quasi-invisible secret compartments. And I thought if this piece of furniture belonged to that school, it might also have such a compartment and I decided to find it. Do you know what? I had to search for three days, groping, measuring, tapping the bottom, and when I was almost sure no such hiding-place existed, I decided to push back a flange at the back of the drawer on the left, and when I tapped it I heard a slight whirr in

187

the wood: almost unawares I had found the spring to lift up the two boards forming the drawer bottom, where someone had built a small cavity in which I found two pieces of paper: a handwritten love poem, with no title or author's name, and most certainly deficient in literary terms, and something that was clearly a map, with references to a house, a fountain, a grille and an avocado bush, and the distance in feet from each of those places to a spot marked with a cross, by the side of which a word had been written that at the time I found both enigmatic and devoid of meaning. Can you guess what it was? Of course, it's easy now: the word written there was 'Buddha'.

"That same night I called Miguel to this room and showed him the map. He laughed and told me it must be pirate treasure, but that he would go and investigate what was there. I didn't see him for three days. We were very busy at the time, myself in the university and Miguel running the Department of Expropriated Property, and when I asked him he said the famous treasure was the corpse of a dog that was probably called Buddha. And we concluded that the spinster aunt who had died of a heart attack had buried her dog and kept the location alongside that poem she had written or received from an old suitor. And I forgot the whole business.

"I forgot so completely that that April day in 1978, when Miguel asked me to come up here and asked me if I remembered the map, I had to dig deep to unearth the story of a dog called Buddha and the love poem. Then Miguel told me the truth: the cross marked the place where a solid gold statue of a Buddha was buried, which he imagined to be particularly valuable not just for the gold, but in and of itself, and that a name was engraved on the marble base: Riva de la Nuez. And after telling me not to tell anyone about it, he confessed that thanks to the map in the bureau he had taken the statue from the Mena y Carbó household and since then it had been buried in the garden of this house. And he handed me a map as rudimentary as the one I'd found in the bureau sixteen years earlier. He asked me to put it back in the escritoire and said that only if something very serious happened to him that made it necessary to use the treasure should I dig it up and sell it. He also told me he intended to stay in Spain on his return from Moscow and it was then that he said if anyone ever asked me about the Buddha in the Boulle bureau, it was a sign I should give them the map and let them dig it up, for that person would take it from wherever it was hidden. And that if I died and Caruca died, my nephew Agustín, Miguel's cousin, should inherit it, so that the bureau with the map stayed in the family.

"The row we had that night is irrelevant, as is my discomfort at the crime my son had committed and the one he was planning to commit. He had confided in me and I couldn't betray him, and that was enough to keep me silent. What I did do was to research for years the gold Buddha that had belonged to Riva de la Nuez and put together this whole story from when it embarked on the Manila Galleon to the day the Mena y Carbós stole it or commissioned its theft in 1951 and buried it under their patio before leaving Cuba . . .

"In all those years I waited for someone to come at night and talk to me about the Buddha in the Boulle escritoire, but I never thought it would be Miguel who would mention it, a week ago. He explained how he had come to prepare the Buddha's removal to the United States and that Fermín, his wife's brother, would be responsible for taking it out on a launch, though Fermín still didn't know what he was taking out or where it was. And he told me that truly elusive Buddha was going to be his salvation . . .

"Are you content, Lieutenant . . .? I think I've told you what you wanted to know: that was what Miguel came to Cuba for: to remove a fifteen-hundred-year-old Buddha that must be worth several million dollars in any art market . . . Please, Lieutenant, open that drawer, yes, the one on the left, and touch the protuberance at the bottom. It's not giving? Push a little harder. Ah, finally the spring to the Buddha in the Boulle escritoire whirred into action. You know, I think I will now finally see with my own eyes that sculpture that has turned so many people crazy over so many centuries . . . including my son Miguel."

Detective Lieutenant Mario Conde couldn't recall many cases in which the prospect of a visible solution produced the emotional charge that shook him when old Alfonso Forcade pointed to the escritoire whose beauty had triggered in him a promising sense of wonder, and that, perhaps impelled by Forcade's incisive mind, the policeman had imagined to be related to the history of the lost Buddha. Consequently, he was looking for more straightforward explanations for that excitement: perhaps his imminent liberation; perhaps the certainty his intuition was proving yet again to be his best ally: everything was food for thought. Nevertheless, the policeman was convinced that if he could get the information to lead him to a magnificent gold Buddha, shaped fifteen centuries ago by an artist whose name would now remain unknown for ever, and whose artistry had withstood every risk posed by greed and history, he had reason enough to feel that excitement now making his hands tremble as he unsuccessfully felt the bottom of the drawer and imagined Rabbit's historical enthusiasms when he told him of that imbroglio of deceit and thieving, the weft of which was threaded by the most basic human motives, driven by ambition. That was why he took a deep breath, tried to calm his nerves, and then persisted with the silent drawer-bottom, until he finally released the spring concealed by a disciple of Boulle.

The map extracted from the quasi-imperceptible drawer bottom had been sketched on a sheet of paper that, despite the years, retained a pale sheen, from which a few marks, letters, numbers and lines drawn in black ink proclaimed their millionaire secret, converging on that precise spot in the patio – almost under a laurel that was surely a hundred years old – where Crespo and el Greco now dug to depths that had begun to dismay the Count.

"Can it really be so far down, Lieutenant?"

"Dig deeper, dig deeper," he insisted, lighting another cigarette and looking at the sky, which had turned into a leaden mantle across which dirty, spongy clouds scurried northwards, laden with water, electricity and evil intent.

A warm, humid breeze from the south was already rustling through the treetops, a prelude to the furies that might assail the city that same morning or, at the very latest, tomorrow morning. The noise of the spade and shovel, striking, moving, extracting earth, brought him right back to a keen awareness of what he was witnessing, but the idea of Miguel Forcade's final dramatic failure, after he'd been preparing himself for almost thirty years to make the leap to the fortune resting on a gold Buddha, concentrated his mind, despite what his eyes could see. Ever since he'd come to possess that Buddha who still refused to put in an appearance, Miguel Forcade must have lived completely in the thrall of a statue endowed with enough magnificence to change his karma in the most radical way: money and power would flow through his hands, the deceased must have dreamed, as he lived in a perpetual state of hypocrisy, waited to seize his moment in a country where millionaires no longer existed and where power, for a man like him, was based solely on capricious decisions that went beyond his will: today you have it, tomorrow you don't . . . The Count imagined the number of deferments that must have altered that desired, attainable fate, while the would-be millionaire lived a diminished life, always looking out for ways to enhance it, as resonantly as he could. Good luck as hell on earth. In fact his fear of the sea must have been a real sickness: because a well-equipped launch would have been the shortest route between that hole in the ground and the financial glory for which he'd betrayed all trust and faith. Then there were the years Fermín had spent in prison, while he worked in an office in Miami for a Cuban who'd got rich somehow or other and who'd die of envy when he discovered his employee's prospect of millions, and that must have been the worst sojourn in hell on earth the Buddha ever prepared for Miguel Forcade, in his desperate confinement to a small house in the South West, while his dreams furnished him the best mansions in New York, Paris or Geneva . . . That pit, which still hadn't given birth, which had in fact been a grave for Miguel Forcade's life, and apparently for his death: a straight line ran from that Buddha for whose appearance the Count prayed to all the gods of the Orient and even the Virgen de la Caridad del Cobre and the corpse found five days earlier in the sea, and in the Count's

192

mind the only person able to trace that line was taciturn Fermín, the man in whom the deceased millionaire who never was had placed all – or part of – his trust, he who, as a result of that elusive Buddha, had entered most unpleasantly, and most physically incomplete, into the perfect state of Nirvana: the one that goes by the common, profane name of death.

"Conde, I don't think there's anything here," protested Crespo, wiping the sweat from his scalp, which got less hairy by the day.

"Did you get the measurements right?" enquired el Greco, leaning breathlessly on the edge of the grave.

The Count looked back at the map, checked each of the references again, took the line and placed it between the roots of the laurel and measured a third time. The centre of the grave fell on the nine-and-a-half-foot spot marked by Miguel Forcade.

"Come on, out of there, for fuck's sake," he told his subordinates, feeling his sweaty hands getting the shakes again. "Come on, Manolo, give me a hand," requested the lieutenant, who threw himself at the ditch and began sinking the pick into the ground at a furious rate, as if his only task in life was to dig to the other side of the world, which in Disney cartoons was always to be found in remote China.

Manolo used the spade to extract the soil dislodged by the Count, who raised the pick once more, when the sergeant asked him: "And what if someone's already been and taken it, Conde?"

"Nobody's taken it, for fuck's sake, nobody!" shouted the lieutenant, and he lifted the pick as high as he could and brought it down with all his remaining might on earth moist because it was so deep and felt the metal point shiver as it hit something solid, compact, definitely metallic, maybe divine. The sergeant's spade dug hurriedly, spurred on by the tenacious Count, until a man-made surface revealed all its opaque brilliance, clouded by twenty-seven years of contact with soil. The Count thrust his hand into the mud and began to extract from the entrails of the world a nylon covering, which in turn contained a cloth wrapping, beneath which a heavy, almost round object slumbered, bound tightly round: the Count managed to retrieve the bag and cut the ropes securing the protective layer of cloth, and there, at the bottom of the pit, he pulled off the gauze that had begun to disintegrate, to reveal before the eyes of the police a yellow gleam capable of dazzling the world. Yes, it was lean and strong, like a real Buddha ready to distance himself from all non-transcendental materiality, and the smile on his face seemed to express sardonic satisfaction: and with good reason, thought the Count, for that pagan god had triumphed over the most incredible vicissitudes for fifteen centuries, and defeated a risk of death by melt-down that had threatened several times. Neatly draped in a metal cloak that fell in the most amazing folds, the body must have been over sixteen inches high, from the feet on the lotus leaf to the final twist of its Hindu headdress. Various men, over countless years, had risked their all for that smiling face, which was able to hallucinate, enrich and even kill those who tried to hold on to it, as if one could grasp the unattainable: old Forcade was right when he stated that the image of the Buddha was merely an illusory reflection of a truth situated beyond all dimensions and categories, because the creator of that powerful religion always recognized that his strength and permanence were rooted in his ultimate spiritual essence, far from the world of the terrestrial and tangible, beyond the realm of appearance: hence

194

the triumphant smile. A right bastard, the Count told himself, keeping his eyes on the sardonic statue, but feeling his waist curse him as he reverted to the vertical. He turned painfully round to the house and on the upper floor balcony saw the old man on his wood and willow chair, and his wife, at his side, also watching the search. Then the policeman yelled at a volume the whole neighbourhood could have heard: "We've got the gold Buddha!"

He looked at his watch and the time gave him a fright: his deadline was running out; it was almost twelve o'clock and, though he had a Buddha, which was almost certainly golden, possibly T'ang dynasty, presumably extremely valuable, he didn't have what he most needed: a murderer who had confessed. Or even a murderess. That's why he decided to move his pawns quickly: while he dispatched Crespo and el Greco to find Fermín Bodes – wherever he is, he insisted – and take him to Headquarters. He called Colonel Molina and asked him to come to that house in Vedado, as they had uncovered something too important for him not to. Then he ordered Manolo to alert the Patrimony people who had authenticated the fakery of the Matisse to send their leading specialist in antique Chinese statuary. Finally, he left his sergeant next to the Buddha, drowsy, but still smiling, at the bottom of the pit, and got into the car they had sent so he could hotfoot it back to Headquarters.

"Step on it, if you like," he told the driver, and, immediately, the Count discovered how much he'd been hijacked by the prickly feeling of shedding his own skin, of seeing himself in the third person, as he was consumed by a hot-blooded character at once admired and intimidating, living in a story already written . . .

From the day he'd become fond of reading and felt a corrosive envy of people able to imagine and tell stories, the Count learned to respect literature as one of the most beautiful things life could create. Perhaps the main reason for that respect was his own inability to throw himself into the ring and live on what literature brought. Because his desire to write was more a challenge than a dream and the extended deferral of his vocation found a unique relief in reading. At the end of the day, the sweet envy he felt of writers who wrote well was not so much a sickness as the conviction that he could perhaps never do it, even poorly.

However, that sublime, literary part of his life rarely connected with a real, everyday existence that was drab and downtrodden, which he tried to soak in rum in order to render it more bearable; consequently he was surprised by a pleasantly aesthetic feeling that he was embodying a literary character: though he had yet to test out the Buddha with a small knife to see if it was gold or lead, as happened with the bird of evil in the story he felt he was reliving.

It was then he remembered Washington Capote, his hot-blooded university friend who, unlike him, could see himself as a literary character, thanks to an astonishing memory for quotations and a facility for performance that allowed him to double theatrically as narrator and character in a novel. Because Washington would have loved to be in the Count's place, repeating confidently and emphatically the eight reasons Sam Spade had to send Brigid O'Shaughnessy to jail: "Listen. This isn't a damn bit of good. This is bad all round", and Washington would review the detective's barbed, cynical monologue till he reached the reason he preferred: "Seventh: I don't even like the idea of thinking that there might be one chance in a hundred that you'd played me for a sucker," said that literary lunatic, smiling for the cameras even better than Bogart.

"'One chance in a hundred that you'd played me for a sucker,'" the Count repeated mentally, able, unusually, to recall that sentence straight off, in order to understand that he really had no right to feel he was a fictional character but should accept he was a sucker: literature's uses in illuminating life were yet again vividly demonstrated to the policeman, who rabidly suspected one thing: almost a hundred per cent chance existed that several people might play him for a sucker.

The duty officer welcomed him with the best possible news: Crespo and el Greco had come in ten minutes ago with a man under arrest by the name of Fermín Bodes. "Good, good," whispered the Count, who at last realized why he was beginning to feel totally in thrall to this case, and not just because of the way it challenged his intellect. From the initial story about an image of the Buddha hidden or transfigured more than a thousand years ago by the faithful who had publicly to deny their faith, if only to guarantee the survival of their god's image, to these sadly contemporary characters waiting for him now, swayed by less altruistic ambitions, the serial deceptions that had dropped into his lap represented a heady mix. Betrayals, frauds, chases, and all manner of lies and fakery had become entangled in a farce that he, Mario Conde, would put an end to. Could this be the end . . .? But when he mentally reviewed the protagonists of the last act, he again felt angry at the insult to his intelligence – and even to his hunches: Miguel Forcade who feared the sea and accepted all the corrupt opportunities power sent his way; Gerardo Gómez de la Peña, the man with ugly feet and the petulance of those blessed by fate, blatantly opportunistic and indefatigably cynical; beautiful Miriam, perchance a blonde, a pawn crowned as queen and equipped with a voracious rapidity of movement that made her distinctly fearsome, with every histrionic resource necessary to live a life of lies, and even to throw her brother into the fire and her beloved husband into the sea; and Fermín Bodes, the sarcastic gymnast, always at half-cock, a joker, some-times at his own expense, at other times at others', only lightly punished for his multifarious crimes and sins . . . The Count had coexisted with such people, same city, same time, same life, looking up at the Forcades, the Gómezes, the Bodes from the lowly spot that they'd assigned him and so many other poor buggers like himself: they were right up at the top, while others were right at the bottom, they were surrounded by Tif-fany lamps and Matisse paintings that might even be genuine, residencies swapped like second-hand books – and he regretted the bibliographical simile – and handled real and putative millions while they acted like implacable judges in tribunals driven by ethical, ideological, political and social purity (where those on trial were almost always the "others"); and silenced and manacled, those "others" suffered from the chronic, incurable disease of life in a hovel, like Candito the Red, or were confined for ever to a wheelchair like his soul brother, or persecuted in the hills for believing the truth of life was to be found in the spurs of a rooster, like his deceased grandfather Rufino; or definitively fucked because they wanted a bit of what was up top, like his old acquaintance Baby-Face Miki, a sinner beyond redemption, who prostituted his scant literary talents by writing self-serving stories of praise. And, what about you, Mario Conde? Better shut up he told himself, as the lift-doors opened.

Before entering his cubicle, the Count took a deep breath and surveyed his appearance: blue jeans mud-stained from bottoms to knee, shoes that might be any colour from brown to black and his shirt, spattered with earth, had lost a button. But he went in without knocking and smiled, as if he were very happy, when he saw the faces of Miriam and Fermin turn round to look at him.

"And you can tell me now . . ." Fermín began aggressively, and the Count was quick to squash him.

"I can tell you lots and lots of things, and you and your sister can tell me lots too. To begin with, I can tell both of you that you are officially under arrest and investigation for homicide. Your status," he pointed to Miriam, "will be communicated to the North American consulate, so no need to worry about that. As you see, you are under arrest until your innocence is proven or you rot in a jail," and he looked at the ex-convict Fermín Bodes, and noticed he flinched slightly as he acknowledged what the notion of rotting in a jail might mean. "Got that clear?"

"But why now?" asked Miriam, and the Count saw her eyes didn't have their usual glint.

"On suspicion of murdering Miguel Forcade . . . Because for starters, I now know what your husband came to Cuba for . . . And right now we are investigating the authenticity and value of a gold Buddha that was buried under the patio of your house."

"A gold Buddha?" Miriam's surprise seemed real and Fermín's silence in keeping with his style.

The Count averted his gaze, and lit up.

"You didn't know? A Buddha more than a thousand years old weighing in at thirty pounds of gold? A statue worth several million dollars?"

"I didn't know, no, I don't know what you're talking about," she denied, her eyelashes fluttering for a reason the Count couldn't pin down: fear, confusion, or disappointment, perhaps. The policeman tried to be credulous and believe the woman to be in nervous shock at the confiscated fortune he'd told her about. But he pulled the rug . . .

"Miriam, I can't believe you didn't know. Please, stop telling me lies; I can't stand liars, and even less those who play me for a sucker."

"But I didn't know . . ." she insisted, tears about to fall from her eyes, as she tried to get her brother's attention. "What's this man talking about, Fermín? What Buddha is it?"

"Tell her, Fermín," suggested the Count, and the man glared: his eyes firing classic sparks of hatred as he said, "It must be something worth a lot of money that your idiot husband wanted to take out of Cuba. But I didn't know what it was or where it was."

"Do you think I'm going to believe that?"

Fermín bared his fangs once again and seemed to recover some of his poise.

"You can think whatever you want, but that's the truth: I never found out what it was or where it was . . . I've just found out from you."

"My God, a gold Buddha, gold . . ." whispered Miriam, but the Count preferred to scrutinize the man and thought he might be telling the truth. It would be in keeping with his character and that of his partners if Miguel had kept his secret to the end, as the best defence against a possible betrayal that might snatch his fortune away. But any excuse was likely from those professional liars, he told himself, fearing now that neither was Miguel Forcade's murderer and that the case might be slipping from his grasp once more. Then he decided to change tactic, hoping he might glean a grain of truth.

"Let's see," he suggested, looking from one to the other, until his gaze settled on Fermín. "If you didn't know what your brother-in-law was after in Cuba and you didn't kill him, you are free of any charges. It is no crime to plan a secret exit from the country. And as for you, Miriam, if you didn't know about the gold Buddha either and you simply accompanied your husband to Cuba, you haven't done anything heinous either and you can go and cry in Miami as soon as all this is cleared up. But listen for a moment: if you want me to believe this, you will need to have something really convincing to tell me and I don't think either of you is about to spill that kind of story, or are you?"

"When Miguel stayed in Spain, the idea was that my sister and I would leave later in a boat. I was to find the money to buy the motor, the launch and everything we needed and Miguel would send a letter telling me where he had hidden something that would make the three of us rich. And although Miguel was always a tricky customer, I knew he wasn't going to pull a fast one: we'd known each other a long time, we'd worked together and he'd trusted me enough to tell me that he was going to stay in Madrid when he came back: and that was something so serious most people wouldn't even tell their shadow; not even Miriam could have known. But it was then I had that problem and was jailed. Afterwards Miguel told me he almost went mad when he found out, although he had no choice but to wait and what he did was to take Miriam out of Cuba with a visa he'd got from Panama. As you can imagine, the ten years I was inside felt like five hundred, because I knew that if I'd been outside, if I'd got to the United States, I could be living the life of a millionaire, because whatever Miguel wanted to get out of Cuba had to be worth millions: you can't imagine some of the things that passed through his hands, and whatever it was must have been much more valuable than anything he had in his house. In order to resist without going mad I spent ten years doing exercises and behaving like a model prisoner, so as to earn the right to a reduction in my sentence, until they finally released me three months ago. Then I called Miguel and he told me that as soon as they gave him the humanitarian visa he'd requested he'd get on a plane and come to help me organize my departure again. And that's what he did. When he got here we sat underneath the oleander in the patio of his house and he told me he'd brought enough money for me to buy a launch and for us to leave Cuba with whatever it was that was worth millions. I asked him what it was and he told me it was something very close by and worth at least five million dollars, but he couldn't tell me until everything was ready. It was then I suggested we find a third person to help. I explained that as I'd been inside and because of the precautions being taken after they'd caught police involved in drug trafficking and more besides, I might not have much freedom of movement and it would be safer if someone else was responsible for getting the launch, motor and whatever else was needed. On top of that, I reminded him it was a risky business crossing the Straits of Florida alone, however good the boat. He was convinced by the argument about crossing the sea solo, and although he didn't like the idea of involving somebody else we reached an agreement: the value of what I was going to take out would be shared out at fifty per cent for him, forty per cent for me and ten per cent for the man I contracted. If what he told me was true, I'd still be getting some two million dollars and I wasn't bothered about giving half a million to someone else. We were agreed and I told him who I was thinking of: Adrian Riverón . . . I knew they'd had their quarrels a time ago; I was also sure he was the only person I could trust, because I've known him almost since he was born, and he was Miriam's first boyfriend. Also, as a lad he'd been a rower and he'd lived for a while in Guanabo, he knew something about sailing and had friends on the beach who would get him a good yacht. Miguel really didn't like the idea, because of the rivalries over Miriam, and Miguel was always jealous of Adrian. And there was also the business of the dirty tricks he played on Adrian to get him out the way when they were working in Planning. You know about that? Well, Miguel wrote a report saying Adrian was a Catholic and wasn't to be trusted. And a statement like that, signed by him, was enough to disappear anyone in this country. They sent him off to Moa, as was the custom then, to be purified among the working-class. And he knew Adrian hadn't forgotten that, as he hadn't forgotten Miriam either. Precisely for that reason I even thought if he was given the possibility of being near her, in the United States, Adrian would be up for anything, because he was head over heels in love with her and because he never got another important post despite being a respected economist . . . Well, it wasn't easy, but Miguel finally accepted Adrian could be the third man in the plan and we agreed I'd talk to him. I explained to Adrian what we wanted to do and he accepted, without a moment's hesitation. He said he knew people in Guanabo who could sell him what we needed for us to leave Cuba and we agreed to see Miguel at Adrian's house last Thursday night . . . But something very strange happened: we'd agreed nine o'clock and Miguel didn't appear then or ever. As he'd told Caruca he was going to see Gómez de la Peña, I called Gómez just after nine and the old man told me Miguel had left his house at around half past seven, saying he was off to see a relative of his about an important matter. Although it was late, we thought he'd arrive any minute, but he still hadn't appeared at ten thirty and that was when I rang Caruca again and she told me Miguel hadn't come home. You know, it was as if the earth had swallowed him up . . . although later we discovered it was the sea that had devoured him. Are you convinced by my story? Or do you still think that I killed him because I already knew about the Buddha and was such a stupid shit that I left it where he'd hidden it, in spite of the risk you or some-one like you would end up finding it? Just think for a moment, Lieutenant, because I don't consider myself a sucker either . . ."

And he thought: of course not, you're nobody's sucker, but he resisted giving his verdict. He thought it delightfully cinematic that there should be a third man, particularly as he'd always enjoyed that dark, sordid film so full of twists, like the story he was mixed up in . . . And the Count thought on and thought it would make no sense to ask Miriam what her present relationship was with the omniscient Adrian Riverón: the woman, who had stopped crying while listening to her brother, would rattle her eternal armour and give the first reply to come to mind, and it would be sketchy and implausible. So he thought on and on and was disturbed by what he was thinking: between the perennially duped Gómez de la Peña and the only ever half-informed Fermín Bodes stood Adrian Riverón, rent with hatred and jealousy accumulated over years, to whose house Miguel Forcade should have got to, but never did? Another hunch, the policeman told himself, but sharper now, drilling painfully into his chest, just beneath the left nipple. These bastards will be the death of me, he concluded and stood up.

"Wait here," he told brother and sister and, addressing the policemen, "Crespo, you come with me. Greco, you stay here."

He went into the corridor, looking for the nearest door. He opened it and went in the archive, proclaiming: "I need to use your telephone," and dialled Major Rangel's number. It rang three times before his old chief said "Hello, Hello," as he always did. "It's me, Boss. I've got a question for you."

"Out with it then, where's the pain now?"

"The chest, beneath the left nipple."

"And? Could it be a heart attack?"

"No, I've got a hunch that's really hurting my chest. What do you advise for real pain?"

"You've got two options: either go to a cardiologist or follow your hunch."

"I'll take the second. Thanks for the advice. I'll see you later and remember it's my birthday," he said, hanging up. But the pain was still creasing him up, and he began to seek relief. "Crespo, go downstairs and ask for a warrant to search Adrián Riverón's house. Then find someone who can stay with little brother and sister and tell Greco to come with us. I'll ring Manolo. But we'll leave in ten minutes, got that?"

"Of course, Conde. Hey, you really in pain?"

"I swear on my mother I am. Right here," and he touched the spot where his strong hunches pained him.

The city seemed to be on a war footing or the eve of a carnival. Or were the wondrous vessels of the Royal Fleet returning to the town of San Cristóbal de la Habana, laden with gold and luxury? The latest news spoke of the imminent arrival of hurricane Felix, which at that very moment in the afternoon was gusting across the seas south of Batabanó and, in all certainty, would lash the island capital the following morning, with blasts of more than a hundred and twenty-five miles an hour and soddening deluges that would begin in the small hours, according to the radio channels, which sandwiched their message between festive *guarachas* and tearful boleros. Workplaces had finished off at two p.m., so people could get home ready to receive as best they could that meteorological curse that held them in its unerring sights.

A tempest culture, acquired over centuries of co-existing with those predatory weather phenomena, surfaced whenever a hurricane came near the country. Ever since Columbus heard about them, and heard the name uttered by the jittery Arahuacan Indians that month of October in 1492, thousand of tempests had swept the Caribbean, changing its topography, destroying the works of gods and men, altering the configuration of their coasts, transforming fertile fields into interminable lakes, and people had learned to live with them as you do with a bad neighbour it's impossible to be rid of. Every year Cubans expected a tempest just as they expected winter colds and summer

206

diarrhoea: it was something certain, inevitable and cyclical, with which you must spend a few days, out of pure and immutable geographical fatalism. The recurrence of these phenomena had the singular virtue of reviving the bad memories of people prone to forget the slightest incident: and they recalled the visitation of the mythical 1926 hurricane, the horrific 1944 hurricane, and the unforgettable Flora, thanks to which there was a reduction in coffee rations they were still living with twenty-five years later. But no hurricane, after all, had been able to sweep the island away – as some dreamed – or change the character of its people – as others would have wished. And so people even relished the rather festive atmosphere, the morbid expectancy before the hurricane hit, and they shouted at each other in the streets: "Hey, you, where you going to spend the hurricane?" as if it were like choosing somewhere to dine on Christmas Eve. The devastation would be inevitable, that they already knew, and had learned from their ancestors' rehearsal of the lessons of history, and the Cubans tried to extract from the hurricane's visit the strongest possible dosage of emotions they shared as a society. Later would come the time to bewail losses and forget hurricanes till the next round.

Without a doubt, the macabre carnival seemed to have begun: some people, on their roof terraces, strapped down the lids on their water tanks; others cut down trees, with a furious intensity that anticipated the hurricane's; others preferred to shore up mattresses, televisions, drawers full of things in the slim hope they might save something that otherwise would take them years to recover, and they did so with incredible broad smiles on their faces; and others took sensible precautions that grated on Mario Conde's nerves, buying up the stocks of rum in markets and liquor stores, convinced that drowning their sorrows in alcohol was the best way to await Felix, or whatever this year's blasted tempest was called. Everything was done at a frantic pace and, while his car advanced towards Adrian Riverón's house, in the old neighbourhood of Palatino, the Count recalled his father's visceral fear of hurricanes. It was an irrepressible fright that had apparently infected him from the cradle (so they said), because ten days after he was born the city was swept by the 1926 hurricane, the most memorable in all the city's chronicles of meteorological catastrophe. Grandad Rufino would recount how the wooden house where they lived had been lifted clean out of the ground by the force of the wind and the family was saved thanks to a small shed driven far into the ground, which he had built to store maize for his fighting cocks and feed for the pigs he also reared. The Count had always tried to imagine that tiny space giving shelter to his two grandparents, their six children, two dogs, twenty handsome roosters, the milking goat, pack-mule and three pigs, while outside the refuge the hurricane changed the face of the earth and left them homeless.

"Of all the terrible tempests there are in all the seas of the world, the worst are those in the seas around these islands and Tierra Firma," wrote Padre Las Casas, half a millennium earlier, astonished by the onslaught of the first Caribbean cyclone described by a European, and the Count thought the friar was right: the tropical hurricane reigned supreme over other terrible storms; it was so persistently hard-hitting, stubborn and predictable . . . And I feel you coming, he told himself, because he felt it coming, inside and out, and he wanted it here now: "Get here now, for fuck's sake," he repeated softly as he lit up a cigarette.

They found an external peace in Adrian Riverón's house that was alien to the tragic festivities of the preparations for the hurricane. As they approached the front door, the Count wondered again what exactly he was hoping to find there, and he still couldn't find an answer. Something, he thought, as he opened the door and Adrian Riverón flashed a smile seasoned with a cough at the sight of the four policemen. Although the wind already lashed, drenched and gusted, the fellow wore only shorts and seemed calm and relaxed, when he said: "And what are you doing in these parts, Lieutenant?" and he coughed again, as persistently as ever, which made the Count doubt once more whether Adrián was a fully paid up member of the select club of non-smokers.

Mario Conde looked at him almost tenderly: a feeling of relief spread across his chest, though he would be sorry if Adrian Riverón turned out to be Miguel Forcade's executor. In his heart of hearts, his skin and even his toes, he'd have preferred to put the blame on a character like Gómez de la Peña or, if that proved impossible, someone like Fermín Bodes; both carried a burden of age-old guilt they'd never atoned for. And what about Miriam? He hesitated for a moment and decided he preferred her to her eternal suitor, the victim of an ancient passion. Unjust justice.

"We've come to search your house," he finally replied, and Adrian Riverón's smile withered at the policeman's words.

"And what's it all about?"

"According to Fermín Bodes you were preparing a clandestine departure from the country. We want to see whether you've begun your shopping. Look, here's the search warrant. And two neighbours are coming as witnesses."

"But this is madness . . ."

"No, it's just a hunch," retorted the Count, and he pointed Adrian Riverón to one of his own armchairs. "Manolo, you talk to him and see if he has anything useful to say," added the lieutenant and, when the neighbours came, he explained the reasons for the search and went into the house followed by Crespo and el Greco.

"What are we looking for, Conde?" El Greco seemed confused and the lieutenant stopped in his tracks. He looked at the policeman, remained silent for a few seconds, then responded: "Whatever, how do I know? Something useful for making a secret departure, but above all a sign that Miguel Forcade was here the day he was killed."

"But what might that be, Conde?"

"I told you, whatever, for fuck's sake. Let's just take a look and forget everything else. Use your heads . . . Oh, and see if you can find a box of cigars."

While his helpers searched the garage, the Count started on Riverón's bedroom. He looked in the wardrobe, under the bed, and reviewed a few books of socialist economics somnolently gathering dust on a small bookcase, as abandoned as the planned ideal they had proposed for their real, near, dialectically historical future. Then he opened the chest of drawers: Adrián Riverón was an organized man despite his prolonged bachelordom, and the Count envied a quality he had never possessed. Pullovers, underpants and handkerchiefs were clean and neatly folded, and his socks were inside each other, like small soft balls. Towels and sheets were also clean and neatly folded, looked almost ironed, and the envious policeman greeted them with a look of displeasure, noticing a slight shininess at the bottom of the second drawer. He lifted the linen up and took out two disturbing and conflicting photographs: the bigger one was a black and white enlargement of a young couple at what must have been a coming-of-age birthday party: she, wearing a long, lacy, light-coloured dress, already stared with the provocative eyes that had stirred the Count's fear and desire. By Miriam's side – green fruit, but already edible at fifteen – smiled her dancing partner, a pitifully thin Adrian Riverón, hair combed over forehead and growing down under his ears, stuffed into the worst cut, even worse worn suit Mario Conde had ever clapped eyes on. Everything was ingenuous, youthful, distant and even slightly squalid in that photo of lost innocence. But the other snapshot was raucous and risqué: there, in full-colour, on card three by two, was a naked Miriam, looking slightly surprised at the camera she'd perhaps set up herself. The woman lay there, lifting her arms over her head to secure a more provocative pose and project her breasts more pointedly, breasts crowned by nipples that exceeded the Count's wildest imaginings. At the same time, her legs were slightly parted to reveal to the eyes of the recipient the dramatic darkness of her sex. I knew it, thought the Count, this fucking piece isn't blonde, and he turned over the card and read: TILL I'M YOURS AGAIN IN FLESH AND BLOOD. YOUR MIRIAM, and at the bottom a date: 12–7–84. He couldn't avoid taking another look at the woman who had undressed for the photo and thought it was a pity he hadn't had better opportunities with her: she was food for the gods without a doubt, as the progressive hardening he felt between his legs told him, forcing him to turn the photos over and leave them on the bed, feeling he'd peeped through a keyhole at an act of rapturous love meant for someone else.

211

"Nothing in the garage, Conde," announced Crespo, and got the reply, "One of you go to the kitchen and the other to the bathroom."

He went out in search of the back door, and, when he saw Adrian, he commented: "A pretty set of photos," and carried on to the patio, imagining what the fellow must be thinking.

There was a covered terrace at the back of the house, with a clothes sink, and a small cupboard for cleaning tools. The rest of the patio had been covered in cement, except for two circles of earth where clumps of seemingly ancient mangos were growing. There was a small shed against the back wall separating Adrian's patio from his neighbours' that the Count supposed must be ideal for storing tools and things for use in the house. An open padlock, hanging from a ring, alerted him to the possibility that something of value might be kept there and the policeman took a deep breath before going in. There he saw shelves as well organized as the bedroom drawers, with boxes for nails, clips, parts for the plumbing and electricity: what you'd expect in a place like that. In one corner he found two gloves and a baseball helmet. So he was a baseball player as well, he thought and couldn't stop himself picking up one of the gloves, putting it on his hand and hitting it against the other, as if he were anticipating some really big hits. Feeling nostalgia aroused by memories of his happy days as a street baseball player, the lieutenant put the glove back in its place and crouched down to see what was in some jute bags, when the two policeman came up behind him.

"Zilch, zilch to filch: not even a cigar," quipped el Greco and the Count turned round to look at him from where he was crouching.

"So, you'll be filching zilch, as usual. Well, it seems there's no lead here. The bags contain stuffing for cushions," he confessed, standing up, feeling the threat of defeat deal a blow to his knees.

After all it didn't make much sense for anything to turn up there linking Miguel and his death to Adrian Riverón – beyond the links to be drawn from those nostalgia-provoking photos, real desire and hatred, and the gloves, which betrayed a dangerous liking for baseball shared with millions of Cubans – so his painful hunch would have to contain itself till it found richer pastures. But which ones? He couldn't see any offering themselves and quaked at the idea of having to shut himself up with Miriam – now he knew her better and could testify to her state as an apocryphal, almost pornographic blonde – or with Fermín and Gómez de la Peña to find some light at the end of the tunnel, he thought, as he abandoned that small room and grabbed the door in order to shut it behind him.

"Wait a minute, Conde," said el Greco, who took one look in the room and then stared at his boss: "What was the instrument the forensic said the dead man was beaten with?"

The Count looked at him and the pain from his hunch vanished as if by magic, for the words spoken by that lad were like the wave of a wand and he would put him forward as the Most Intelligent Policeman of the Month, so that the Union would place him on its wall display for labour rewards and bear him in mind for the next handout of electrical goods: yes, he deserved a freezer and a week on the beach that genius of a policeman who made him yell: "Fucking hell, Greco, have you seen the bat?"

"Well, I can see a bat, Lieutenant: look up there," replied the policeman and the Count looked up:

between roof-tiles and iron beams there lay a wooden bat, crouching as conclusive as death itself.

The last time Mario Conde had played baseball was at university. He was in the third year of his degree and, as usual, volunteered to be part of the worst baseball team in the whole history of Cuban university sport. It was as if the central-European scientific model for the planning of economic and social life proposed by Gómez de la Peña had also penetrated the hidden recesses of the student body, and it was considered necessary, one fine day, to restructure – yet again – the country's universities and their faculties. That's why one morning the School of Psychology, which had always been part of the science faculty, was transformed, through some mysterious administrative design, into an independent faculty, as rigorous as all the other university faculties. Then, in order to meet all the necessary norms and obligations, the faculty had to participate in the University Games with its own teams, in which inevitably the names of the same athletes cropped up again and again because of the lack of students matriculated in that new faculty, more renowned for its intellectual activities than its crude physical aptitudes. And that last year when the Count played baseball he also kept goal for the football eleven, defended for the basketball team, ran for the 4×400 relay team, as well as playing first base and third bat in the baseball team . . . The Count as third bat . . .! Because the Psychologists' only sporting virtue was their enthusiasm: although they were doomed to come last in almost all competitions, they were proud to hold aloft the Olympic motto that competing was more important than winning – for they almost never won;

among other reasons because of the exhaustion their sportsmen accumulated over a week of non-stop action.

The last day he played baseball, the Count felt he could hardly lift his arms up and failed three times with the bat when it was his turn at the end of the eighth innings and they were trailing two zero to the Philology Tigers. Because of a mistake, a base and a dead ball, the Count had a historic opportunity to enter the batter's box with the possibility of an advantage at first base, even though two of his team were out and it was at that precise moment that he suffered one of his first memorable hunches: like all his colleagues, the Count now preferred to use one of those new-fangled aluminium bats, which were considered more efficient and sturdier than the old wooden bats. But his hunch warned him that perhaps the old scorned bat made of green-veined *majagua* hardwood that nobody now used might be the only one able to achieve the miracle and save that last championship game – which, without his imagining it, would also be the last time he'd play. Before the astonished gaze of his colleagues and shouts of alarm from Skinny Carlos, who was still skinny and who almost hurled himself from the terraces to stop his friend committing such an idiocy, the Count slung his aluminium bat to the ground, went over to the bench for the wooden bat and got ready to bat. After passing on two hits, making no attempt to strike the ball, in spite of Skinny shouting, "Hit it, for fuck's sake," the Count looked towards Carlos and calmly executed the dramatic ritual he'd practised in his years as an amateur playing for fun: he asked the referee for some time, moved away from the home-plate, picked up some earth in one hand and spat in the other, rubbed them both together and wiped them on the backside of his trousers. After that he placed the blade of the bat between his legs and cleansed it of impurities, rubbing it on the material, before he spat once more on the ground and returned to the batter's box, where he played out the final act of his *mise en scène*: he scratched his balls and looked Dog, the Philology Tigers' best pitcher, in the face . . . Only someone whose wrists have felt the crisp thud of solid ball against compact wood, produced in a microfraction of a second, one that can send the white sphere flying amazing distances, is endowed with the understanding of what Mario Conde felt at that moment when he steadied himself, carried through his swing and the blade of the bat hit the ball and sent it hurtling into the far depths of the park on the right, so he could run like crazy round the bases, as if he hadn't been doing baseball, football, basketball and athletics for almost twenty-four hours a day throughout the whole week, and calmly reach third base, to the jubilant cries of a skinny Carlos, who had thrown himself on the pitch shouting: "Fuck, what you need is real balls!" and hugged the Count's three companions who had scored thanks to his great batting, which put the game at three–two in favour of the Psychologists, who finally won their only game the day Mario Conde played baseball for the last time, in the 1977 University Games.

"So what's the story on the bat?"

Sergeant Manuel Palacios nodded and the Count felt a shiver run down his spine: the adrenalin hoping that that bat might tell the whole story, ending up in the hands of Adrian Riverón, a batter of forbidden balls, was similar to the adrenalin hoping the other guy would be guilty and not that useful suitor. Once again

216

his policeman's craft confronted him with the sordid evidence of human intrigue that transcended the limits of what was permissible and wrecked people's lives for ever: and he started to function again as the choreographer of that performance, giving it a final structure, finding a sadly satisfactory end before the definitive fall of the curtain.

"That was the bat," said Manolo, flopping into the armchair where Miriam had been sitting.

The sergeant, who was always alert, now seemed tired, bored or disappointed.

"What's the matter, Manolo?"

"You've found Miguel Forcade's killer. Now you'll leave the force. Hey, is that really what you want to do?"

"Uh-huh," mumbled Mario Conde after a moment, and he tried to redirect the conversation. "What did they find in the laboratory?"

"First of all, the fingerprints are all Riverón's, so he was the only one to touch the bat. Secondly, the blood: although the blade of the bat was wiped with a cloth soaked in spirit, there were blood cells on the wood fibres. The blood group was O, the same as Forcade's. Finally, other traces of blood were found on the bath-room floor that the water hadn't washed away and they are also O, and it's almost certain they belonged to the dead man."

The Count left his armchair to look out of the window: gusts of wind were beginning to comb the tops of the trees, as a precursor of worse evils to come. In the churchyard, on the other side of the street, skirts and coifs blowing in the wind, nuns were nailing planks on the doors to the holy precinct, to prevent the tentacles of the Evil One entering the Lord's house in the form of rain and wind. This was an autumn landscape different from the one imagined by Matisse, in rational, measured Europe: the tropical sign of autumn had nothing in common with leaves that fell at a precise change in the seasons or light filtered through high clouds. The trees the Count could see never let go of their leaves if a force superior to gravity didn't snatch them away, and the light in the country had only two real dimensions: either the intense blue of a clear sky, able to flatten objects and perspectives, or the deep grey of the storm, which mired the atmosphere and brought on nightfall. But the hurricane now pushing against the island's southern coast, wanting to take it with her, was the most tragic climax to autumn in that part of the world where nature was dispensed in exaggerated measures: rain, wind, heat, thunder and waves, and where evergreen leaves only fell under the weight of those catastrophic arguments. It was a nature that periodically decided to demonstrate to man his inability to control her and warn of her infinite scope for revenge.

"I don't really understand why the asshole never got rid of the damned bat . . . Well, Adrian is well and truly fucked now," was the verdict delivered by the Count, and he asked him to bring in the man who'd been Miriam's first boyfriend, her great love for more than fifteen years, to ask him to tell the truth. A truth perhaps beyond fake pictures and authentic statues, and able to drive ambition and deceit: because Adrian had perhaps only killed for love. In the end the truth was pathetic.

A pale and sweaty Adrian Riverón coughed as he always coughed, and asked the Count: "What do you want to know?"

"You really don't want a cigarette?"

218

"I told you I never smoke . . ."

"Just as well."

"Go on, tell me . . ."

"No, you tell me: how and why did you kill him?"

The man still found the energy to smile, and lifted up the packet, asking the lieutenant's permission to take a cigarette. The Count nodded, with the knowledge that he was finally nearing the truth, and also raised a cigarette to his lips.

"The fact is Miriam doesn't like me smoking. It's not good for me, you know. I had to give up rowing because of tobacco." He paused, adding: "I killed him because he tried to hit Miriam."

"Don't try to justify yourself, Adrian. I only require the truth, please."

"That is the truth: Miguel and Fermín were coming to my place at nine. Fermín spoke to me about possibly leaving the country on a motor launch, taking something out that would earn me in the region of a hundred thousand dollars in Miami. I agreed right away. And I told him I had two reasons: because if I went I could be near Miriam, and because, ever since Miguel Forcade threw me out of Planning, I'd never been able to lift my head in this country. It didn't matter if afterwards Miguel defected to Spain or Gómez de la Peña was defenestrated: my file says I'm not to be trusted and no boss of any important enterprise will take a risk with me, do you understand? Well, you know what my line of business is . . . That was why I wasn't bothered if I had to deal with Miguel Forcade and see his cynical face again, if it was a means to get what I wanted.

"But it seems my fate is marked by this man. If not, you tell me, how is it possible he gets to my place an hour early, on the very first day Miriam and I got together after so many years? All I can imagine is that he was coming to suggest a way to betray Fermín, because that was his style. The fact is Miriam knew we had the meeting with Miguel at nine, and as Fermín had arranged to be at my house at eight thirty to talk to me first, she thought if things got messy and her husband saw her there, she could always say she'd come with her brother. Consequently, when Miguel left to see Gómez, she came over here to my place and we went to bed after all these years . . . Because she was on a high now she'd finally found out what Miguel wanted to take out of Cuba."

"So she knew?"

"No, she found out that day. For some time she'd been on at Miguel to get him to say what it was, and that afternoon, before going to see Gómez de la Peña, he finally told her they were going to take out a Matisse painting Gómez de la Peña had kept for him."

The Count couldn't stop himself: he smiled.

"The Matisse painting?"

"Yes, one that Miguel had left that bastard . . ."

"I'm more convinced by the day: Miguel Forcade was a man of many talents."

"He was just one big son of a bitch, Lieutenant."

"I already knew that. Carry on with your story, Adrian."

"That night Miriam swore that if I went to the United States she would leave Miguel, because she couldn't stand any more of his depressions, his envy and even his impotence, and she proposed a real act of madness: that we should steal the painting after Miguel and Gómez had done their business. We were talking about that when Miguel knocked on the door . . . You know, when I saw it was him through the window, I felt my whole world collapse. It didn't make any sense for him to find out Miriam was there, so I told her to hide in the bathroom until I thought of a way to get her out of the house, perhaps with Fermín's help. But when I opened the door the first thing Miguel did was to ask me where the treacherous whore Miriam was; he pushed past me and went into the room. I don't know if he'd been spying through the windows, or had heard her talking, I don't know, but he knew she was with me, and he walked in shouting her name. And then something happened that made me see red, drove me mad, because the mere thought that Miguel might touch Miriam drove me crazy and I grabbed the bat in my room and shouted to him not to take another step. Then he tried to grab me and I hit him on the head. It was horrific: the guy fell to the ground and started to convulse, foaming at the mouth and pissing himself, but hardly losing any blood, until he started to go stiff and then still. Miriam had come out of the bathroom and saw the grand finale. We both stood there speechless for a time and she said the best thing would be to hide the body and act as if Miguel had never arrived. The first thing we decided was to hide him and she helped me take him to the outhouse and then she went off in Fermín's car, which Miguel was using, and parked it in Old Havana.

"I stayed at home waiting for Fermín, who arrived at nine fifteen, and I talked to him as if nothing had happened. What he wanted to tell me before his brother-in-law got there was simple: if what we were about to take out of Cuba was really worth several million, there was no reason to share them with Miguel Forcade, because after all he must have stolen it when he worked for Expropriated Property. Of course, I said yes to everything, without letting on I knew about the painting, and then at ten Fermín began to ring to find out why Miguel hadn't come, and when he didn't show he decided to leave at about ten thirty.

"My problem was how to get a corpse out of my house. The only way I could think of was Fermín's car and I called Miriam. She told me where she'd left it and that she'd thrown the keys in a rubbish container on the corner. I waited till midnight and went to Old Havana and when I saw the street was empty I shifted the things in the container and got the keys, drove the car to my house and removed the body from the outhouse and wrapped sacks around it. You know what most upset me? The way the son of a bitch smelled of shit and the way the stench stuck to my hands. You know, I think I can still smell it . . ."

The Count, who had been imagining the stages in the tragedy Adrian Riverón was now relating, quickly put the rest together: a corpse swathed in sacks, dragged to the garage, placed in the car boot . . . What about the castration?

"And why did you mutilate him before throwing him into the sea?"

"I don't know. I think I thought I could put you lot off the scent if the corpse appeared . . . It came out of the blue, but it was if I'd had the idea in the back of my mind for years, because I enjoyed doing it," he said, and squashed the ash of his cigarette, which had been burning his fingers. "Then I drove the car back to Old Havana, gave it a thorough clean and left it where you found it. And I went home and went to bed . . . May I have another cigarette?"

"Help yourself," said the Count, who could hear the powerful whistle of the wind through the window.

It seemed the hurricane had arrived. And he looked up at the sky, over the church tower, afraid he might see a nun fly by.

"Adrian, everything you did was very intelligent . . . What I don't understand is why you kept the bat . . ."

The man coughed, as he took another cigarette and lifted it to his lips. When he went to light up, he hesitated, as if ashamed by what he was doing.

"I'd owned that bat for twenty years . . . Miriam gave it to me as a present when we got engaged and it was in the bedroom because I'd just showed it to her . . . I couldn't throw it out, could I?"

"I think I understand. But I'm not sure if Miriam would . . . Look, keep those cigarettes and smoke if you want," whispered the Count as he left his cubicle.

He switched off his recorder just as Adrian Riverón was declaring "I couldn't throw it out" and he contemplated Miriam's eyes and saw they were still beautiful, with that diffuse, changing colour, dominated by poisonous lashes that had been the ruination of two men. But her eyes were too dry.

"The bit I saw was as Adrian described it. I don't know about the rest," she affirmed, and the Count was not surprised she was still the strong, confident woman he'd been struggling with for three days. That was why he looked at Manolo to deal the final blow.

"Are you sure you two didn't plan to kill your husband in order to make off with the painting?" began the sergeant, bending over in his chair so his face almost struck Miriam's.

"No, because I was going to separate from him . . . as soon as I had the painting."

"Which turned out to be fake."

"Yes, he deceived me over the painting as well."

"And why did you try to make us suspicious of your brother Fermín?"

"Because he was innocent. You wouldn't be able to implicate him, and that would give me time to leave and then it would difficult for you to think of Adrian."

"But you already knew about the gold Buddha?"

"How many times do I have to tell you I didn't. Miguel deceived me because he trusted no one. Or haven't you realized he didn't have a single friend?"

"The poor man," whispered the Count, and fell back into the requisite silence.

"And what did you and Riverón expect to live on in the United States?"

"On the money he'd get from what we were going to take out of Cuba . . . from the painting. But in the end I wasn't particularly worried. I was going to leave Miguel even if it meant sleeping under a bridge. Nobody can imagine what it's like to live with a man like that . . . It's a pity it's all turned out like this."

"Who's it a pity for?" the Count interjected, unable to restrain himself.

"For Adrian . . . and for me."

And the policeman saw the armour of a thousand skirmishes fall from Miriam's shoulders, the woman with the perverse eyes. She was now going to cry, from her own eyes and with real reason. And it would be better if she did cry a lot, and bellowed if she wanted to, at the loss of her last chance to be happy.

"Let her be, Manolo," said the lieutenant, bored. "Let her cry. It's the best thing she can do."

He had to run and lock himself in the bathroom. He turned on the tap in the washbasin and watched the water flow crystalline and pure, before putting his hands in the jet and wetting his face, again and again, in an attempt to wipe away the oppressive filth and angst: the knowledge that he'd just witnessed the definitive collapse of several lives had provided him with the most glaring evidence of why he hadn't been able to write that squalid and moving story he'd been dreaming of for years: his real experiences instinctively headed elsewhere, far from beauty, and he realized he should first rid himself of his frustrations and hatred if he was ever to be – or had been – able to engender something beautiful. It was only then that he grasped the realm of fear that prevented him from letting rip on paper, from making real, alive, independent, and perhaps everlasting, the dark flow of lava that had swept away his life and his friends', and transformed them into what they were: less than nothing, nothing at all, nothingness itself. Candito was right: cynicism had become the antibody that allowed him to carry on, and Andrés had also discovered his double-think: irony, alcohol, sadness and a few doses of scepticism provided a carapace, while the rationale he had fabricated for his inability to write what he wanted served as a soothing, enduring wall of self-deception.

Finally he dared look up and contemplate himself in the mirror: once again he didn't like what he saw. It wasn't his face, which was beginning to line; nor his hair, beginning to thin out; nor his teeth, beginning to yellow: nor any of those first signs of predictable decline, but the feeling that the end was already cast in stone, and a painful conviction: only a miracle could bring him back to his true path – if miracles existed, and if that path existed – and only one decision could set him on the road to redemption: we're either saved or fucked together: he just had to write, squeeze the seed, lance the boil, empty his intestines, spit out the bitter saliva, execute that radical operation, begin to be himself.

He didn't think about it: his cupped hands splashed water over the mirror and his image became elusive and difficult to retain: transfigured and blurred, with no definite outline and always half hidden, that had been his real face, the policeman's face he'd been showing to the world for the last ten years: and with it he must finish this story of ambition and hate, until he could finally relinquish the shards of that battered carapace.

The Count looked at his watch again: now it indicated five twenty-five.

"Please forgive me, Colonel. I promised I'd deliver the case at five ten and I'm fifteen minutes late. But the fact is the typewriter ribbon jammed."

"Is everything here?" asked the new chief of Headquarters, licking his lips, and Mario handed him the folder of preliminary case-findings.

"All that's missing is the authentication certificate for the Buddha. The people at Patrimony need to seek more advice, but it is definitely gold, Chinese and pretty old. And also worth much more than the five million Miguel told everybody."

"But that's incredible, over five million," responded Colonel Molina, laughing nervously.

His new boss, thought the Count, was no doubt already savouring the congratulations that he would receive for his evident efficiency as a leader of efficient criminal investigators.

"Are you pleased?"

"Of course I am, Lieutenant. I've very happy I wasn't mistaken when I sent for you and gave you all the freedom you required for this case. It seems incredible: in three days you discovered a fake painting, you found a

226

sculpture that had been lost for forty years and which is worth millions and millions and you even solved the story of a murder that at the end of the day had nothing to do with the sculpture worth millions.

"I'd hardly say that," suggested the Count.

"Well, not directly," agreed the Colonel, smiling again.

If I call his mother a whore, he'll split his sides, thought the Count and went on the offensive.

"Now I hope you'll keep your promise, as I did mine."

Alberto Molina's broad smile faded quickly.

"But, Lieutenant, have you thought it through? I think your future lies here," and his gesture, which indicated the boss's office, rapidly extended, to other less specific limits within the building. "You've shown me what an excellent policeman you are, and I'm going to promote you here and now."

"Don't harp on, Colonel. I want my release, not a promotion. I'm done with all this."

And Molina still couldn't understand.

"But why?"

The Count mentally fanned out before him the possible reasons and decided to select the least aggressive.

"I just don't like solving cases like this one; the most innocent character in the whole story is the one who will rot in jail . . . First, I'm fed up with wallowing in shit, lies and deception. Second, I can't stand the idea that half the police who were my colleagues for ten years, including people I really believed in, have been kicked out, rightly or wrongly. Third, I want a house by the sea, where I can start to write. I want to write a story that is squalid and moving.

"Squalid?"

"And moving" added the Count, elaborating.

"Because I want to speak of love between men. That's what I want. Over to you, Colonel."

"I swear by my mother I really don't understand you. Love between men, Lieutenant?"

Molina left the folder on his desk and preened his magnificent officer's jacket. He edged round his desk and opened the centre drawer.

"Here you are," he said, and opened out the sheet of paper on to the table.

The other stood up and grasped it. He read the opening sentences and felt satisfied, but he continued to the end: Lieutenant Mario Conde was granted the discharge he had requested for personal reasons, and it stated, in the second paragraph, that he had shown an exemplary attitude in ten years of service, demonstrating through his efficiency that he had been the best detective at Headquarters and an excellent work colleague, among other praises sung single-spaced. The Count swallowed, he didn't know if it was because he felt emotional or full of doubt, and dared to ask: "Colonel, why did you write these things about me?"

"Which things?" came his reply.

"The stuff under the granting of permission . . ."

Molina smiled again and flopped into his comfortable armchair.

"Did you notice the date on the letter?"

The Count looked and understood even less.

"It says October 4, and it's the 9th today . . ."

"Yes, it says the 4th. Did you look at the signatures?"

He glanced back at the paper and couldn't believe what he saw: there, on that same horizontal line, sat the signatures of Colonel Alberto Molina and Major Antonio Rangel. No, that was impossible, he thought.

"When you told me you were going to hand in your file on the crime solved within the hour, I realized it was a pity to lose you as a policeman, but that I had no right to hold on to you. I thought it through, took a decision and went to see Major Rangel to ask him to write this letter, backdated a week, and for it to carry two signatures. You owe the praise to him. My role was to grant you the discharge that you'd asked for."

The Count was taken aback: flattery came his way very rarely and that sweet-smelling colonel, in cahoots with the Boss, was praising him and had even managed to move him. So he had been a good policeman, had he?

"Thanks, Colonel," he said, and began to prepare his best salute, knowing it would never satisfy the rules and regs. For fuck's sake, he said to himself, stretching his hand over the desk, ready to make a run for it. Like Miriam, though for different reasons, the Count wanted to cry.

Wanted to, really: and from his own eyes.

Violins accompanied the oboe, pianissimo, bathed dreamily in the agony of the passage, before yielding to the vigorous instrumental crescendo and choir rapturously singing Schiller's verses to joy. By some phonetic or poetic miracle, the German voices were not at all the harsh growl usually associated with that language, and they grew into an expansive cantata that, like few human creations, succeeded in communicating, in an ecstatic epiphany, the feeling of life, the certainty of hope and possibility of optimism: for the first time the Count thought that ode was like a primitive song to fruitfulness, an invocation to the hidden gods of heaven and earth in order to gain their favour.

His eyes turned towards the garden: the old man, Alfonso Forcade, seemed impervious to the music

229

booming out from the cassette recorder perched on the iron bench, at maximum volume so it reached the remotest corner of that arbour. Nonetheless, as the Count observed him more leisurely, he noticed slight tremors in the neck of the old man, who naturally carried within him the whole chorus and orchestra, perhaps under the orders of Beethoven himself: Forcade tried to communicate his own emotion to the plants, to make them share in the redeeming spirit. That was why the Count waited for the choir to end before he interrupted the concert.

"You like Beethoven?"

"They like him . . . As well as Wagner, Mozart and Vivaldi. It is well known that wheat is particularly sensitive to the sonatas of Bach. And no secret that plants grow and produce more when they are given symphonic music to listen to."

"Wouldn't it be a cruel shame if the hurricane put an end to all this?"

"No, you are quite wrong. Nature is never cruel, because she doesn't know how to be. Cruelty is a sad privilege of human beings. That is why the pre-Hispanic cultures of the Caribbean personified the hurricane and gave it a human figure. For them it was the terrible god of the Tempest, and they called it 'hurracane', 'yurricane' or 'yoracane', according to their dialect, but in each and every case the word meant Malign Spirit, more or less what the devil is to Christians, and that's why they gave songs and dances as peace-offerings . . . as I'm doing now . . . The fact these disasters occur never ceases to be regrettable: perhaps tomorrow all of this garden that I have planted and tended for nigh on thirty years will be gone. That also makes one want to weep."

Leaning on his wooden crutches, old Forcade got up

and walked slowly between the garden paths where a threatening breeze was already rising, and Mario Conde puffed on his cigarette. The policeman waited for the symphony to finish before telling him how the investigation had ended. He didn't seem overly surprised by the news that his son had died at the hands of Adrian Riverón and because of Miriam. Perhaps he mind-read one of them? wondered the Count, knowing that any answer would be unimportant. As a scientist, Dr Forcade knew Miguel's death was irreversible and merely commented: "Do you know something? I was right to let you do the thinking, because you're much more intelligent than I am . . . I thought Miriam might have done the whole lot . . . And look who it was, the poor man. Well, I'm glad I was able to be of some help. And that justice has been done. May God be merciful . . ."

Then they began to walk slowly back to the wrought-iron bench, as if making a final tour of a landscape that would be definitively different after the god of the Winds had passed by.

"At the end of the day these plants and I will suffer the same experience: that is where we surely share the same destiny of birth and death. What is terrible is to see the beings one has begat and loved die before oneself."

The Count felt a desire to remind him that there were many other differences between Miguel and those plants, but concluded it would be too cruel on his part. A privilege of human nature. And he also thought how Alfonso Forcade knew precisely what manner of man his son had been. And then decided to think no more: the old man might read his thoughts again.

"But the silk-cotton tree, the baobab and the laurel

will resist. They might lose the odd branch, but they will resist," commented the old man, indifferent to the Count's thoughts, and his voice lilted joyously. He even smiled, and his teeth stayed exposed to the elements, until the curtain of his lip fell.

"I expect it's because they are sacred trees, isn't it?"

"No, I don't believe any of that . . . They will resist because they're stronger and that's another of Nature's laws. The wiliest and the strongest survive. The rest go to the dogs, Lieutenant."

"Take it easy, Manolo," begged the Count, though he had no intention of looking out of the window.

If the hurricane came, many of those building would cease to exist, like old Forcade's music-loving trees, and his day's charge of emotions already seemed on the high side.

"I'm just upset, Conde."

"How come?"

"I'm upset because you're leaving the police."

"Well, I've got a cure for that: jerk yourself off twice, stand on your head and take a diazepam with a lime infusion and you'll see how relaxed you get."

"Fuck off, you always come out with the same shit," his colleague protested, as he drove round the corner and parked the car in front of Major Antonio Rangel's house.

While Manolo disconnected the aerial, the Count contemplated that idyllic image: in the foreground a bonfire was burning, dry leaves that had certainly been cut because of the imminent tempest, and, further back, up a ladder, a man nailing down wooden panels over the windows at the front of the house. And the Count wondered: if he'd still been the chief, who the

232

fuck would have done this? because the Major would have been at Headquarters, giving orders, supervising, listening to cases and tying up all the loose ends so the final knot fell right into his hands.

"Can I be of help?"

"Quiet, Mario, look where the hell I am," said Rangel, from his ladder, not turning round to look at his visitors and abandoning his domestic chore, almost pleased with what he'd done. "Let's go inside. I'll finish this later."

"Ana Luisa will kill you," the Count warned, and at last the Major smiled.

It was perhaps the first time his teeth had been visible out of sheer glee. Maybe in his mere five days out of the police, awesome Major Rangel had recovered a capacity that had seemed lost for ever.

"Well, you know, I'm really happy with everything I've done at home today. And as the store advanced us oil because of the hurricane, we're having fried yucca for lunch . . . Come on, let's go in," he said, as he let them through into the library. "Sit down."

The Count and Manolo sat in the armchairs and the Boss opened up his small humidor, which was packed to bursting with cigars.

"Go on, pick one. Careful, they're Davidoff Cinco Mil Gran Corona."

"Now you really have gone mad," declared the Count, who in ten years had only ever extracted one Davidoff from the Boss: his meanness as a cigar-smoker climbed its most selfish peak with Davidoff Cinco Mils.

"But there's more," Rangel assured him, as he opened up a desk drawer and brought out the unthinkable: the shine on the black label of that Johnny Walker went way beyond the Count's expectations and all of Major Rangel's traditions. The Boss set three glasses on the table, put ice in each, and poured out three generous helpings of amber liquid. He gave a glass to each guest, raised his own, and said: "Congratulations, Mario Conde."

The Count looked at him and told himself yet again how lucky he had been to work with a man like that.

"Thanks, Boss," and they chinked glasses, drank, and lit their cigars, so the library ceiling was soon covered with that blue perfumed cloud that only a trio of Davidoff Cinco Mil could form when enjoyed in the company of a vintage whisky.

The Count's second gulp emptied his glass and he asked for more fuel.

"But that's the last you'll get from me today. You know, my daughter sent me this bottle from Vienna and I'm not going to polish it off in this session with you . . . Well, how did the letter strike you?" Rangel asked incisively, allowing himself another smile that surpassed all his usual limits. Alhough this time it wasn't possible to see his teeth.

"You almost made me weep."

"Molina seems a good fellow. It was his idea."

"But you put the words to it. Why did you write that when you'd never said anything like it to me?"

"So you didn't get too big-headed . . . any more than you were already. Because I can tell you one thing, Mario Conde, before you get drunk and start saying ridiculous things. I suffered a lot in my life as a policeman and putting up with you was one of my worst trials. You can't imagine how much I wanted to kill you whenever you did something stupid or turned up at Headquarters looking like you do today or disappeared for a couple of days because you were drunk . . . I could have kicked you out a hundred times, and I think I could have even had you shot because you were so irresponsible, undisciplined and badly behaved. But I decided it was best to tolerate you as you are, because you also showed me something you don't find every day: that you are a man and a friend, and you know what that means, whatever the place or situation. And I liked having that kind of friend."

The Count thought this declaration of love way over the top. He never imagined that imposing man, excessively conscientious in his work, and monogamous to boot, might distinguish him only for those qualities he thought he saw in him . . . Could it be true he was like that? he wondered and gulped down more whisky, to try to become a little more credulous.

"And I'll tell you something else . . ." The Boss returned to his theme, but the Count gestured to him to stop.

"Don't go on, or I'll have to kiss you."

"You see . . .? I was on the same wavelength . . . What I meant was I'm pleased you're leaving the force. If you want, I'll talk to a friend of mine and get you work in a circus."

"That's not a bad idea. I'd already thought of it: the police clown. I've always thought that sounded good, you know. Or do you prefer the clowning policeman . . .?"

"Don't fuck around, Conde. What I was about to say was quite simple: it's better you leave the police before it's too late. Before you end up a cynic, insensitive, or a fellow who reacts the same to the sight of a dead body as a cold drink. If you really want to write, get on with it, but don't ever say again you don't have time. Do it now, right away, and forget everything else."

"Well, we're well and truly fucked there, Boss. I can only forget everything when I'm pickled in alcohol."

"Don't forget anything then, but get on with your life. You've still got time."

"Do you think so?"

"I do, but the rest is down to you. So, what do you make of this tobacco then?"

"The best in the world."

"Almost, almost, because now the Davidoffs are Dominican, made with tobacco from Cibao. My friend Freddy Ginebra sent me these . . . And the whisky?"

"The best I've drunk all day."

"That's certainly true."

"And is it also true you're not going to pour me another drop?"

"Most definitely."

"Why do you need so much? You've got more than half a bottle left."

"Yes, but it's mine. How else do you think I can wait for the hurricane?"

It was only when the Boss congratulated him that the Count again grasped the chilling certainty that his age had changed. The precise time of the mutation, one forty-five in the afternoon, had gone by in the middle of his hurried investigations, and the hours passed without his feeling anything special, not even physically. Nevertheless, the evidence that his liberation was nigh seemed more visible after he'd had that hunch that led him to the truth. Poor Adrian Riverón, he thought yet again, trying desperately to forget the story of a murderous bat romantically preserved, as he opened the door to his wardrobe, by now bathed, shaved and perfumed, and realized he had nothing new to wear on his birthday. Even in the harshest of times, when the ration book for industrial products barely allotted each Cuban male one pair of trousers, two shirts and a pair of shoes a year, his mother had always sorted things so he had some new item of clothing to wear on the momentous occasion of his birthday. But recently the Count had denied that tradition and the paucity of options offered by his wardrobe was the most striking evidence of the long period of neglect his clothing had suffered at his hands. There on the floor, curled up like an old dog feeling the cold, were the jeans he preferred to all his other trousers, and the Count lamented yet again that the dark mud where the Buddha slept had stained them so dramatically that they were desperate to visit the public laundry before embarking on new battles.

As it really was a notable occasion, the Count decided to wear that night the trousers to the only suit he had possessed in his adult life, the one he'd bought for that ever more distant occurrence, his marriage to Maritza, seven years ago. Even though they stank because of the long rest to which they had been subjected, he preferred to believe it wasn't too bad, and he thwacked them several times, hoping to improve their odiferous state. He never once thought of submitting them to the iron in order to remove the wrinkles they'd acquired from the hanger. He pulled on his trousers in front of the mirror to make sure they weren't that awful: other people wore trousers with creases and pleats, and if he adjusted the waist no one would notice that the garment's original owner weighed a good fifteen pounds more than their almost stick-like present-day wearer. It was much easier to select the rest of his apparel: he took out the only shirt hanging up, preserved in dusty splendour by the fact he'd never liked it, and reclaimed his everyday shoes, rendered opaque by the film of limescale left by the water he'd used to wipe off the mud stains. You are elegance itself, just look at your profile, Mario Conde, he encouraged himself, contemplating his figure in the mirror: a desirable thirty-six year-old bachelor, ex-policeman, pre-alcoholic, pseudo-writer, practically skeletal and post-romantic, incipiently bald, ulcerous and depressed, and in the final stages of chronic melancholia, insomnia and coffee stocks, ready to share his body, fortune and intellect with any woman, white, black, mulatta, Chinese or non-Muslim Arab, able to cook, wash, iron and, three times a week, accept his tender labours of love.

He lit a cigarette, allowed himself a second dose of cologne and went into the street to confront warm, wet gusts of wind, black heralds of Felix the Ravager, who was already throwing out advance warnings of a predictable destruction of the city. The blacked-out streetlights on the Calzada, bolted and barred doors of houses, the emptiness of the streets swept by the gusts and the drizzle accompanied him to the bus stop, where his heart was almost broken by the sight of a dirty woolly dog dozing on a pile of rubbish, under one of the benches, and fortunately unaware of the approaching tempest. The Count looked at the dog and, for some reason or other, whistled. The animal lifted its head and peered at the man out of a sleepy, hungry haze. "Tell me, Rubbish," he said, and the animal wagged its tail, as if that were its only real name. "You don't know a hurricane's on its way, do you, Rubbish?" he went on, as the dog got up and took two steps towards that speaking being, still wagging its tail. "And it's a fucking evil hurricane," he went on, and the animal padded a little nearer. Its eyes were round, like shiny, sweet nuts, and its hair, matted with dirt, fell over its face, as if once combed into a fringe. The

Count smiled when the dog stopped in front of him and touched his leg with its warm snout and he couldn't contain himself any longer: he ran his hand over the animal's dirty head, repeating his defining epithet: "Rubbish, what can you tell me about your life?" he enquired, thinking perhaps that the animal had been driven from its home by cruel, slightly mad owners, the kind that prefer to kick out their dog rather than relieve it of a couple of lice. Grateful for this gesture of affection, the animal moved its head and licked the man's hand and the former policeman felt that wet warmth demolish all his feeble anti-street-dog defences. It was an irrational, irrevocable relapse, which forced him to say: "OK, come with me," and he began to retrace the three blocks separating him from home, with Rubbish as his travelling companion. When they arrived, the Count opened the door and the dog went in as if he'd lived there all his life and he suspected Rubbish must have been having a good laugh. Almost afraid he'd made a mistake, the Count searched his refrigerator and was pleased to find a dark-coloured fish, age unknown, hibernating there, which he put in a casserole with leftover rice and placed over the flame. The smell of food gave a new rhythm to the tail of Rubbish, who even barked twice at the Count, urging him on. "What, are you hurt?" he asked and stroked his head again, until he saw steam rise from the saucepan and switched off the flame. The Count used a fork and knife plucked from the depths of the sink to chop up the fish as best he could and scrape out the rice stuck to the sides of the saucepan." OK, Rubbish, I apologize for not laying a clean table-cloth, but this is an emergency," he warned, and took the saucepan out to the terrace and poured the meal into a tin he'd thrown out. "Hey, watch out for bones, and blow first, because it's hot." The dog was so patently happy its tail seemed as though it might drop off and, between mouthfuls, it looked up at the extra-terrestrial being that had saved it from starvation, the rain and loneliness. While the dog chewed its food, Mario Conde looked for an old rag under the clothes sink and put it next to the door to the terrace, where the animal would be well protected from rain and wind. When Rubbish finished giving a shine to the tin, he pointed to the rag and the animal obeyed: licking its whiskers, the dog turned round three times on the rag before stretching out and crossing its front legs. "Look," the Count explained slowly: "I've got to go out. Stay here if you like. But if you want to go out into the street again, use that passageway. Do whatever you want. I can tell you we don't always have food here, that if you stay I'll have to give you a bath, that I spend the day out in the street and am sometimes lonelier than you, but as I've not had a dog for many a year, perhaps I'll take to doggishness again with you ... What do you reckon, Rubbish? Well, I'm off. Do whatever you want, and long live freedom!" He concluded his speech and shut the door, with Rubbish's sincere thanks expressed in the look that accompanied him till man and animal lost sight of each other. "I'm raving mad," was the Count's self-diagnosis, and he left the building at a run, as it was almost eight thirty and he hadn't drunk anything for two hours: on that day when he celebrated his thirty-sixth birthday, became a dog-owner again and gave up being a policeman.

"You finally got here, wild man. Well, what's your verdict on life?" Skinny greeted him from his wheelchair. The Count saw anxiety ride across the face of his best friend, who was peering out of the front door scrutinizing the horizon for a sight of the birthday boy who was so late. "I called your place twice but no sign of you."

"Fact was I was buying a dog," replied the Count as he crossed Josefina's garden, planted with *picualas, malangas,* violets and white *vicarias,* ideal for all eye illnesses, and he promised himself that he too would have a musical dialogue one of these evenings. Would these *picualas* like la Aragón's cha-cha-cha or would they prefer a ballad by The Mamas and the Papas?

"Buying . . .? A dog . . .? Mario, don't give me any more of that shit and give me a hug. Congratulations, my brother," said Skinny, who'd not been skinny for some time, and spread his tentacles out in order to squeeze a skeletal Mario Conde.

"Thanks, brother."

"Come on then, your fans are waiting inside."

"Wait a minute, Skinny, let me ask you a question, and give it me straight: if I write about you, about me, and about the guys in there, and mention a few fucking things, will you get angry with me?"

"What sort of fucking things?"

"I'm not sure . . . Like you were left handicapped by the war you went to fight, for example."

Skinny Carlos glanced at his legs and smiled when he returned his friend's look. "That's not the worst fucking thing, Mario. The worst came after: thinking what might have been if this hadn't happened . . . But it happened, and don't fucking go on about it anymore, I'm not in the mood today. You write whatever comes to you, but make sure you do it well. Come on, let's go inside."

With the experience of years, the Count stood behind the wheelchair and turned it round to go back in the house. They went down a passageway, already hearing the Beatles music with which the Count's friends were beginning to stir their nostalgia, and entered the dining room, where the last of the faithful on earth were waiting. Josefina was the first to congratulate him and kissed him on the forehead, Rabbit copied in his best style, and gave way to a hug from Andrés, a precise, strong handshake from Candito, a kiss on the almost childlike cheek of Niuris – the girlfriend Rabbit was sporting that day – a competitive slap on the back from Baby-Face Miki and a liquid look from Tamara the twin, whom the Count kissed with a restraint that expressed his fear at the closeness of her skin, always prone to alarm him down to the last male hormone in his body.

"How come the miracle? What made you come?" the Count asked, looking into the woman's moist almond eyes.

"Could I *not* come? Carlos called me and told me to be here and I . . ."

"Of course you could, Tamara. Thanks."

"All right, enough of that," shouted Skinny, giving the Count a glass. "If you want lovey-dovey, get off to the park."

"Hey, matchmaker, quit the joking," retorted the Count threateningly, aiming a finger between his eyebrows. "Or are you never going to grow up?"

"Me? No. And you?"

"Well, as today's a special day I didn't start on any great innovations and decided to follow a traditional recipe of steak with bacon and gruyère cheese, which goes like this: buy fresh fillets in the market, on the long and thin side, and cut to the same size. Spread the

242

steaks out and lightly salt them; put a strip of bacon down the middle and the gruyère on the bacon. Then dust everything in herbs: personally I add thyme, basil, oregano and rosemary . . . Then fold over each fillet, as if it were a pasty, and join the ends with a couple of toothpicks, which I only managed to get today, to stop the stuffing leaking out. With me so far?"

"Uh-huh," replied the Count, all his gastric juices rising up in a proletarian rebellion. "Uh-huh, uh-huh, with toothpicks, go on . . ."

"Well, then let them sit, so the smells of the cheese, the meat and the bacon infiltrate each other and are then impregnated with the smells from the herbs. After that, heat equal measures of oil and butter in the frying pan, fry the steaks on a full flame for a couple of minutes on each side, so they go brown, and then leave them for another eight minutes on a low flame . . . Then put the fillets in a dish and place them in the oven, but on the lowest heat possible, so they don't go cold or cook too much. Meanwhile, remove the fat left in the pan and put in butter, mixed with the juice of a Seville orange, which is better than the lemon in the traditional recipe. Remove the orange and butter sauce from the burner when it's hot and add two spoonfuls of cream. Next you take the steaks from the oven, sprinkle on a good amount of parsley and pour the sauce over them, and now it's ready to serve or you can put it back in the oven for a short time, but on very, very low, until the guest of honour arrives, who may even go by the name of Mario Conde."

"And who has now arrived, Jose. Tell us what else you've done?"

"What, you want more . . .? Right, well, there is more, because the fillets are served with potato puree, made with the oil and butter fat we separated out after frying the fillets, you remember . . .? But, as I know the scene, I took the necessary precautions: it's only one fillet per head, so be warned: though you can have as much as you want of rice, mushy black beans, stewed yucca, flash-fried green bananas, onions in bread-crumbs, tomato, watercress, lettuce and avocado salad, guava shells with cream cheese and coconut jelly in fruit juice with savoury cheese."

"I do not believe it, I do not believe it: gentlemen, the age of abundance is upon us!" quipped Rabbit.

"And don't we have any coffee?" asked Andrés.

"Café from Oriente roasted and ground by yours truly," the woman confirmed, looking into the feverish eyes of the Count, whose stomach, used to thirty years of strict food rationing, refused to believe what his ears had heard.

"Hey, Jose, now I'm no longer a policeman, you can damn well tell me: where the fuck do you find all these things?"

Carlos's mother looked at the Count, then at her son and glanced at all the other friends, before turning to the Count, who was now in no doubt at all: Josefina was like the circus magician who conjured from nowhere an elephant dressed as a sailor.

"You really want to know, Condesito? Well, I get it out of here," she said after a pause, and touched her temple: "out of this imagination of mine."

From the first swig the Count's experience of drinking had warned him that this mixture of rum, friends and old Beatles songs might be explosive. The special dinner served up by Josefina had prepared their stomachs to accept a larger intake of alcohol and bottles were emptying at a dangerous rate. After the meal Skinny had insisted on moving on to the presentation of the gifts that each guest had had to bring, including the two compulsory bottles of rum – a tax only Candito the Red had been spared because of his new religious affiliations. Seated at the head of the table, the Count received the presents in turn from his friends, and they catered for each and every one of his physical, material and spiritual cravings and desires. The first was Carlos, who gave him a small goldfish bowl with a fighting fish, for he'd heard of the death of his most recent Rufino.

"Great, now I've got a dog and a fish," commented the Count, as he watched the fish's slow, purplish flight.

Candito the Red presented him with a Bible with black, bound covers that, according to him, had more commentaries and maps than any other published in Spanish. Ever subtle and material, Tamara gave the Count the checked shirt he had always wanted: seemingly straight out of a Wild West film, and made of soft wool, just the job for the approaching winter, and in the pocket, behind the Levi's label, a Schaeffer pen, ideal for the aspiring writer. Perhaps paying all his nicotine debts at once, Baby-Face Miki handed over a pack of twenty boxes of Popular cigarettes, and along with it, or so he said, the monthly allowance of one of the several children he'd scattered over the face of the earth. Gentle Niuris, in the full freshness of her sixteen years and obviously guided by Rabbit, gave him two cassettes of Chicago's *Greatest Hits*, which the Count read from the top down: from "Make me Smile" to "Beginnings", from "Saturday in the Park" to "Colour My World", the titles sounded like cries of alarm at the huge number of years that had passed between the days when they'd listened to those songs together and that hurricane-force birthday-party night. With his loving eye for detail, Rabbit unfolded before the Count's eyes a poster of Marilyn, asleep on a red sheet that emphasized the glow from her yellow (dyed, to be sure) hair, the precise undulations of her black woman's buttocks and the magnetic pink of a single visible nipple. Andrés, who had patiently waited his turn, faithful to his profession as a medic, placed in the Count's hands two jars of Chinese pomade – one from the tiger, the other the lion – and an envelope with a hundred analgesics, a combination of pills and ointment that would save the Count from death by migraine during his next hangovers. Last in the queue, Josefina walked over to the thirty-six-year-old she'd known for twenty, when her son was skinny and walked on two legs and shut himself in with the Count to listen to music at full volume and dream of a future in which war did not figure; and, without uttering a word, she gripped his cheeks, made him feel the roughness of hands ravaged by washing up, cooking and laundering, and then kissed him on his forehead.

"Thanks, Jose," the Count stammered, moved by the burden of tenderness that kiss carried.

Rabbit rescued him this time, insisting on a full account of the Count's last case. Mario tried to refuse, but the screams from his audience won the day. Before starting, he looked at Tamara, at the opposite corner of the table, and tried to imagine how much of the story he was about to relate would remind her of the episode in which they had both been embroiled as a result of the death and disappearance of Rafael Morín, a man immaculate only in appearance, who married the twin and shattered Mario Conde's heart into a thousand pieces.

"Once upon a time in China, at least fifteen or twenty centuries ago . . ." began the Count, preparing to begin at the beginning, and spoke for an hour to the best audience he'd ever known.

"Conde, Conde, how amazing," exclaimed Rabbit when he heard the end of Adrian Riverón's murderous confession. "Can you imagine, if the Hindu monks hadn't gone to China, Miguel Forcade would have died differently."

"Why don't you write this down?" queried Baby-Face Miki, the only published writer among the Count's friends.

"I might do one day," replied the ex-policeman, thinking that yes, maybe he did have a story here that was at least moving, if not squalid.

But now, right now, for fuck's sake, he wanted to write about a wounded man and the other scars left by less solid, but equally lethal bullets.

"More rum, more rum," Skinny shouted from his wheelchair, and after helping himself, he asked: "And what the fuck are we going to do now?"

"Carry on drinking," posited the Count.

"No, better that I tell you a story, another story," interjected Andrés from his chair, with such conviction in his voice that the others fell silent for a moment, and the doctor jumped in to fulfil his promise. "It's a story that began long ago, but I can only tell you now . . . because I told the people at work today I wanted to leave Cuba . . ."

He suddenly threw down the dice, and glasses clattered on to the table, alcohol-scented mouths gawped, corks returned to the necks of their bottles and, beyond the walls, gusts of wind whistled no more, as if on orders from a higher command.

"Twenty-six years ago, when my father left and my

mother refused to follow, something was broken for ever in our family. You remember, Rabbit, how my little sister Katia had died two years before and if there could have been any solution to that unjust death, my Dad's departure took it with him: we'd never again be the family we'd once been and the best we could do was to start sharing out the blame for what had happened and what now would never happen . . . Dad was the most to blame, because he abandoned us just when we needed most to be together, and left his country and turned into a contemptible *gusano*, living in Miami . . . Life fucked me up and I was full of fears and reproaches, and if anything saved me it was finding a group of friends like you, who became as important to me as my family and never criticized me for my father's decision. Then things began to go down a path that seemed for the best: my mother took it into her head that I should study medicine and I thought I should please her and was really happy that I could choose my career and become a doctor and I think I've been a good doctor, haven't I? On my way I made a good marriage with a woman I still like, I had two children, I became a specialist and everything seemed so ideal that you even started to envy me: you said everything had turned out right for me, that I had a good family, a good job and even a good future . . . But there were things that weren't as I wanted them and I don't know if I am right or have a right to ask for those other things. I wanted my life to be more than getting up in the morning, helping to dress the children, going off to the hospital, working all day, coming back in the evening and sitting down to see how my children do their homework while my wife cooks, and then having a bath, eating, watching television for a while and going to bed in order to get up the following day and do the same as I'd done the day before, and so on and so forth . . . Perhaps one of you thinks that is what life is about, but if that's true, then life is shit. Because it's a routine that's got nothing to do with what I want . . . The worst thing is, when you start to think you discover that this routine began much earlier, when other people, other necessities, other turning points decided your life should follow one pattern and not another, without your really having the right to choose and write the story you wanted to write, don't you agree, Rabbit . . .? What would have happened if I hadn't let Cristina go, if I'd gone after her, carried on with her, even though she was ten years older than me, and even you lot thought she was a whore because she'd had several husbands? Or if I hadn't given up baseball to devote more time to my schooling and become a good student of medicine, as I had to? Who would I be now if I'd done what I wanted to do and not what you were supposed to do and what everyone forced me to do . . .? Because some ten years ago something happened that stirred me up and I started asking myself some of these questions: my father wrote me a letter, after I had heard nothing from him for a long time, and he said he was sorry for abandoning me and explained why he had left: he told me that there had come a moment after my sister's death when he needed to change his life and that he would have preferred to take us with him, but dear Consuelo was opposed and insisted on staying where she was rather than follow him wherever he was bound. As far as I was concerned that explanation didn't in any way justify his selfishness, although I saw my father differently for the first time, not as the guilty man I, my mother and the world around us had created . . . Now he seemed a man, with his own needs, anguish and hopes, a man

249

like any other who'd sacrificed part of his life to have another, the one he thought he needed and had decided to choose, you know? Perhaps it's all stupid, but that's how I felt, and I told him so, and he replied by saying that if he could help me in any way, I could count on him, that despite what he'd done, he was still my father. That made me feel better towards him, but that was all, because my life continued to be perfect, almost impossible to improve on, until one morning I got up not wanting to go to work, or dress the children, or do any of what I was supposed to do and I felt as though my life was all a big mistake. Does this ring any bells, Conde? The knowledge that something diverted the route you should have taken, that something pushed you along a path that was not yours. The dreadful feeling when you discover you don't know how you've got where you are, but that you are somewhere you don't want to be. It was all shit. Why did it have to be like this? And my first thought was to run out of the house, as I did when I fell in love with Cristina and ended up drunk on wasteland in Old Havana: but now I'd have to run much further, to throw off myself and that feeling of claustrophobia and routine I couldn't stand a minute longer. But one thing held me back: the sight of my two children dressing themselves to go to school. If I left, I'd be leaving them just as my father left me and I didn't want them to suffer that. But if I didn't break out of my own routine I was condemning them to live like me, teaching them to obey and be people who'd receive orders for the rest of their lives, to become a second round of the hidden generation. Miki, do you remember the hidden generation? In the end they'd be as fucked as I was, faceless no-hopers with nothing to tell their own children. There and then I took the decision to leave, to go anywhere, but with them, and when I returned from the hospital that evening I told my wife, and she said I was mad, understood fuck all, and what the hell were we going to do and I said: 'I don't know, but I've made up my mind,' and I asked her: 'Will you come?' And she said she would. She said yes straight away . . . Then I wrote to my old man and explained how I now needed the help he had promised . . . That was the only way I could get far away, try to change my life, and if I was making a mistake I might as well be mistaken big-time, right? And for once in my life make my own mistakes. That was a year and a half ago, and all this time I've been doing the necessary paperwork to leave, without anyone finding out till something was for sure. I couldn't even tell you lot, who are my brothers and will understand me, and if you don't understand me you won't condemn me, will you, Carlos? Red? And you, Miki, would you dare write this story in one of your books . . .? Today, when I went to see the director of the hospital, a man who was a comrade in the faculty, he couldn't believe what I was saying and he even tried to dissuade me, but when I told him it was a decision I wouldn't go back on and even had the letters asking for permission to leave, he put his hands to his head and said: 'Andrés, you know I'll have to take this upstairs,' and he even looked up, when he should really have been looking down, because I now know I've got to work in a Policlinic in a barrio till they give me my letter of liberation, yes that's what it's called, a letter of liberation, and they let me leave, and it will take one or two years, maybe more, but I'm not worried: it is my decision, my madness, my mistake, and for the first time I feel as if I own my decisions, my acts of madness and my mistakes, even the fact that I've acted like shit with you and not told you before what I wanted to do, but you know I couldn't tell you, more for your good than mine, because you're staying and, if Jehovah wishes, as Candito says, in two years I might be right off the map . . . But right now, though I feel calm I'm also afraid I'm shooting myself in the foot, because I'm probably doing to my own children what my father did to me, except in reverse. And I'm going to miss you people, because I love you from my heart and balls . . ." he said this, then started to cry, as was right, as he needed and wanted to do, and he moved Tamara and Niuris to weep, provoked a tear in Skinny Carlos's eyes, a blasphemy in the mouth of Candito, who shat on Jehovah, and a sigh from the Count, who stood up, hugged Andrés's head, and told him: "And we love you too, you pansy," and pressed him hard against his chest, which seethed with a bunch of shared stories, mixed up with political prejudices, fear of the future, reproaches against the past and tot after tot of rum: the horrific sum of their flawed lives.

Andrés's confession killed off the impact of alcohol on the Count's brain. An unhealthy lucidity spread through his mind, placing a question mark over his own life, now reflected in the mirror of Carlos's life, which he intended to write up, and Andrés's, which Andrés himself had just outlined: his own frustrations took on a sharper relief in the light of his friend's words, and the Count totally understood why he had left the police: he needed to escape, even though he was incapable of changing location. Too many nostalgic memories tied him to the house where he was born and lived, to the neighbourhood where he grew up and where his father and Grandad Rufino grew up, to the friends he had left, whom he could never abandon, to certain smells and plagues, to many fears and epiphanies: his anchor was fixed in such a way he almost didn't need to know how it was secured: he simply possessed irrevocably a physiological need to feel that he belonged in one place.

The bitter burden of Andrés's words had decreed an end to the fiesta, and the break-up began, sadly and with everyone feeling they'd experienced something final and beyond appeal. Today it could be Andrés's departure, tomorrow it might be the death of Carlos, sentenced to his infamous wheelchair; another day would bring Miki's betrayal, another Rabbit's lunacy till they reached the apocalypse, he thought, as Tamara's car advanced along Santa Catalina on the way to her house. The Count, who had so wanted her to ask him to provide the company he longed to give, was hardly surprised when she said: "Will you come home with me?"

"Of course," he'd answered, convinced Andrés was provoking all this, and not entertaining the possibility that Tamara might have wanted it long ago, perhaps even as much as he had.

The wind had risen with nightfall and an opaque drizzle hit the car windscreen, blinding the couple's vision.

"The world is coming to an end."

"Or already has," she corrected him, turning the car towards the garage entrance.

"I'll open up," he offered, stepping out into the rain and out of the way of the car, which shone the full beam of its headlights on the amalgam of shapes that recalled Lam's and Picasso's bestiaries, hybrid animals, ready to leap, terrified by the machine bearing down on them.

"Did you get very wet?" she asked, getting out of the car after she'd locked its doors.

"Hardly at all."

"Come in, I'll put the coffee on," she suggested as she opened the door to her house.

He recalled the last time he was there: that morning they'd made love with the fatal sensation that a divergent past had come between them, along with a future in which it would be difficult for them to get along: because nobody loved a loser, because she'd be unable to share his sad policeman's life, because he'd never overcome the phantom of a dead husband called Rafael Morín asleep, perhaps, between their bodies, he thought that day, and today, too, when he wondered why he was there, although he knew the answer.

Tamara returned to the living room with two cups and settled down on the sofa, very close.

"Why didn't you ring again, Mario?"

He smiled and sipped his coffee.

"Just what I was thinking . . . Because I thought it best for you."

"But you never asked me my opinion."

"I thought I was right."

"Perhaps you were wrong."

"You reckon?"

"I said perhaps . . ." and she took a sip as well.

He looked at the huge house and supposed she left her son at his grandmother's. Everything in that house could be for him, that night, to round off his birthday.

"I was probably wrong, as usual. But the fact is, Tamara, I don't want to fall in love. And even less so if it's with you . . ."

"Why?"

"Because I've already fallen in love once. Because I

only suffer afterwards . . . and because I start singing boleros."

"Don't fuck around, Mario."

"I swear I do."

He thought he must protect himself, because he liked that woman and her coffee too much, and worst of all she knew it, he also thought, looking into her eyes that were still moist, at the shape of the breasts he'd once kissed, and now tried to remember her naked, as he'd had her that day he consummated the dream he'd postponed for fifteen years. But something missing between his legs told him it had been a very long day too over-burdened with reminiscences for him to try and finish on a glorious note, when he would no doubt have to show off his panoply of amatory skills. So, with a heavy heart, he stood up and finished his coffee, then put his cup on the table in the middle of the room.

"What's the matter, Mario?"

"I'll try to explain: I really like you a lot, more than anyone else, I love going to bed with you, I'd even marry you in church and I'd like to have eight children with you, but today is a bad day. A hurricane is on its way . . . What Andrés said has knocked me out. Just imagine, if he thinks that about his life, what can I say about mine? That's why I'd better go . . . Can I come back another day?"

She nodded and a lock of hair fell impertinently over her eyes.

"In ten years' time?"

"Or ten hours."

"Better make it ten hours . . . or I can't guarantee a thing," she replied, standing up. She also put her cup on the table and without further ado applied her mouth to the Count's and stuck her torrid tongue between his teeth. When he could eventually speak, the Count looked at her.

"Thanks for the invitation. You bet I'll come, and the first thing I'll do is sing you a bolero."

"Don't be so stupid, Mario: don't you realize that I'm alone, that I need you? You should try to be a little less selfish and put yourself in other people's shoes. Then you wouldn't have been so surprised by what Andrés said . . . You aren't the only one who is fucked. I'm telling you that I need you and –"

"Don't talk that way, Tamara: I'm not used to anybody needing me. Not even myself." Now he was the one kissing her, with the brevity demanded by a farewell as necessary as it was undesired. "Don't worry. I'll be back tomorrow. After the hurricane has come and gone."

As soon as he set foot in the street, he was convinced he'd made a mistake, as usual, and should run to the tree of self-flagellation in order to whip his buttocks. The taste of ripe fruit that Tamara's breath had left in his mouth was something sustained and tangible, like the feel of her breasts against his chest: he was going, leaving behind him a woman full of longings, who even said she needed him, only to meet the sodden hostility of rain and wind, as he floated his melancholy on the air and wondered how many more times he would get it wrong in life. Every time. Now, he told himself, he needed to see the hurricane come and go, to see whether the devastation it wrought would create a new face to pitch against such a vision of failure and frustration and grief and gloom. His whole body soaked by the rain, its force lashing his arms and face, the Count ran down the centre of the street, feeling the rain and air purifying him in those early hurricane hours that were to mark the first day of his new life. As he ran, he realized that the speed was causing his body to abandon his soul, always so ponderous and pretentious, which now chased after him in vain. A strange sensation of purity and total freedom began to flow through him, after so many attempts, ideas, plans and desires to feel free. He ran down the lonely street, savoured the rain racing down his cheeks, broke through the air with his chest, refusing to think: wanting only to wallow in that freedom, but his brain denied his wish and he had to think. And he thought: I'm not the same person anymore. Anymore?

"Yes, fuck you, get here quick," he yelled at the threatening sky, without slowing down, convinced, for the first time in many years, that he was doing exactly what he wanted to do and should be doing: running, and with his last breath, singing against the night:

Finally, fatal world, we go our separate ways,

The hurricane and I stand alone.

The end of the world had come: a strong, insistent blast of wind almost blew out his bedroom window and the Count warily opened his eyes, their lids gripped by fear. No physical pain haunted him, but his uneasy conscience had received scant relief from those brief hours of sleep and oblivion. The window panes filtered a slow, sickly light that didn't fit with that time of the morning, and the wind thrust and beat unceasingly against the city as the hurricane tightened its steely vice, and the rain came in waves, sheet after sheet, like a battering-ram determined to break its way through, demolishing every obstacle, everything that longed for permanence.

The Count was surprised by a long forgotten feeling of worry about someone who was dependent on his tender care. He got up and, without putting his shoes on, quickly made for the back door, opening it a crack for fear Felix might take advantage of the fissure to penetrate his own home. He whistled, and Rubbish's wet, shivering shape appeared before him, his tail drooping between his legs. "Come on, come inside," he said, and before closing up the Count used this moment of courage to take a look at the patio. The old clump of mangos sown over fifty years ago by his grandfather Rufino lay on the ground, its dislocated fragments covered by alien branches, incongruous leaves, come from wherever. The Count imagined the physical pain the tree must have suffered, and not a single bar from Mozart's *Requiem* at the moment of death. But the tops of the trees that were still standing also seemed ready to fly, as if wanting to go far from where they'd been planted. The world bowed in defeat before the presence of a curse that had unleashed its invincible weapons on the city.

He put on the flame a last remaining spoonful of coffee, mixed with the dregs he'd extracted from the coffee pot. While he waited for that dark liquid that might perhaps taste of coffee to come to the boil, he concentrated on drying out Rubbish's filthy coat with a cloth he'd found in the kitchen cupboard. The animal was still scared and kept looking at the windows, rattled in turn by the blasts from water and wind.

Finally the infusion was ready and he drank a cup of greyish brown liquid. It's not so bad, he told himself, and regretted not having a drop of milk to offer the dog. I warned you, my friend, and he stroked the head of the animal, who had taken refuge under the table. Then the power of the wind gusted as mighty as thunder and he heard an explosion. The neighbourhood was being demolished by a gale force of over one hundred and fifty miles an hour and there was little you could do against that perversion from the heavens, except wait and pray.

The Count, who had rejected the second of those options thirty years ago, thought it would probably be best to go back to bed, and he put his head under the sheet while nature performed its macabre purifying ritual. He knew that calm would descend in two hours: the rain would stop and the sun would come out, to throw more light on the disaster. What would be left of that aged, much castigated city the Count carried in his heart, even though his amorous longings went unrequited? What would survive of that neighbourhood from which he couldn't and didn't wish to escape, the only place on the planet where he felt it possible to enjoy a minimal space to drop down dead – or continue with life? Possibly nothing at all: in truth, the devastation had begun long ago, and the hurricane was only the fierce final blow sent to finish off the sentences already begun . . . Memories would perhaps remain, yes, memories, thought the Count, and the certainty of that saving grace made him forsake his bed, walk to the kitchen table and place his old Underwood on a surface stained by cigarette burns, lemon juice and old rum-inspired patches. Yes, now was the time to begin. He placed that promisingly white sheet of paper against the platen and began defiling it with letters, syllables, words, speeches and paragraphs with which he intended to recount the story of a man and his friends, before and after every disaster: be it physical, moral, spiritual, matrimonial, work-related, ideological, religious, emotional or familial, from which the only thing saved was the cell originating friendship, timid yet stubborn like life itself.

And the Count wrote, trusting that his story about a policeman, a wounded youth, a lad who wanted to be a great baseball player and fell in love with a woman ten years older than himself, a man determined to remake history, a beautiful, svelte woman with rock-hard buttocks, a writer prostituted by his environment, and a whole hidden generation, would prove to be so squalid and moving that not even the disaster of that October day and every other day in the year would be able to undermine the magical act of extracting from his brain that chronicle of love and sorrow, experienced in a past so remote that memory tried to paint it in

260

more favorable hues, so it became almost bucolic. *Pasado Perfecto*: yes, that would be the title, he told himself, and another blast reached him from the street, warned the scribbler that the demolition was proceeding apace, but he merely changed the sheet and started a new paragraph, because the end of the world was drawing nigh, but had yet to come, since memories remained.

Mantilla, November 1996–March 1998